Summer
in the
Scottish
Highlands

BOOKS BY DONNA ASHCROFT

Summer at the Castle Cafe
The Little Christmas Teashop of Second Chances
The Little Guesthouse of New Beginnings
The Christmas Countdown
The Little Village of New Starts
If Every Day Was Christmas

Donna Ashcroft

Summer
in the
Scottish
Highlands

Bookouture

Published by Bookouture in 2021

An imprint of Storyfire Ltd.
Carmelite House
50 Victoria Embankment
London EC4Y 0DZ

www.bookouture.com

ISBN: 978-1-80019-349-9
eBook ISBN: 978-1-80019-348-2

To Marike Verhavert
For your kindness

Chapter One

Paige Dougall breathed in a lungful of fresh Scottish air and took a right into Lockton High Street, just as her three-year-old let out a sleepy huff from the back of her ancient Peugeot 505. 'Don't give up,' Paige begged the car as the engine spluttered and coughed.

She let her eyes skim the pavement and cluster of shops to the right of her, tracing the familiar shapes. The village hall with its resplendent new roof; the pathway which led to the school and The Book Barn, the small library where she'd helped out on weekends and evenings in her teens before working there full-time; then the red-brick post office where Morag Dooley collected gossip before embellishing and sharing it with the world. Further in the distance, Paige could just make out Apple Cross Inn and beyond that, the all-year-round Christmas shop where her mam worked, which had opened years after Paige had left her life in Lockton. Framing it all was a huge range of mountains speckled with lush summer grass, and a blue, almost cloudless sky. A bubble of apprehension crept into her throat and she pushed it down, along with the overwhelming desire to turn the car around and head back to London. She was homeless and jobless for the next four weeks and had nowhere else to go – at least until she figured something out.

She started the car again and crawled slowly down the high street, marvelling at how few people were around considering it was Friday afternoon. In her corner of Notting Hill the pavements were always teeming during the summer months, from the crack of dawn to late into the night. Somehow the quiet unsettled her. It took only another five minutes and thirty-two seconds to reach her parents' house and Paige pulled into the gravel driveway, pausing for a beat to take in the pretty double-fronted cottage she'd grown up in. Her mam had obviously been in the garden recently, nurturing the stunning array of summer flowers including begonias, sweet peas, geraniums, pansies and petunias which waved in the wind like a colourful welcoming committee. Paige's gaze rested on the pretty white name-plate that hung to the right of the front door with the words 'Kindness Cottage' painted on it in red lettering. No one knew where the name had come from, but according to legend, years before the owner had had a reputation for delivering food parcels to poorly villagers, who in turn had presented her with the carved name-plate for the house. Paige let out a shuddery sigh, thinking how long it had been since anything resembling kindness had touched her life.

Paige opened the door of the car and swung herself out slowly, taking a moment to stretch. Ignoring the exhaustion dragging at the edges of her mind and limbs, she gritted her teeth and grabbed one of the small suitcases she'd jammed into the footwell of the passenger side, closing the door gently so as not to wake her little girl, Grace. Paige was determined to unpack the boot and talk to her parents before her daughter stirred and wanted to explore. They had no idea about the visit, and she needed to explain that her time with them would be short.

As she approached Kindness Cottage and its bright red door, she heard a sudden patter of footsteps to her right. Then, before she knew what was happening, a ball of beige and cream fur with an enormous set of teeth launched itself at the suitcase and began to tug.

'What are you doing?' Paige yelped at the Golden Retriever, as it pulled at a red bra strap which had somehow caught in the side of the clasp, almost jerking her over. 'Leave it!' She used her mum-voice, the one that always worked on Grace when she misbehaved, and yanked the case towards her, stumbling backwards towards the car. But the dog held on, its brown eyes glittering with playful delight as it waved its head from side to side, intent on continuing their game. It was small, fluffy and as cute as a button, despite its strength – and in any other situation Paige would have dropped to her knees to pet it. But she was tired and it was gnawing on her favourite silk bra. The only one she owned with knickers to match it – not that anyone ever got to see those. It was then that she looked up and saw the man standing on the pavement to the side of her.

He was somewhere in his mid-thirties, tall, probably six foot, with dark brown hair, and eyes that made her think of a clear blue lake on a hot summer's day just before you dived in. His hands were in the pockets of faded jeans, a dog lead was hooked around his large tanned wrist, and a black T-shirt with the words 'Chill Out' stretched across a muscular chest. She ignored the appreciative flutter in the pit of her stomach, which quickly morphed into a hot fizzle of fury when Paige realised he was laughing – worse, his whole body was now shaking with amusement as if he could barely control himself.

'This isn't funny – will you come and get your mutt!' She clenched her fists and yelled as the dog gave one last, enthusiastic tug and the case burst open, flinging her most intimate possessions across the gravel driveway and flower borders. Two of her G-strings landed in her mam's begonias and the rest sprayed across the lavender in a series of vivid Ts. One lacy black bra dangled from the wing mirror of her car; the other two splatted against the windscreen and slid out of sight. The book she'd been trying to read for the last six months, *The Magic of Making it Big*, lay open beside her mam's welly boot stand, and Paige realised with a spurt of irritation that she'd lost her page. Worse, her make-up, hairbrush, toiletries and medicine now lay scattered like multicoloured paint splodges over the pebbles. She stood for a second blinking as the energetic young dog made off with the red bra, bouncing up to its owner before dropping the sliver of silk like a trophy beside his walking boots.

'I'm so sorry.' The man flashed Paige a stunning grin before bending to pick it up. Then the dog whirred around, spinning and almost tumbling over itself as it strained up, waiting to see which way his owner was going to throw it next. Instead the man's eyes danced with amusement as he clipped the lead to the dog's collar before striding onto the drive. 'Yours, I think?' he asked, holding the bra in the air between them, as his grin deepened, exposing dimples under sexy, sharp cheekbones. His accent was from somewhere down south, reminding Paige of everything she'd just been forced to leave behind.

'It hardly belongs to anyone else,' she hissed, snatching her underwear from his fingertips, stuffing it into the back pocket of her trousers, while the dog panted and raked its paws on her smart black slacks as it tried to jump up. 'Will you control your animal, please?' she repeated, bending and pushing the dog away as it strained to lick her. She picked up one of her lipsticks and a couple of small hair clips, looking up as she gathered more. The man pulled his errant pet away from her, laughing at its antics, his limbs loose and easy in sharp contrast to the irritation and stress biting into Paige's shoulders and neck.

'I apologise, he's a pest. Stop it, Mack! Put that down and sit. I've got snacks.' His voice was hoarse, more with amusement than ire. But the hound continued to strain at the lead. 'He's not that good at responding to commands. I'd like to think it's because it's the afternoon and he's tired, but he's been living with me for seven weeks now and I've realised it's the same no matter what time it is. He's not the best listener – our fault. I think we might be a little too lax,' he admitted.

We? Paige wondered, giving herself an internal kick when disappointment tickled the back of her neck.

'Let me help.' The man bent and gathered her hairbrush with one hand, holding the over-excited dog back with the other.

'I can do it,' she snapped, as he picked up the suitcase and placed it on the bonnet of the car, tossing the brush into it before picking up the black and midnight-blue bras which were lying next to the front tyre. Paige felt her cheeks heat as the man tucked them carefully inside the case without ceremony. 'Really, I don't need your help,' she continued, as he grabbed the bra dangling from her wing mirror, and she saw his attention dart to the back seat of the car where Grace was still sleeping.

He turned back to her, more curious now. 'You know the Dougalls?' His tone was languid, but she could see a spark of interest in those blue eyes.

'They're my parents. I grew up here,' Paige answered, because it was easier than telling him to mind his own business.

He nodded slowly, perhaps expecting her to elaborate. 'Good people. You don't have much of an accent.' He put his hands in his pockets, ignoring the dog which was now attacking the laces of his shoes. 'I'm Johnny Becker. I work with my twin brother Davey at Apple Cross Inn. I've lived in Lockton for the last three years and I'm pretty sure we've never met…' He squeezed his lips together as he gradually and thoroughly traced her face, making her whole body shudder in unwelcome response. 'I'd definitely have remembered. Your name is?'

'Paige.' She cleared her suddenly dry throat, surprised that she'd told him. Living in London for so long had made her a little more suspicious than that. Perhaps it was all the fresh air from the mountains befuddling her brain? 'And I haven't been home for a… while.' Not since she'd eloped six years ago, in fact.

He nodded, putting her on guard as something about the slow, lazy movement triggered a hundred different memories she'd spent the last year trying to forget. 'Staying long?'

Paige shook her head. 'No more than a week.' She might have been signed off from work with stress for four, but she was determined to get back sooner.

'Pity.' His lips curved before he sauntered over to the other side of the drive to pick up a jar of her medicine, which was resting next to a rock. Then his smile disappeared as he read the label and his forehead scrunched for the first time since they'd met. 'Yours?' he asked, handing it to her, tugging the dog back as it spotted her best make-up brush lying to his left. 'I used to take this myself,' he added softly, picking up the brush and tossing it into her case. 'For insomnia and stress. If you need someone to talk to while you're here...'

Blushing, Paige snatched it and popped it into her back pocket. 'Thanks for your assistance, but I'm pretty sure I can deal with the rest.' She looked down at the young dog who was now slumped over Johnny's shoes snoring, his small pink tongue lolling out. 'Have you thought about training?'

The easy smile was back, although this time it didn't reach his eyes. 'I tried it, believe it or not, but it didn't work out... The dog's not just mine – my brother and I have divided the chores, and training is my responsibility. This is a timely reminder I need to sort something out.' He grimaced and jerked his chin towards his feet before bending to carefully pick up the fluffy bundle. The dog snorted and pressed its nose into Johnny's chest, its legs flopping this way and that, a picture of cuteness. 'Davey's on a mission to give me something to get serious about, so he got a rescue for us to share. To give my life some purpose, he says,' he confided with a wink. 'Just wait until he meets you.' He smiled again, then turned and waved before loping back onto the pavement and walking in the direction of the high street.

Paige watched him for a moment, her forehead crinkling. His movements were so familiar, the whole don't-give-a-damn, relaxed attitude raising her hackles. But there was still a flicker of interest in her belly which she was doing her best to ignore. Because she wasn't looking for romance or to be swept off her feet by a stranger; she'd been there and done that six years before, and just look how that had turned out. She frowned as an uncomfortable ache of grief settled in her throat. Squeezing her hands into tight fists, ignoring the bone-deep tiredness in her limbs, she took a deep breath, ready now to face her parents and all the memories in Kindness Cottage.

Chapter Two

Cora Dougall stood on the doorstep of Kindness Cottage for almost thirty-three seconds with her jaw wide open, before letting out a shriek and enveloping Paige in a hug which smelled of chocolate cake. 'Paige, it's been so long.' Paige hadn't seen her parents properly since they'd come to London for her husband Carl's funeral a year before – her fault, because she'd kept putting them off. The hug felt good, and she untangled herself quickly before the contact made her unravel.

'We weren't expecting you. You've lost so much weight, lassie, looks like I'm going to be feeding you up.' Her mam was round, with light brown hair, green eyes, and a smile that was sunny enough to warm an entire village. She peered over her shoulder at the car as Paige put the small – now shut – suitcase on the floor. Her mam looked older – the lines on her face had deepened – but her cheeks were still rosy and she looked good. 'Is my wee grandbaby with you?'

'She's sleeping. I thought I'd unload the car before we woke her up.' Paige scanned the familiar floral wallpaper in the hall and the shiny dark wooden floor, remembering Carl telling her how old-fashioned it looked when she'd brought him home just after they'd met. 'Is it okay if we stay? Just for a week?' she added quickly when her mam's cheeks bloomed. 'I can't be away from work for any longer,' she lied. 'You know how busy it gets in the summer, all those events.'

'I'm happy to have you for however long you'd like to stay.' Her mam's eyes twinkled with a sheen of happy tears, and she picked up Paige's suitcase and put it into the hall before Paige could stop her.

'Your da's working, but he'll be back later. He's going to be as delighted to see you both as me. Let's get you settled. We'll put you in your old room and Grace in the spare, it's all made up.' She headed for the car at speed and paused by the back window so she could stare through the glass. 'The bairn's grown.' Her voice was soft, but there was an ache in it and Paige forced down the feelings of guilt.

'Grace is a good girl,' she said softly. 'She'll be happy to see you.' Paige crossed the driveway to open the boot and grabbed a couple of the larger suitcases before her mam could get to them. Then she heaved them towards the house, stretching muscles that felt like they hadn't been used in months.

'There's a lot in here for a week, lassie,' Cora said, picking up a couple of the small remaining bags and following her.

'I was meant to exchange on the house I'm buying last week, but the owners delayed.' *For the fourth time in four weeks.* 'I'd given notice on the place I've been renting. We finished moving out this morning, and most of our stuff is in storage.'

Her mam cocked her head. 'Is there a problem?'

'No…' Paige soothed. 'It should all go through next week. I've been told that number forty-two is already empty. Mr and Mrs Easton are about to move to Dubai and are visiting their parents before they leave, so we can move in as soon as we complete.' She rubbed her forehead, trying to soothe the pain stabbing at her temples. It was just another thing in a long line of irritations she was having to deal with. 'It'll all work out,' she promised herself.

'Ach, you always were on top of things, lassie,' Cora chuckled, as she dumped the bags in the hallway and turned back to the car. 'Shall I wake the wee one now?'

Paige paused before nodding. 'Sure. She'll be happy to see you. She always loves your FaceTime calls.' She watched as her mam practically skipped in the direction of the car. Then Paige leaned her shoulder against the doorframe of the house, letting it hold her up for a moment. It had taken hours yesterday to move out of the rented house. She and Grace had slept on mattresses overnight, then they'd had the long drive up from London. Her stomach rumbled, reminding her she hadn't eaten for almost twenty-four hours. She just hadn't fancied anything. Eating had become more an act of survival than anything else.

Paige wandered into the house and veered right into the sitting room. Nothing much had changed since she'd left. The dark floors still shone as sunlight burst in through the deep windows, which were framed by thick pink patterned curtains. Two chesterfield sofas faced a fire and Paige remembered roasting marshmallows on it in the winter. To the right was her father's favourite leather chair, which looked a little more wrinkled and worn. Next to it was an oak bookcase, packed with all his treasured reads. She went over to the mantelpiece so she could check out the pictures in the frames. In one, her brother Matt stood beaming – he wore a black cape and mortarboard and was waving a PhD certificate in the air. Behind him, Paige recognised an arch from one of the colleges she knew he now lectured in at Cambridge. Beside that was a photo of her sister Rachel dressed in her judge's attire – she was frowning at the camera, her expression tense. There was an old picture of Paige in The Book Barn, surrounded by books, and another of her and Carl in a small silver frame. She was holding Grace; it had been taken the day she'd left hospital after giving birth and Carl had been late to pick her up. There had been a reason – she couldn't remember it now – he'd always had one of those. But even now she could remember the crushing disappointment as she kept checking her watch, desperately trying to soothe the fitful newborn.

'Mummy!' Paige heard the squeal from Grace as her feet thundered on the hall floor. Fixing a smile on her face, Paige turned just in time to see her mam and daughter enter the sitting room. 'I'm hungry,' Grace said, running up to hug Paige's legs, her curls bouncing around her shoulders.

'You're always hungry,' Paige teased, brushing a hand across her head, marvelling at where all those thick blonde locks had come from. Her own hair was shoulder length and reddish brown, without a wave in sight. Grace was beautiful, with light blue eyes, the same colour as Carl's. She'd been a good baby, had slept through from six weeks, gone to a childminder without complaint, ate everything that was put in front of her. She'd been the one thing Paige had excelled at in her life. She swept her daughter up and gave her a big hug before placing her wriggling feet back onto the floor. 'Let's sort out some lunch,' she murmured. 'I probably need to pop to the shops for something, I didn't have much food to bring from the house.'

'There's no need, lass. I've pasta and cake. They were always your favourites.' Paige watched as Grace grabbed her mam's hand, who smiled before leading her into the kitchen. Then she took one last look at the mantelpiece before following them both.

Paige lay on her bed an hour later, listening out for her daughter who was downstairs painting pictures with her mam. Cora had insisted she have a lie-down and Paige had reluctantly promised to have a quick nap, knowing Grace would be safe and occupied. Cora had been a teacher for years before she'd retired and started to work at the Christmas shop in Lockton. Her mam had a creative eye, so the house was filled with everything you could want for collaging, painting, knitting, colouring in, or pretty much any type of art. Grace had squealed with delight when she'd seen the supplies. Paige rubbed her forehead, wishing she had a magic wand to wipe away her constant headache. If she was in London she'd still be working, with one eye on the clock so she didn't miss Grace's six o'clock pick-up. Having nothing to do felt odd.

She let herself sink into the soft mattress and pillows, and took a deep breath, feeling sleepy. The bedding smelled of mountain air with a hint of wild lavender – the result of some kind of laundry alchemy she'd never learned. Her mind began to wander as she forced herself to relax and emptied it of her multiple to-do lists. But then her head filled with the house sale, job and all the ways she'd failed with Carl, and stress made her blood thunder in her ears until her eyes popped open and she sat up. She reached for her suitcase as she remembered she hadn't taken her pills, popped two and washed them down with the water she'd brought up from the kitchen. Then she got up and paced the space between the end of the pretty double bed with its silver bedposts and the large pine wardrobe. Her bags were still sitting beside it because she hadn't unpacked. She wouldn't be in Lockton for long enough to make it worthwhile.

She heard her da's voice in the hall as the front door slammed and she headed into the hallway, ignoring the weariness in her limbs, feeling excited but oddly concerned.

'Paige!' Marcus Dougall shouted as she ran down the stairs. He was a round man with a jolly smile – a policeman who had served Lockton and the local area for almost thirty years. He was wearing his uniform, having just finished work, and was currently on his knees hugging Grace, a picture of delight and surprise. 'Your nana called to say you'd both arrived and I've been so looking forward to coming home. We weren't expecting a visit.' He pulled back so he could look at his grandbaby. 'You've grown so much.' Grace giggled and hugged him back, her chubby arms circling his shoulders, making Paige wish she was three again. Her da looked up and their eyes met – his grin widened. He looked so much older than he had the last time she'd seen him, and her stomach squeezed with guilt again. 'Ah lass, aren't you a picture.' He scooped Grace up as he stood and walked over to give Paige a hug. He smelled of mountains and doughnuts – probably Cora had sent him to work with a lunchbox of his favourite treats. 'But you're way too skinny. Good job your mam's a genius at fattening her family up.' His features softened as he took in her face, and she could see the instant he noted the tiredness. He'd always been able to read her. When she'd been growing up, he'd been the one person she'd confided in. But when she'd eloped with Carl, the connection had broken and sometimes it felt like she had no one to talk to at all.

'I'm fine,' she said.

'Aye.' He frowned and she hugged herself, uncomfortable with his scrutiny. 'A holiday wouldn't go amiss. Your mam says you wouldn't even let her take your cases to the bedrooms and insisted on washing up after lunch.' He shook his head. 'You were always so independent, lass. Perhaps now you're here, you'll let us both fuss over you for a while. Aye, it's good to see you.' He turned back to Grace and ruffled her curls. 'Did you bring some books? Your mam always had her nose buried in one when she was a wee lass – are you a bookworm too?'

'Worm!' Grace squealed with delight, and Marcus tickled her tummy. 'Story, please?'

'She loves her books,' Paige said quietly. 'I brought all her favourites.'

'Excellent.' With Paige following behind, her da carried Grace towards the kitchen where the smell of her mam's chicken casserole wafted through the door. 'Then that's me set for the next few hours.' He laughed as Grace giggled again and leaned her head on his shoulder, and Paige felt an odd tug of gratitude mixed with guilt. When was the last time her daughter had relaxed in her arms like that? She was always too busy, trying to do so much.

'Perhaps after this wee one goes to bed, we can take one of our walks? It's been an age since we caught up.' Her da looked at her with far too much understanding.

'I still need to unpack.' Paige cleared her throat. Tomorrow, when tears weren't threatening to pour, she'd walk with him.

He smiled. 'Your mam and I can help with that – then we can take a short stroll after we eat. I've missed our walks. There's so much I don't know about your life now.'

Paige smiled as she followed her da to the dining room, knowing they'd go for that walk, but she wouldn't be confiding anything in him. Her secrets were all her own these days.

The sun was still high when Paige followed her da through the wooden gate at the end of Kindness Cottage's garden, into the lush open moorland that led to one of the sets of mountains which flanked the town. She stopped for a moment, taking in the view, and drew in a long breath.

'Aye, it gets you, doesn't it?' her da murmured, stopping to watch her. 'Every time I leave Lockton, I get a kick out of coming back. There's pink in your cheeks already, lass, must be the air.' He squinted. 'Not so pale, but too thin. You ate barely anything at dinner.'

'I wasn't hungry. I ate plenty on the drive here,' Paige lied, almost jumping as something brushed her leg. 'Braveheart.' She grinned, kneeling to tickle the enormous black cat under the chin as he whacked his plump tail across her calves, purring like a lawnmower. 'I almost forgot you'd be here,' she murmured. 'You remember me, boy? It's been years.' The cat was almost fifteen, but his coat still shone and from the looks of him, he still had his huge appetite. Braveheart nudged her leg once, then trotted back towards the garden, most likely in search of food.

'Do you remember when we got him?' her da asked, his expression brightening. 'You were around fifteen, and you borrowed all those books on cats from The Book Barn. You always had your head buried in something. Aileen Dalhousie said you were born to be a librarian. I know you felt the same for a while.' He coughed as Paige's cheeks flamed. It was a touchy subject. When she'd eloped with Carl, she'd left a lot of dreams behind – hers and those of Aileen, the old librarian who'd mentored her. She'd disappointed a lot of people. The guilt was still surprisingly fresh. When Aileen had passed away the year before, Paige had felt it keenly – and for an unhappy while she'd dwelled on what might have been, until she'd forced herself to stop. 'You read much these days?'

The change in subject was a relief and Paige began to walk, staring at the ground so her da couldn't see her face. It was bumpy, but the grass was so green, and in between scraggy tufts, pretty wildflowers sprouted. 'Not much, I don't have time.' She'd bought *The Magic of Making it Big* six months ago and still hadn't got past the first few chapters. 'What about you?' Books were a safe subject; her da could talk about them for hours. Back when Paige had lived at home, they often had.

'I'm still waiting for Charlie Adaire to write a new one.' The author was famous for his series of detective novels featuring a cantankerous shopkeeper/private eye. She was feisty, intelligent, relentless and always managed to catch the killer, no matter how devious or clever they were. His stories had become particular favourites of her da's after Aileen had introduced him to the series, and Paige had bought him a few of the older novels for Christmas the year before. 'Your mam got me some by a different writer from the library in Morridon, but…' He pulled a face. 'I couldn't get into them. Tell me about your job.'

'It's great.' Paige's cheeks burned with the lie. 'Busy – you know how it is. What's the latest from Morag Dooley and the Lockton grapevine?' She changed the subject again as something throbbed in her windpipe. That need to confess all, to talk about Carl, how she wanted to make up for all her failures. But she wouldn't give in to it.

Marcus paused before answering, and when Paige sneaked a look at his face, she saw disappointment. 'Ah, nothing much. She's got a cat, she'll bend your ear about that if you visit. I think Morag was lonely before Zora moved in. You should go and see her in the post office – she'll be bursting to interrogate you so she can spread the latest to the village.'

Paige laughed, knowing she wouldn't be going anywhere near the red-brick building.

'Your mam said the new house hasn't gone through?'

Paige shrugged. 'It will soon. As soon as we exchange, I'll head back to London. The solicitor told me it'll be within the week.' Her shoulders stiffened. The sale had been dragging on for months now, and Paige had a suspicion the solicitor had been lying.

'And… how are you coping, after Carl?' her da probed. Paige wiped her palms on her trousers, growing weary.

'Oh, you know, these things take time.' She forced out a bright smile. 'Shall we head home? It's almost time for Grace's bath.'

'Aye.' Her da turned. 'Let's do that.' He glanced back towards the mountains. 'We can walk again tomorrow, lass, there's still a lot I'd like to know.' His eyes caught hers. They were filled with concern and Paige swallowed, wishing for a moment that she could give in to the swell of emotion burning in her throat. Knowing if she did, she might not be able to stop…

Chapter Three

Johnny Becker sliced a cucumber in the large kitchen of Apple Cross Inn. The simple chopping motion was relaxing, and he ran his eyes over the metal countertops which were littered with dirty pots, pans, fresh herbs and other paraphernalia. The shiny silver cupboards above them were still hanging open from when he'd been gathering ingredients. When Johnny had run the chef's table in one of the finest restaurants in New York, every surface had shone like glass – and if anyone had left so much as a rosemary sprig on the floor, it would have resulted in a twenty-minute rant. He'd overseen a spotless kitchen and his team had spent most of their working hours stressed out and tense. Despite that, he'd had a reputation for being inspirational, if a little highly strung. Those words would probably have graced his epitaph if he hadn't had to crash out of the career he'd spent his twenties building after he'd collapsed and almost died: a heart attack brought on by stress and a faulty valve. He was well now, but the awareness of his fragile mortality was something that haunted him every day.

His insides clenched and then stretched out as he reminded himself those days were long gone. His mind strayed to the red-haired beauty he'd met on the Dougalls' drive almost a week before, to that visceral tug of attraction, before he remembered the bottle of pills that had spilled from her suitcase – a stark reminder of the life he'd once led, and a warning to keep things exactly as they were.

'What's the special?' Matilda Tome, who occasionally helped out in the pub, interrupted, dancing into the kitchen and winking lasciviously. She was in her early thirties, with curly red hair that she'd tied into bunches which trailed down her back.

'Prawn cocktail. Plus, we've got the usual baked potatoes, sandwiches and ploughman's lunch,' Johnny said, ticking the menu off on his fingers, feeling strangely flat. Three years ago he'd have been making dishes like cheese gougères, quail with caramelised onion and truffles, or lobster ravioli, which would have been accompanied by a glass or bottle of something from his restaurant's cellar of fine wines. The contrast hadn't jarred until recently. Why was that?

Matilda grinned. 'Of course, it's a Wednesday, I should have known – it's always prawn cocktail on a Wednesday.' She gave him another cheeky wink.

The door leading to the flat upstairs suddenly burst open and Johnny's twin, Davey Becker, came marching into the kitchen holding a white trainer with half the side ripped off.

'You didn't put Mack in his cage – he's been chewing everything he can get his teeth into.' Davey had the same blue eyes as Johnny, but a more wiry, athletic build. Their expressions were identical, so Johnny knew his brother was upset.

'I walked him over from my house and he was pooped when we arrived, so I didn't bother putting him in the cage. Plus, I checked on him a couple of times. We've been working on the chewing.' Johnny grimaced, remembering how many of his shoes now featured bite-marks. 'I wasn't expecting him to wake up and I wasn't expecting to be long. I don't like locking him up.' He checked the clock on the wall. 'I'm sorry. I guess it took me more time to get everything ready than I expected.' In truth, he hadn't exactly rushed.

Davey frowned as he surveyed the mess. 'Did you change the menu?'

Matilda snorted and smiled.

'Nope.' Johnny took in the cluttered metal counters. It would probably take him more time to tidy up than he'd spent on prep, but he didn't mind, he wasn't in a rush. Once he'd finished lunch, he planned to spend the rest of the day sketching before walking Mack again later.

Davey sighed. 'Well, this isn't the only thing that dog's eaten.' His brother's mouth flattened. 'Two of the cushions on the sofa have been annihilated. There are feathers everywhere and you're clearing them up.' He waved the shoe in the air like a weapon. 'I know you're trying to keep your life stress-free, John, but there's a difference between being relaxed and imitating the dead – I think you might have strayed too far in the wrong direction. I still don't understand why you weren't happy with the dog training course we set up…'

Johnny shrugged. 'I hated those classes. The whole thing was so rigid and strict. Mack hated them too, it just made him stressed. I've been trying some classes on YouTube.'

Davey glowered. 'Well, they obviously haven't worked. You promised you were going to talk to Agnes Stuart if I sorted out

Mack's check-up at the vet, which I've done. She got a rescue dog from the same place two months ago – roughly the same time as us. I've heard hers can even sit up and beg.' Davey glared at his ruined trainer.

'Fine. I promise to talk to Agnes,' Johnny said reluctantly, remembering how Mack had embarrassed himself on the Dougalls' drive. The hot burst of fury on Paige's face as he'd made off with her bra. And how attracted he'd been to the mystery woman. 'And I'll clear up the feathers.'

'Thanks,' Davey said.

'Before I forget.' Matilda, who'd been listening, spun on her heel as she headed for the door to the bar. 'Fergus McKenzie popped in earlier. He mentioned Tony Silver from that annual review guide, *Best Pubs*, is doing the rounds in the area soon. He heard it from one of his customers at the whisky distillery. Thought you'd want to know.' She gave them both a dazzling smile before disappearing.

'Wow, that is news.' Davey scrubbed a hand through his dark hair. 'Perhaps you could think about jazzing the menu up in preparation?' He shrugged when Johnny didn't comment. 'It would be great for the pub to get featured in that book. You know I've been thinking of adding onto the back, maybe opening a restaurant… This kind of endorsement could be exactly what we need.'

Johnny let out a long exhale. 'I'll think about it.'

Davey cleared his throat. 'I'm not expecting anything radical. But I hear Tony's partial to fish and likes it when pubs use local ingredients. We could get some salmon. Wasn't that in one of your signature dishes once?' He raised an eyebrow as Johnny felt a flare of interest, which he quickly shut down.

'There's no pressure, mate, but you might enjoy cooking something different? I know I've asked you a thousand times, but I'll say it again – I want you to be a full partner in the pub. Make it a family business.' There was a clattering sound above them and Davey looked up. 'Looks like Houdini might have broken out of his cage again.' He shook his head, half smiling. 'I'll see to him before he chews through the rest of my flat. Perhaps you could come up when you've finished and take him and those feathers off my hands.' With that he turned and left the kitchen, with the half-eaten shoe swinging by his side.

Johnny stood for a few moments, looking at the clutter on the worktops as his mind sifted through his favourite recipes. He had about a hundred things he could do with salmon – make fishcakes, poach, steam, grill, or fry it, adding various spices, fresh herbs, butter or a mixture of all of them, until it would melt in the mouth. But if he did that, and the pub made it into the guide, their clientele would expect something far more exciting than soup or a baked spud. Worse, Davey would keep pushing and pushing him to become a full partner. Then he'd be back to performing, driving himself to be better and better, stressing about everything being just right.

Did he really want to risk it? Weren't they fine as they were? He shook his head, then opened the dishwasher with a thump, before starting to pile the carnage inside.

Davey's flat was large and covered the whole of the pub's top floor. There was a huge sitting room, kitchen, bathroom and three bedrooms, one of which Johnny had occupied until about five months before. At that point, the tenant in the house Davey owned just outside the village had left, and Johnny had decided to take on the rental. It had been time for him to find somewhere for himself, away from the bustle of the pub and the siren call of the kitchen.

Johnny entered the sitting room and came to a sudden stop. The dark grey sofas and off-white carpet were covered in a mass of white feathers which stuck to every surface, including the mantelpiece, fireplace, windowsills and black lampshade hanging from the ceiling. 'Oh boy,' he murmured, stepping further inside. Mack was in a cage set back from the sofa, and as soon as he heard movement he let out a low whine. Johnny crouched and gave him a stroke through the metal criss-cross of bars, feeling a punch of emotion as the dog blinked his large brown eyes. 'I'm guessing if I leave you in there much longer, you're going to figure out how to escape again.' He sighed as he glanced around, marvelling at the scale of the mess. 'Way to go.' He shook his head. 'Looks like I won't be sketching this afternoon –instead I need to find the hoover and a seamstress to fix this lot.' Two of the dark grey sofa cushions had chunks taken out of them, but they could probably be mended by someone with the right skills. He'd pop into the post office later to get a number from Morag Dooley, as she had the inside track on everyone in the village.

Mack gave another low whimper and put his paw up to the cage, and Johnny felt a tug in his belly. He got up quickly and backed away. 'Oh no…' he murmured when the dog whined again. 'Stop trying to get around me because it's not going to work. We'll go for walks and have a good time – but I'm not falling for you. Don't expect that.' He frowned as Mack bared his teeth, mimicking a smile. 'Not going there,' Johnny said gruffly, clearing his throat. Then he turned and headed to the kitchen to find the vacuum, wondering exactly when he'd started to lose control of his safe and easy life.

Chapter Four

Paige blew out a long breath and shut *The Magic of Making it Big* on the same page she'd opened it to an hour before, placing the paperback onto the pine bedside cabinet and taking a moment to look around her bedroom. The curtains were still open but the sun had almost set, and the pretty pink colours of dusk made the mountains look almost magical. Her mam had put a vase of wildflowers on the windowsill yesterday afternoon, and the gorgeous smell from her small act of kindness had penetrated the space.

Paige breathed in their fragrance, wishing she could sleep. Grace had gone to bed at seven o'clock, and she'd heard the floorboards in the hallway squeak as her parents had headed up later in the evening. She got out of bed so she could look for something to distract her. Her clothes were still piled next to the wardrobe. She'd refused to hang them – somehow it would be an admission that she wasn't going back to London yet. She'd been in Lockton almost a full week. There was still no news on her house, and the HR manager at Premier Events wouldn't take her calls. Probably because she knew Paige would insist she was ready to return to the office. Paige stopped at the small white bookshelf to the left of the door and crouched, running a fingertip over the book spines. *Lord of the Rings*; *The Lion, the Witch and the Wardrobe*; the complete Harry Potter series; *Charlotte's Web*; *Wuthering Heights*; *The Great Gatsby*; *The Hitchhiker's Guide to the Galaxy*. It was like tracing a huge chunk of her life. All the places Aileen had introduced her to, all the adventures she'd taken, until Carl had appeared in her life. She sighed and picked up *Charlotte's Web* just as Braveheart sauntered through the door. He sniffed the air and hopped onto the bed, settling himself into the centre. Paige grinned and climbed in too, taking care not to unsettle him. Then she opened the book, yawning a little, and for the first time in six years, began to read. Moments later, her eyes began to droop.

*

It was dark, and the rain was coming down in thick sheets, obscuring the road. Paige looked out of the window of the car, feeling tears prick her eyes. 'I'm just asking you to help a little more,' she said carefully, using her calm voice so as not to upset Carl. He was driving the car despite the fact that she'd offered, frowning as he peered out into the rain. 'Grace is two and she needs her da. You're never at home.' She felt tired, bone-tired, and her stomach was hurting. She'd seen the doctor last week and he'd prescribed pills to help her sleep, but they hadn't worked.

'You know what it's like to work in events,' Carl snapped. He sounded annoyed and Paige wondered if this was the wrong time to have this conversation. He'd been rude at the party, disappearing frequently into the garden, taking shelter under a marquee his friends had put up so he could have a cigarette. Chatting with a pretty woman with bright red lipstick who looked about twenty.

Then again, he'd always sought out a woman at every opportunity – much like he had the first time they'd met. She put the radio on, deciding to park the whole thing until later, or tomorrow. But as the dulcet tones of Coldplay filled the car, Carl reached across to switch it off. 'It's not okay to walk away when the crew are still working. Just because you leave to collect Grace, doesn't mean the rest of us can.'

Paige pushed down the instant flare of annoyance. 'I have an arrangement, and I put the hours in, Carl, more than most. When Grace is sleeping, early in the morning, even at the weekends.'

'Putting your career before our daughter,' he hissed, shaking his head.

Paige let out a long exhale as the words wounded, glad he couldn't see her expression in the darkness. 'Grace is my priority – that's the reason I work when she's asleep or at the childminder. I also clean, cook, buy the food, do the bins, mow the lawns, take care of paying the bills because you never seem to have any money…' She felt a tear tumble down her cheek and swiped it away.

'Here we go again…' Carl grumbled, and Paige shook her head. There was no point in discussing it. She didn't even know why she'd brought it up. Carl had never wanted to be involved in the practical day-to-day running of their lives. He wasn't interested in fatherhood, and was even less interested in her. Recently, it felt like he barely wanted to work at all. Carl continued to stare at the road. 'I'm bored, Paige. You've changed and the work, I've been doing it for too long. This isn't the life I wanted. Before we met I was always out, working up and down the country. Living the kind of life I've always dreamed of. I spent months abroad. It's just the same thing every day now – the same person in my bed – and I'm finding it harder and harder to adapt.'

It took Paige a moment to absorb the stab of hurt. 'Being a parent can be difficult. I have days—'

'I love Grace, but I never wanted kids. I know you say she was an accident, so I don't blame you.' Paige bit back her retort. 'But I need time to think, to work on my creativity. Now it's all bedtime routines, story time with the same damn book over and over, getting her to nursery, child-friendly food, toys all over the house. We never go out.' He shook his head and put his foot down as they hit a B road, then whizzed around a corner without slowing. Paige decided not to comment, or ask when he'd ever so much as run their daughter's bath.

'You're out most nights,' she said quietly.

'What's the point in staying in? You either have your head buried in that laptop of yours or you're looking after Grace,' Carl moaned.

'Because there's no one else at home willing to do it!' Paige shouted, suddenly flooded with a hot spurt of fury. Carl turned his head in her direction, his face signalling pure annoyance. He opened his mouth and she knew he was going to settle into one of his familiar rants about how useless she was. Then a set of headlights flashed from the other direction and his head snapped back. That's when the whole world seemed to slow. Paige saw another pair of headlights and the lone rabbit in the middle of the road, its eyes shining white as they hurtled towards it.

'Shit.' The expletive said it all – Carl never swore – and he jerked the wheel to the left, swerving to avoid the stunned creature. Paige couldn't say what happened next. There was a crunch and a loud snap, a wild rocking motion like the ones you get on a theme park ride. She felt a sharp pain in her side, a strange sensation on her arm, and the world went black.

*

Paige woke and checked her watch. It was five a.m. and the house was totally silent. She felt hot and clammy, and reached up to swipe away the tear on her cheek. Her eyes began to focus and she looked around. There was the window to her right, the vase of flowers, the floral curtains that framed the sun coming up. She pushed back the covers and got out of bed, quickly shoving on a pair of shorts and a T-shirt. Her stomach grumbled and she grabbed her pills, creeping to the next bedroom to check on Grace, who was asleep, surrounded by a cloud of blonde curls.

Paige knew she had at least an hour before her daughter or parents woke, so she crept downstairs, intent on keeping herself occupied by going for a walk. The kitchen was at the back of the house. Her parents had put in new units since Paige had moved out. They were blue – her mum's favourite colour – and the counters and breakfast bar were a mottled granite. A window above the butler sink let in the morning sunlight, picking out about fifty empty jam jars lined up along the counters on each of the four sides of the room. By the end of the summer, Paige knew they'd all be full and her mam would have gifted at least half to friends around the village. She ignored the ache in her throat as she recalled sitting and reading at the edge of the counter while her mam pickled onions and made her famous chutneys and jams. She remembered the delicious scents that drifted from the large pots as they bubbled on the stove. Those were the days when the merest sniff could whet her appetite. She hadn't eaten jam for years, or spent quality time with her mam in just as long. Coming home – let's just say it was the equivalent of taking a can opener to the emotions she worked so hard to contain.

Paige opened the fridge and frowned at the contents, assessing the huge selection of food before closing the door and grabbing a banana. She ate a few bites as she washed the pills down, jumping as something fluttered against her leg. 'Braveheart.' She grinned, kneeling to tickle him under the chin. As soon as the cat's bowl was full, he flipped up his tail and ignored her. Paige watched him eat for a few moments, then grabbed her handbag and stepped out.

The air smelled fresh, and Paige could instantly pick out some of the summer fragrances: strawberries from her mam's small allotment in the back garden; lavender that lined the front border of the house, attracting bees; and honey. Her da kept beehives at the back end of the garden to the right of the gate which led to the mountains, tucked away behind his potting shed. Paige had often helped him gather the harvest when she'd lived at home. She frowned when the memory made her think of Carl, who'd hated anything that wasn't in fancy packaging with a price tag to match.

She picked her way along the narrow pathway to the iron gate, opening it carefully so as not to make a noise, then headed right towards Lockton High Street. Her insides were still churning from the dream, her head filled with all kinds of regrets. She took a deep breath as she walked, switching her speed from sluggish to her usual brisk pace. The sky was a pretty bright blue that highlighted the mountains in the distance and on both sides, and the whole view made her feel like she was strolling into a warm hug. Buttermead Farm was on her left now, and she knew it would only take about another fifteen minutes to reach the first shop on the high street. When she did, everything was closed and the pavements were empty. She strode past Meg's Christmas shop and cafe, stopping to peer in through the window. Her mam had worked here part-time for eighteen months now and had a soft spot for the owner, Meg Scott. Cora sent decorations down to Grace on a regular basis; small, sparkly packages filled with glittery magic that her daughter loved. A little act of kindness Paige barely noticed in her busy life.

Next was Apple Cross Inn, the pub where Johnny had said he worked. Paige felt a tug in her chest when she thought about his sharp blue eyes and the way he'd laughed. How angry she'd been when his dog had scattered all her possessions. Had she over-reacted? Carl had once accused her of having no sense of humour; had he been right?

The pub was double-fronted with a white facade, and there were colourful flower baskets hanging from hooks on either side of the navy door. Fairy lights had been strung across the front and Paige imagined they would light up prettily when the sun went down in the evening. Further along the high street was the village hall which had recently been renovated. She stopped to watch a starling sweep overhead, flying towards the back of the village hall where Paige knew the primary school was located. Behind that sat The Book Barn, where she'd worked with Aileen. Curious, Paige followed the pathway which ran parallel to the village hall and ducked behind the school. There was a narrow entrance surrounded by foliage – much like Sleeping Beauty's castle might have looked after a hundred years.

She pushed through leaves to find an open doorway and pursed her lips. Surely the library should have been locked?

'Hello…' Paige stepped into the large entrance. The building smelled of fresh paint, and as she moved further inside she could see one of the high walls gleaming a vibrant white, which was highlighted by the sun streaming in from rectangular skylights positioned across the vaulted ceiling. The rest of the walls hadn't been touched, and were still the dirty beige colour Paige remembered from six years before. A stepladder stood on a large white sheet but there was no sign that anyone had been working recently. She felt a warm draught on the back of her neck as she wandered further inside, turning to see if she could work out where it had come from, but the door had already blown shut. She looked around the room. Gone were the rickety old bookshelves she'd spent hours poring over, and in their place were boxes and boxes of flat-packed shelves in a rustic wood. Paige spun on her heels – where were the books? There were no posters, rugs, beanbags, or quiet nooks for readers to while away the hours in either. Had someone sneaked in and stolen the lot overnight? Her forehead scrunched; daylight robbery didn't happen in Lockton, and night-time robbery didn't either. She reached for her mobile just as the door to the small office behind the reception desk opened and Morag Dooley strolled out.

'Ach lassie, you scared me half to death.' Morag tapped her brown cane on the floor and leaned on it before checking her watch and fluffing up her mass of grey curls. She was wearing a bright pink dress with long sleeves in almost the exact shade of her lipstick. 'I heard from your mam you were visiting. It's early, is everything all right?'

Paige shook her head. 'Where are the books?' she asked, spinning a finger in the air, taking in the floors and walls.

Morag's mouth crinkled into something resembling a smile and she tipped her head in the direction of the office. 'Packed away in there, along with everything else. It's very cramped.'

'Why?' Paige asked, looking around and frowning. The counter between them was the same one she'd worked at once, scanning books, music and movies, chatting with visitors. She'd loved her shifts in the library; the smell of paper, meeting the people who'd come in to borrow something or just to seek solace amongst the books for an hour. You could learn so much about a person from the things they read. She took a deep breath; she hadn't realised how much she'd missed being here.

'It's been cleared so we can redecorate.' Morag frowned at the unpainted walls. 'It's taking a little longer than we anticipated. Ach, it's been looking tired for years, lassie. When Aileen passed just over a year ago, the library shut. There was no one here to look after it.' She perused their surroundings as Paige nodded. Now she was here, she could remember the old woman so clearly, her long, white hair and sharp brown eyes. Aileen had been kind and intelligent, and a living encyclopaedia of books. There wasn't a person alive who the librarian couldn't find the perfect book for – she'd often said the right choice had the power to change someone's life. Occasionally, when Paige was in London, feeling stressed out and worn down, her mind would wander to The Book Barn. She'd conjure its smell, memories of chatting with Aileen, and think about all the books she'd read and recommended. 'The Book Barn was too shabby to reopen,' Morag continued. 'A few of us applied for a grant from

Creative Scotland, which we got. Your mam, Agnes and I are the trustees. Tom Riley-Clark, who does odd jobs around the area, has been helping with the painting as a favour, but he keeps being pulled off to other projects and he's working on a huge one now. I've no idea when he'll be back.' Morag's eyes lit up as she focused on Paige.

'It's great you're trying to get the library reopened.' Paige cleared her throat, backing up a little. 'Do you have a new librarian?'

'Ach, we've advertised a few times, but the right person hasn't materialised. Your mam, Agnes and I planned to set aside some time to work on getting this place open, and to advertise again, but with the annual Jampionships coming up, we haven't had a moment. I expect we'll get to it eventually.'

Paige looked around the half-finished room.

'We need a person who knows what they're doing, with an interest in reading.' Morag waggled her eyebrows.

'I hardly ever read now,' Paige muttered.

'Someone who could organise events, really bring the place to life. We're offering a fair salary… and Aileen's cottage is for sale at a good price if the new librarian needs a place to stay. There's plenty of room for a wee bairn.' She stared pointedly at Paige, who began to shake her head.

'I wish you luck,' Paige said, looking around and imagining the shelves filled, the way the place might smell. Remembering how she'd set up story time, and read to children on Saturday afternoons. How much pleasure it had given her to hear them giggle and see their faces light up. Much like Grace's did when she opened a book. But she didn't have time for things like that now; she had to create a secure future in London for her and Grace. To pursue the career she'd been building. 'I'm sure someone will be interested.'

'Aye, lassie. I expect they will. If you can think of anyone in the meantime, you give me a shout.' With that Morag winked, turned on her heel and headed back into the office, leaving Paige staring after her, wondering what the strange fluttering feeling in the pit of her stomach was all about.

Grace was giggling, and Paige forced herself awake as she realised she'd fallen asleep reading *The Hitchhiker's Guide to the Galaxy* in her parents' garden, lying on a sun lounger on the edge of the round patio. It was early afternoon and her daughter was playing chase with her granda, dodging between the sunflowers Cora grew in pots which lined the edges of the flower beds, shrieking as he caught and tickled her. 'Stop, Granda,' she chortled, before running back to a small table on the patio that Cora had set up, which was covered with paper and crayons. 'Mummy!' Grace must have noticed Paige was awake, because she picked up Paws – her greying floppy bear. Paws had been a constant companion since her first birthday, and a security blanket since her father had died. The toy had a zipped compartment in the front in which Grace kept her special treasures. She unzipped it now, pulling out a folded piece of paper which she shoved towards Paige, watching as her mother carefully unfolded the drawing. It featured a series of colourful squiggles and a large black box.

'It's beautiful,' Paige cooed.

'Cat!' Grace pointed to the largest black squiggle before twirling around and pointing at Braveheart, who was sleeping on top of the garden shed. His ears pricked but he didn't move. 'Mummy!' There was a long pink rectangle lying in what Paige guessed was grass, because the scribbles were green. 'House!' Grace finished, prodding the black box, before running squealing back to where Marcus was waiting, ready to chase her.

'Yes, our new house – it's not quite ready for us to move into yet.' Paige traced a fingertip over the box, smiling as her daughter giggled again when Marcus swept her up. Then she sighed, remembering her conversation with the estate agent two hours earlier.

'I'm sorry,' the man had said in his no-nonsense voice. 'The sellers still haven't signed the paperwork. They're on holiday now so it could be another two weeks.'

'I haven't got two weeks,' Paige had grumbled.

'It's out of my hands,' the man had declared, before taking another call.

Paige traced a finger over the square box again. Number forty-two was small, but big enough for the two of them. She hadn't fallen in love with it, but it represented the first rung on the ladder to security and success. The foundation of her new life with Grace. She looked up when her daughter squealed again; it had been a long time since she'd heard her laugh so often. It was the only silver lining to staying in Lockton for longer. Paige let out a long exhale, wondering what she was going to do for the next two weeks to stop herself from going mad.

Chapter Five

The Jam Club met every Thursday evening in the village hall, which was situated halfway up Lockton High Street. The group had met in Apple Cross Inn during the summer months the year before, continuing right into February because the hall's roof had leaked, soaking the carpets and paintwork until the building had become unusable. The villagers had put on a concert on Christmas Eve, raising enough money to replace the whole thing, so now they were back in their rightful place.

Johnny had joined the Jam Club in the summer the year before, and since then had made sure his Thursday nights were free and Davey was available to sit for Mack. He wasn't sure why he kept attending. Perhaps because it was the one time he gave his creativity in the kitchen free rein? Although he rarely shared his attempts with anyone; seeking approval was a slippery slope. He arrived late, so there was only one seat left at the front of the room. Four rows of chairs faced the top table and almost all of them were full. He ignored Morag's frown as he slumped into the vacant space, immediately noticing Paige Dougall who was sitting on the seat beside him. He hadn't seen her since the Friday before, but had heard on the Lockton grapevine that she hadn't left the village yet and he'd had to stop himself from seeking her out. There was something about her that he was drawn to – a fragility he wanted to fix. He'd not felt this pull for years and the sensation unsettled him.

She had a pad resting on one knee and a pen poised above it. Her shoulders were tense and her forehead looked scrunched – reminding him of his own reflection in the mirror just three years ago. She didn't turn to look at him, but Johnny could feel the tension coming off her in waves and had another urge to reach out, which he ignored.

'Thank you to everyone who arrived on time…' Morag said pointedly, her eyes skimming over the crowd and resting on Johnny. The founding members of the Jam Club – Morag Dooley, Agnes Stuart and Cora Dougall – were all sitting on the top table, with a selection of unlabelled jams on display in front of them. Johnny knew from past meetings that everyone would have a chance to sample them during the evening. It was one of his favourite parts of the meeting. He enjoyed trying different flavours and discussing the various tastes, picking out ingredients and getting excited about unusual combinations that worked.

A door slammed and Johnny guessed who the latest visitor was without turning because of the way Morag's face dropped. Jason Beckett ran the large library in Morridon, a town situated fifteen miles outside Lockton. He'd visited the Jam Club just over a year before when he'd been dating Evie Stuart, who was currently sitting in the second row. Evie was now married to American firefighter Callum Ryder, who'd moved to Lockton to be with her, and they'd recently started a family. But Jason still turned up to the Jam Club meetings from time to time, intent on impressing them all with his vast knowledge, newly acquired from whichever book had caught his eye. He scoured the crowd before he sought out a chair at the back of the hall and grabbed it, bringing it to the front of the room and arranging it next to Johnny's.

Morag linked her fingers on the table and he could see her knuckles were white. 'Now we're all here…' she said, frowning. 'Perhaps we can kick off the meeting by talking about this year's Jampionships.' Lockton hosted an annual competition which brought hopeful jam makers from far and wide across Scotland, intent on winning the prestigious first prize. She glanced at a folder on the table. 'The tickets are selling well, despite it being just over three weeks away. The judges have been selected, including our very own expert.' She winked at Cora, who blushed, her attention darting to Paige who was staring at her skirt.

Where was the little girl Johnny had seen in the car a week before? He glanced around, but the rest of the hall was empty. Probably Paige's father, Marcus Dougall, was on babysitting duty. Or perhaps the child's own dad, Paige's husband or partner, had arrived? The thought made Johnny uncomfortable and he glanced at her left hand, which was bare of jewellery, feeling a flare of irritation when the knot in his stomach smoothed out.

'I'm seeking volunteers to direct people to the marquee when they arrive. I'm sure you'll all be happy to offer to help out.' Morag glared at the assembly, daring them not to put their hands up. Johnny chuckled, and found himself raising his. 'I'm also expecting a lot of you to enter. You can take a form at the end of the evening, or fill one in online. Meg and Evie, as last year's winners you're exempt.'

She pointed to the middle row, where Evie and Meg sat shoulder to shoulder. 'Paige, perhaps you'd like to have a go as you're here?'

Paige's head jerked up in surprise, her auburn hair shining under the overhead lights. What was her story and why was she still here? 'I'm… I think, hope, I'll be back in London by then.' Johnny could hear a thread of uncertainty in her tone. She looked back at her knees as she avoided Morag's searching gaze.

'That's a shame, lass.' Morag turned to him. 'Johnny, I'd like to see an entry from you. Something a little more ambitious than the last attempt.' She raised an eyebrow, but he didn't comment. He was used to Morag nagging about his boring menu in the pub, and in truth his strawberry jam the year before had been very average, despite the last-minute addition of fresh mint. Even as he'd been decanting it into a glass jar, he'd known his old self would have been pouring it into the compost bin, muttering in disgust.

'I'll be entering,' Jason said loftily, folding his arms. 'I've been reading a lot of books on making jam. My library is full of them. There are some cutting-edge techniques you might not be aware of?' His voice lifted at the end, as if he were hoping one of them would ask him to elaborate. 'I suppose, with the library still being shut, you don't get the same opportunity as me to do research?' He surveyed the top table.

'Aye, but if we get really stuck, there's always the internet. I find there's a fair amount of material on there if you know where to look.' Agnes gave Jason a wide smile as Johnny tried to suppress a chuckle. Beside him Paige let out a soft laugh. Perhaps there was a sense of humour under that solemn expression after all?

'Nothing beats a book though, does it?' Jason pressed, his brow furrowing. 'Is there any news on The Book Barn opening again?' He smoothed his brown hair, patting his wayward curls into submission. He had a cherubic face, which Johnny had heard a customer in the pub call handsome once – at least until Jason had ruined the illusion by opening his mouth. 'I've a friend who works for Creative Scotland. She mentioned you'd had trouble finding someone suitable to run it. Must be a pain for you after getting all that grant money?'

Morag's lips tightened, her pink lipstick puckering into an 'o' shape, making Johnny lean back in his chair as he waited for the explosion. 'We've had plenty of interest.' Her voice was ice. 'But we're waiting for the right person. We don't want just any old eejit running the show.' She paused for a beat, glaring at him. 'It's only a matter of time before we find someone.'

He shrugged. 'Remember where I am if you need a hand with interviewing or getting the place up and running. As I mentioned to my friend, I've plenty of experience. In many ways, I'm surprised no one has asked me to help. I've lots of ideas.' He looked around at the crowd, his expression earnest. 'For instance, I've implemented a zero-tolerance policy in my library, including fines for laughing or talking during story time – and lifetime bans for bending the corners of pages.' He shuddered. 'It's made a huge difference in just a few months, particularly amongst our younger members.' His lips puckered. 'Although attendance has been down in that demographic recently, probably because of it being holiday season.' He smiled again. 'That's just one of the many things I could bring to a library like Lockton's. Don't forget I'm here if you need any assistance.'

Cora rubbed Morag's shoulder as the air around her seemed to fizzle and crack, and there was a low murmur of concern from the back row. 'Why don't you tell us more about those jam recipes, Jason?' Cora said.

Jason's forehead wrinkled in concentration. 'I found all sorts of tips. The correct temperature for heating sugar, for instance – 140 Centigrade or 284 Fahrenheit – so many people get that wrong.' He shook his head. 'Also, there are a huge number of ingredients no one ever thinks of using.' He puffed up his chest, seemingly oblivious to the waves of resentment coming off the top table. 'There were some easy fruit recipes if you're looking to improve your basic skills.' Jason turned back to Johnny, who had a sudden urge to bark out a laugh as he remembered some of the chutneys and jams he'd created in New York. Then again, few people in the village knew much about his past beyond that he'd worked in some large restaurants before moving here. It wasn't common knowledge that an article in the *New York Times* had referred to him as a rising Daniel Boulud, and another as Gordon Ramsay without the potty mouth. 'There's the most amazing recipe for Prosecco and pomegranate jam, with a twist for when you've a little more experience. Perhaps you'd like to see it, as inspiration for when you're a bit more advanced?' He paused until Johnny nodded, concealing his grin. 'There are another few recipes I won't be sharing until after the Jampionships, of course.'

'Um, thanks,' Johnny murmured, his tone barely hiding his mirth. 'I'll bear that in mind.'

They were saved from any more of Jason's advice by a door slamming. Johnny turned as Lilith Romano, head chef at Lockton Hotel, which was located a few miles out of the village, came marching in. Lilith was Italian, with coal-black eyes and a glossy mane of dark hair that she'd wound in a large bun on the top of her head. She wore jeans and spiky heels which rapped on the floor, and a silky red shirt that shimmered next to her olive skin. She was a beautiful woman and Johnny's brother, Davey, was crazy about her. Until just after Christmas, Johnny had suspected she'd felt the same about him. But while their relationship had progressed slowly over the festive period and into the New Year, they'd suddenly stopped dating the day after Valentine's Day and Lilith had avoided the pub ever since. Word was, Davey had asked Lilith to move in with him and Matilda had overheard them arguing about it; but the rest of the fight had been muffled, suggesting they'd moved rooms. News of the end of their fledgling relationship had spread across the village – although no one, not even Morag, knew the full details. His brother had flatly refused to discuss it even with him.

'Will you be entering the Jampionships this year, Lilith?' Morag asked, as the chef grabbed another chair and started her own row for one at the back of the hall.

'No.' Lilith shook her head. 'My parents have announced they are sending a manager to help with my work at the hotel – he arrives tomorrow morning. I've no time for competitions…' She blew out a breath and shifted awkwardly in the chair. Johnny knew from Davey that Lilith's relationship with her family was complicated, and they'd threatened to send someone in to take over the hotel from her at Christmas, citing concern at the lack of guests. 'It's not busy at work at the moment, so I thought I'd see what the plans for the Jampionships are in case they affect our clients.' Lilith's eyes darted to Johnny, before skimming across the rest of the chairs. Then her mouth dipped, perhaps because Davey wasn't there?

'Then I think it's about time we all stopped blathering and I told you more,' Morag said loudly, and clapped her hands.

Johnny watched the various members of the Jam Club wave goodbye before filing out of the village hall, as he picked up his empty tea cup and carried it to the kitchen. He should probably leave, but he wanted to check Paige was okay. She'd been quiet during the rest of the meeting, but he'd seen her pressing the pencil between her fingertips so tightly against the pad that the lead had broken in two, then surreptitiously scraping the flakes onto the floor. He knew that feeling of stress, how sometimes it felt like the world was squeezing your shoulders until the tension made you want to scream. He knew he should probably avoid her, but he couldn't stand by and watch someone go through that without offering a kind word.

'I could have strangled the eejit,' Morag grumbled, as he entered the bright yellow room. She chucked a dark blue mug into a bowl of bubbly water and attacked it with a cloth. 'Coming into the meeting, offering his advice…' She slammed the mug onto the stainless-steel draining board, splashing water and bubbles onto the tiles behind the sink, then picked up a side plate.

Agnes patted Morag on the arm and gave her a bright smile. 'Ach, there's no point in getting yourself in a tizz about it. Jason's a fool.'

'A fool with friends in high places,' Cora said quietly, frowning. 'At least if he's telling the truth.'

'He is,' Morag growled, thumping the plate down, making Johnny stand back in case it shattered. 'I had a call from a Ms J. Martin at the post office this morning. Apparently she works for Creative Scotland. She wants to visit The Book Barn in a week – she'd like an update on the redevelopment and launch plans. She suggested it would be good if we gave her a tour. She mentioned Jason, and I've the strangest feeling' – she pressed a hand covered in soap suds against her chest – 'that when she sees how behind we are, she might suggest he gets involved. There's a clause in our grant contract which says she can appoint a supervisor...'

'Then we need to get the library open before she arrives,' Agnes snapped. 'Jason's a harmless enough soul, but I don't want him implementing all sorts of rules and regulations here. No one in the village will want to go to The Book Barn if he does.' She rolled her eyes. 'Aileen would be turning in her grave if she got wind of it – and you know how I feel about troubled souls.'

'I agree, but how can we open in a week?' Morag shrugged. 'The Jampionships are taking up so much of our attention at the moment. I could do a few hours in the evenings, but I'm sure that won't be enough.'

'If only there was someone in Lockton who was at a loose end,' Agnes murmured, looking around the assembled group and stopping when she got to Paige.

'The lass is having some time off,' Cora said firmly. 'She's owed holiday from work; she's only here until her new house goes through. Marcus and I are enjoying our wee grandbaby, and she's supposed to be relaxing and having fun.'

'Helping get the library open could be both relaxing and fun,' Johnny said, wondering what had possessed him when all four women turned to ogle him. What Paige did with her time was none of his business, but her cheeks flushed and she seemed to perk up.

'I... I am free at the moment,' Paige said, looking at him strangely. 'In all honesty, I could do with a project. I'm going to be here for at least another week and I'm not used to having so much free time. I've got experience of working in the library and putting on events, so I'm sure there's lots I could do to help set things up.' She looked more animated. 'But it has to be on the understanding that I'll be going back to London as soon as I exchange on my house.'

'Of course,' Agnes said, winking at Morag and Cora.

'If you want to do it, I can keep Grace busy,' Cora said. 'I've been promising her a visit to Meg's shop. She can spend a few hours helping me put baubles out tomorrow. There's plenty we can do in the next week.'

'That's a good plan.' Morag finished washing up, emptied the bowl and leaned back against the sink unit, her attention switching to Johnny.

He held up his palms to indicate he wasn't getting involved, amused by the spark of determination in her eyes. He knew he'd lost even before he opened his mouth, but the game amused him. Morag was appalled by his aimless existence, and along with Davey, she was one of the harshest critics of the way he lived his life. 'I'm busy, I have a job,' he said.

Morag dismissed the comment with a flick of her wrist. 'That doesn't take you more than a few hours, lad. The lassie can't do everything in the library by herself.'

'I can,' Paige said firmly, glancing at Johnny before she blushed.

'There's painting, building the bookshelves – and there are about a hundred of those. Tom was supposed to do it but he's working at the McKenzie Distillery – and I happen to know that's urgent work. There are tables, computers and books that need putting out – I can't make head nor tail of Aileen's filing system. But I do know it used to work.'

Johnny frowned, wondering why the idea of spending time with Paige appealed so much.

Beside him, the woman in question let out a long-suffering sigh. 'I'll be fine. I remember the filing system and don't need any help. I'm sure Mr Becker has more important things to spend his time on. Dog training, perhaps?' Her tone was light but Johnny felt a little put out by the obvious dismissal. He watched as Paige turned away and put her pad on the counter so she could scribble on her notepad.

'Ach.' Morag let out a puff of disgust. 'The lad's always at a loose end. He spends half his days walking up mountains and the rest in the pub kitchen, stirring the soup he bought from my shop.' She gave Johnny a stern glare, which would have withered a lesser man, but her comments still stung. 'I can't believe you'd turn us down, laddie.'

Johnny looked at Paige, who was still hunched over, scribbling. 'Of course I'll help.' It would be interesting to get to know her a little more. To learn the story behind those tight shoulders and the permanent frown that darkened her looks. He wasn't going to acknowledge the strong pull he felt towards her – the intense desire to spend more time in her company. 'I enjoy painting.' He cleared this throat. The easy flow of the brush, the impact a new colour could bring to a wall. The process was relaxing. 'But I'll need to have Mack with me,' he added. 'I can only imagine the mischief he'd get up to if I left him home alone.'

'So can I,' Paige murmured. 'I'll make sure to keep my underwear out of sight.'

'Not on my account,' he joked, earning himself another dark glare.

'That's settled then.' Agnes's attention ping-ponged between Paige and Johnny, and a sparkle began to form in her eyes.

'I'm really happy to do it myself.' Paige turned, her voice sharp with annoyance. 'I work best alone.'

'It's fine,' Johnny said, smiling despite himself. 'Morag's right, I do have time.'

'Then I'll drop in the keys off for you later, lass.' Agnes grinned, her expression filled with mischief – and Johnny wondered in that moment if he'd just made a very big mistake.

Chapter Six

Paige watched as Grace pored over her picture book at the table, the morning sunlight from the window in her parents' kitchen picking out golden flecks in her blonde hair. The moment her daughter had been born, Paige had fallen for her. The fact that Carl hadn't felt the same had filled her with sadness, and it had been the first hint that their marriage was in trouble – a truth that Paige had never been able to fix, no matter how hard she'd tried.

Grace looked up from her book and studied the table, which was empty aside from her empty glass and plate. 'Where's your work, Mam?' she asked, looking serious. 'You look sad,' she murmured, her light blue eyes filling with concern. 'Do you want to cuddle Paws?' She pointed to the bear sitting on the chair to her right.

'I'm okay.' Paige forced a smile, fighting the tiredness which made even talking feel like hard work. She still wasn't sleeping and the dreams about Carl were haunting her every night.

'Your mam's going to help set up the library in the village, it's a very important job. She's probably just thinking about what she has to do first.' Cora walked into the kitchen carrying a wicker basket under one arm. 'I'm heading off to work myself in a moment, cherub, do you fancy coming to help?'

'At the Christmas shop?' Grace gasped, her body shuddering with delight.

'Aye.' Cora smiled.

'Yes!' Grace jumped up from the table before grabbing Paws and running to her nana. 'Will I see Santa?'

Cora laughed and stroked her head. 'I'm not sure if he'll visit today, but there'll be a hot chocolate and as many Christmas decorations as you can carry, if you're a good lass.'

'I missed Santa last year – Mummy had to work,' Grace confided. 'But he didn't forget me on Christmas Day.'

Paige swallowed the guilt. She'd been planning to take the afternoon off, but there'd been a problem at one of the events and she'd ended up working late, begging her childminder to keep Grace a little longer than usual. Then when she'd tried to rebook a slot in their local grotto, she hadn't been able to get one and it had all been too late. Grace had been fine about it, but Paige still hadn't forgiven herself. She'd thought her daughter had forgotten, but clearly three-year-olds' memories were long.

Cora gave Paige a quick nod of understanding. 'Ach, that wouldn't have been the real Santa anyway – I hear in December he never leaves the North Pole.'

'Really?' Grace's mouth pursed with the kind of derision only a toddler could muster.

'Meg knows him personally. She'd love to meet you,' Cora said. 'And I'm sure we can find you a few important jobs to be getting on with at the shop.' Paige watched as her daughter grabbed her mam's hand, trying to remember the last time Grace's face had lit up like that. Their days had become a long list of chores and structured routines with little time for fun. Her mam stopped by her side before they left, and gently patted her shoulder. 'I left some lavender oil in your bathroom, lass, in case you wanted to have a wee soak before you head out.'

'Thanks,' Paige murmured, as the unexpected kindness made her well up. 'See you later,' she called as they headed out of the door. Then she cleared the dishes from the table, thanking fate that the library had come along to fill her long days so she didn't have too much time to think.

Paige pulled another box out of the small office in The Book Barn and let out an audible sigh as she perused the beige walls of the large room, taking in the piles of bookshelves which had to be set up. She should have known Johnny wouldn't turn up. She'd told him she'd be there at nine a.m. sharp and it was already half past ten. The whole thing sparked another hundred memories of Carl, far too many to shut out – late arrivals, unexplained hours when he vanished into thin air, how carelessly he'd treated any plans that involved her or Grace. How worthless he'd made her feel. She shook her head. It didn't matter that Johnny wasn't here. Hadn't she learned the hard way that she had to rely on herself?

She went to grab a second box of books, wishing she'd packed a screwdriver for the shelves, and came to an abrupt halt as she noticed two paperbacks stacked on the library counter next to the till she'd set up earlier. Their spines faced outwards so she couldn't read the titles. Had they been there the whole time? She took a steadying breath, wondering if she was losing her mind, or if the pills were making her head fuzzy.

Dappled sunlight from the skylights drew Paige's attention to the ladder which was still set up in the corner. She sighed – if she was working alone, the walls would need to be finished before she put the shelves up. Paige marched into the back office where she'd seen a pot of white emulsion, a tray and some rollers. The dark green overalls piled next to them were far too big, but she'd brought an apron from her mam's kitchen which she tugged on. She ground her teeth as she marched back into the main room, kicking off her shoes before popping the tin of paint open and giving it a thorough stir. She poured a small measure into the tray, then pushed the ladder closer to the wall, making sure it was still on the sheet. She picked up the tray and roller again and climbed carefully, pleased she'd worn a pair of old trousers and a tatty shirt. Irritation made her skin prickle and she took a deep breath as the acid in her gut burned. Then she leaned forwards and swiped the roller across the wall, working quickly through the thin layer of paint in the tray, covering over what felt like a thousand good memories.

There was a bark from the entrance and suddenly Mack came bounding inside, skidding through the library before haring like a greyhound around the empty space. Johnny sauntered after him as if he had all the time in the world. He wore jeans and a dark T-shirt with 'Take Time to Smell the Roses' emblazoned across the front. It stretched across his chest, picking out muscles Paige wouldn't have expected, which triggered an unwelcome flutter in the pit of her belly. He came to an abrupt stop when he saw her on the ladder, then his eyes shot to Mack as the dog, clearly bored of tearing around the carpet, spotted her.

'No, Mack. Stop!' Johnny shouted as the dog made a beeline for the ladder, and his paws connected with the bottom rung. He might be small, but the impact made the ladder wobble and Paige's foot slipped. Then she started to tip backwards because she hadn't been holding on.

'No!' she shrieked as she fell down, gripping the roller and paint tray as if she somehow expected them to help. She stiffened, bracing for the crash, when suddenly Johnny swept her up, pulling her away from the ladder as the breath was knocked out of her lungs and she hugged the paint tray to her chest. 'Woah,' she said, as his arms tightened around her shoulders and legs. The sensation of being held released a bubble of awareness. 'Put me down.' Overwhelmed, she started to push at Johnny's arms.

'You're welcome,' he said, smiling, dropping her to her feet. He looked a little off balance himself as he shoved his hands into the pockets of his jeans and shook his head at the dog, who was watching them. 'Apologies for being late and sorry about Mack. You didn't need to start without me.' He looked at the ladder before glancing down again. 'You read the books – you don't eat them,' he said to Mack, clipping a lead onto the Retriever's collar before dragging him away from the pile of paperbacks. 'Sit!' The dog remained standing and stared upwards with his tongue lolling out.

'I didn't think you were coming,' Paige said primly.

Johnny shrugged. 'I had to prep for lunch in the pub. It's a simple menu and one of the bar staff, Matilda, has agreed to take over serving, plating and heating everything up – so I'm all yours until this evening, and it'll be the same for the rest of the week.'

'You're the chef?' Paige asked, surprised. She would have expected him to spend his time on the other side of the bar.

Johnny frowned. 'Chef is a very fancy word for what I do, loaded with all kinds of expectations. My shepherd's pie always goes down well.' He went quiet for a moment, as something like disappointment swept across his face.

'Oh…' Paige searched for a response. 'I wasn't expecting you to be here that much.' The jolts of attraction, the way her body reacted to his, was irritating, and at odds with everything her head was telling her to feel.

Johnny grinned. 'I'm far too scared of Morag not to put in the hours.' He glanced around the room. 'I'm guessing if we want to open next week we've got our work cut out.' He smiled when Paige frowned, surveying the small tower of fiction, cookery and travel books she'd set out earlier before glancing again at the ladder and the paint tray and roller she was still holding. 'Looks like you got started early.'

'I was here at nine as agreed,' she said archly, choosing not to admit she'd arrived well before the appointed time. 'If you're serious about helping with the painting, there's a set of overalls in the office.' She held out the painting equipment and he grinned before taking it.

'Sit!' Johnny tugged Mack back again as the dog crept closer to one of the cookery books, perhaps attracted by the glossy cupcake on the spine. 'I'll change and take this rascal with me.' As he headed past the counter with the pooch in tow, he paused to pick up one of the mystery books. '*Best Pubs.*' He shook his head as he leafed through the pages, stopping to read a few of the entries. 'Fish, fish, fish – should have figured as much. Was my brother Davey here earlier?' His expression soured.

'No, why?' Paige asked, surprised by the sharp look of annoyance that flared across Johnny's face, which seemed so out of character.

'No reason.' He put the book on the counter again and grabbed the other one, holding it up so Paige could see it. '*An Idiot's Guide to Relaxation.*' His face transformed as a grin took over. 'I borrowed this just after I moved in with Davey – you don't need to be an idiot to follow it, but it probably helps. It definitely didn't mention anything about getting a rescue dog.' He scowled at Mack, but even Paige could see the spark of baffled affection in his blue eyes. 'I'm guessing someone decided to play a joke on us.'

'Or it's a coincidence. Morag probably left them out. I noticed one of the boxes had been opened in the office.' Paige watched as Johnny turned and headed into the back room, before she opened one of the boxes she'd carried out earlier. She scribbled into a notebook, adding each book to the inventory as she unpacked.

Johnny returned a few minutes later, dressed in the overalls which fitted him like a glove. He tied Mack to one of the legs of the main counter and tossed him a chew toy in the shape of a bone. 'That should keep him occupied for' – he checked his watch – 'at least four minutes. After that it's every man and woman for themselves.' He grinned again, returning to the office to pick up a larger roller before placing it on the floor beside the tin of paint.

Then he pulled a screwdriver from the pocket of the overalls and passed it to her. 'I thought this might come in handy.'

Paige took it and twisted it between her fingers, surprised he'd thought of it. Carl had never been observant. But perhaps not all men were like him after all?

Johnny turned back to the ladder. 'I've not done this in years. I think the last time was when I redecorated my first restaurant.' Mack barked as Johnny moved the ladder to the right and poured more paint into the tray. 'A team of us worked day and night for a week.'

'Restaurant?' Paige asked, turning to look at him.

Johnny shook his head. 'Another life.' He was on the fifth rung balancing both the tray and roller on the edge of it. He looked like he knew what he was doing, but Paige wondered how long it would be before he got bored. He pulled out his mobile. 'Mind if I put on some music?'

Paige shrugged and he pressed a button. Something soothing filled the room; it was quiet because he didn't have speakers, but the low buzz made her feel oddly relaxed. They worked in silence, with Paige unpacking more of the books while Johnny painted, doing a surprisingly decent job of covering the beige. After what felt like ten minutes, he climbed down from the ladder. 'Looks good, and it won't take much longer until I've finished the first coat on this wall. Mack needs a quick walk. I was thinking of grabbing us coffees – and I could pick up something for lunch?'

'Already?' Paige squeaked, checking her watch and doing a double-take. They'd been working for an hour and a half, and even the wayward mutt had been quiet for most of it. She got up and stretched, trying to work the kinks out of her neck from when she'd fallen. 'I'd like a coffee, please, but nothing to eat.'

Johnny frowned. 'I'll hunt something down – I'm sure I'll find some food you fancy. Feeding people is kind of my thing.'

'I'm fine,' she muttered as he grabbed the dog lead and walked out, still wearing the overalls – Paige found herself lingering on his long limbs and the curve of his bum before she realised what she was doing and turned away. She grabbed the two books from the counter and added them to one of the piles on the floor, before heading into the office to grab another box. She paused to scan the little room. It was the same beige as the main library, with a small desk and filing cabinet. Lined up against it were fifteen boxes of books still waiting to be unpacked, two computers, a stack of chairs and a set of tables which would need to be set up. Beanbags and poster rolls had been placed beside them.

'*Ciao?*' Paige heard a shout from the front of the library. The Italian woman who'd been at the Jam Club meeting was kneeling beside the pile of books. She looked up as Paige approached. '*Sì*, you are here.' She pointed to the mounds on the floor. 'I heard the library would be open soon – I thought you'd be further ahead.' She rose slowly; her dark skirt showed off a pair of legs that Carl would have described as shapely, and a set of heels that were almost half the height of Paige's calves.

'There's a lot to do.' Paige folded her arms. 'You're Lilith?'

The woman nodded, her dark eyes glittering as she scanned the room. 'Lilith Romano, I run Lockton Hotel.' She paused and her shoulders drooped. 'Ran. It's under new management as of today, courtesy of my papa. I found these when I was creating space for the eejit in my office.' She held out a bag to Paige. It contained three books: a paperback edition of *Surrounded by Idiots*, a colourful tome on Italian desserts with a picture of a tiramisu on the cover, and a book from the non-fiction section on difficult family relationships. 'I borrowed these from Aileen.' Lilith looked around. 'I thought I'd return them since I was passing. You have some help getting things ready to open?' She shook her head when Paige began to open her mouth. 'I wasn't offering. I need to use one of the computers, *sì*?'

'Don't you have any at the hotel?' Paige asked, almost biting her tongue when she realised the question was a little rude.

Lilith shrugged. 'I... need privacy.' She gazed at the empty space where the computer tables used to be. 'Will everything be set up soon?'

'Yes,' Paige said. 'We'll be open next week and at least one computer will be ready to use.' She'd make sure of it. 'Feel free to drop by then. It's going to be a soft launch; we'll organise something bigger when the new librarian's been recruited.'

Lilith frowned as she spotted the ladder. 'Tom is helping you paint?'

'Nope. Johnny Becker from the pub. Long story,' she added when Lilith raised an eyebrow.

'Is Davey helping too?' Lilith's lips parted a little.

'No.' Paige shook her head.

Lilith let out a long sigh. 'I will see you again next week.' With that she left.

Johnny returned ten minutes later with a subdued Mack, two coffees and a hamper. He handed Paige a coffee and whipped a bright red blanket out of the square box then placed it on the floor, tying Mack up at the counter where the dog settled down to sleep. Johnny began to unpack the food, serving it up onto plates. There were sandwiches, sausage rolls, crisps and grapes. 'I couldn't rustle much up with so little time. I thought if I brought a few different things, something might whet your appetite.' He looked up as Paige began to unwrap the cardboard from one of the shelving units, placing the instructions to one side. 'You need to stop if you're going to eat.'

'Thanks, but I'm fine.' Paige took a sip from her coffee. It was hot and strong, and the sudden shot of caffeine made her feel a little lightheaded. She placed the cup on the floor beside her and opened a pack of screws which had been attached to the flat-packed shelves.

'No appetite?'

Butterflies swirled around Paige's body as she realised he was watching her. 'I ate a big breakfast,' she lied.

'Want to talk about it?' he asked quietly. 'I have it on good authority that talking helps.'

'Nope.' Paige turned to look at him and lifted her chin. 'You're a stranger, why would I?'

Johnny shrugged. 'Sometimes strangers are the best people to open up to.'

Paige frowned. He was sitting on the large blanket, watching her. There were piles of food around him, far too much for both of them to eat.

She checked her watch. 'Exactly how long do you expect to spend on lunch?' Her tone was sharp, but instead of being offended he grinned.

'I've always enjoyed taking my time over food. But if you join me, I promise not to take too long.' He picked up an empty plate and held it out to her. Paige sighed and took it, then sat on the opposite end of the blanket, selecting a sandwich and nibbling at the corner. It tasted of cardboard; nothing seemed to taste good these days. She put the plate down as he bit into a sausage roll. 'What's your favourite food?' Johnny asked, staring at her fingers, which were drumming on the blanket.

Paige shrugged. 'I eat on the run. Look, we haven't got time—'

'To eat?' His eyes were clear and a little too penetrating. 'You really don't like to let yourself relax, do you? Why is that?'

'Because…' She stopped, wondering why she felt this sudden need to unburden herself. It was like something was building inside her, had been since she'd arrived in Lockton and walked with her da. It was probably being so far away from London. But she had no intention of letting anything spill out. 'Not everyone cares about food,' she said bluntly, wiping invisible crumbs from her clothes.

Johnny quirked an eyebrow. 'Now that's just not true. I feel like I've been thrown a gauntlet. As a former chef, I've got to tell you that's going to be difficult to resist. Food can be very seductive if you let yourself go…'

Paige felt something deep inside her knot as her eyes met his. 'A sandwich is not seductive, neither is a sausage roll. The cereal I grab when I'm on the run is about filling an empty stomach, routine and necessity. You're not going to convince me otherwise.'

Johnny gave her a playful smile and leaned forwards. 'Depends on who gets their hands on the ingredients.' He stared at her for a moment and then his forehead furrowed. He jerked back and took a long breath, breaking eye contact.

'Hello!' Paige almost clapped when she heard Morag's shout from the entrance. 'Ach, you've done well…' The old woman glanced at their picnic as she walked over, before taking in the freshly painted wall. 'I popped in to see how you were getting on, and to tell you the events company has arrived in town to put the marquee up for the summer dance – just in case you notice a lot more people in the village. They're setting it up extra early this year because the preschool want to use it for sports day to stop the wee ones getting burnt in the sun.' Morag's gaze drifted to Paige and she felt a prickle at the back of her scalp. She grabbed her coffee and took a sip so she had something to do with her hands. 'There are a few hot toddies amongst the team; there've been a lot of fluttering hearts in the post office.' Paige's throat pulsed as she blinked, waiting for Morag to continue. 'It made me think about when you met your Carl.'

'I'm sorry,' Paige murmured, jerking to her feet, feeling dizzy as she stood. 'I've just remembered something I have to do.' She didn't wait for a response, and instead headed out of the library and into the warm air.

'I didn't mean anything by that, lass.' Morag's voice followed her out. 'Where are you going?'

But Paige didn't want to stop. Her stomach was roiling; it was as if all the emotions she'd spent the last year trying to suppress were threatening to spill out – and she wanted to be alone when they finally did.

Chapter Seven

It was light outside and warm. The sky was blue, and there were ribbons of cloud scattered across the sky and horizon. Johnny stood at the end of the narrow pathway at the edge of the high street, looking around before he spotted Paige. She was sitting on a small bench facing the road, which had stunning views of the mountains. Her chest was heaving and she was staring at the ground. He dropped onto the bench beside her, and she jumped. Her eyebrows rose to her hairline as she turned to look at him. She had pretty eyes; he hadn't had a chance to look at them properly before. Probably because she'd been shooting *I want to kill you* vibes in his direction since they'd met. Now he could see them up close, he realised they were brown with flecks of gold. 'You okay?' he asked. 'I feel like something just happened in there. Morag felt bad – she offered to take Mack to the post office so we could talk.'

'You don't know? I thought Morag would have given you the full lowdown. She probably has a PowerPoint presentation and leaflets to give out.' For the first time, Johnny heard the faintest hint of a Scottish accent in the lilt of Paige's voice.

He chuckled. 'I'm sure I'll get to see those in the post office tomorrow. If not there, someone will show me in the pub. It's the way of village life. None of us get to keep our secrets. Do you want to tell me the story yourself?' He shrugged, taking care not to sound too interested.

Paige's shoulders straightened. 'It's not a secret. I met my husband when he was here putting up the marquee for the Jampionships six years ago. He was from London and he worked for the events company. That's why Morag mentioned him just now. I fell head over heels, and we eloped. I was twenty-four, and he was ten years older. It was a bit of a scandal, the whole village was up in arms. I think that gossip kept my ears burning for at least three years.' She crushed her hands into fists, put them to either side of her and leaned forwards. She was very slim, and seemed impossibly small next to him.

His mind wandered to the moment she'd fallen from the ladder and he'd caught her in his arms. How good she'd felt… He pushed the memory away and smiled. 'I can't see your ears, but they aren't glowing through your hair, so Morag's definitely not talking about you now – besides, Mack's not much of a conversationalist.' Paige didn't look up and she didn't laugh. 'Small communities like to talk and that's quite a story.' Her mouth compressed. Was that why she took the pills? A bad marriage, or guilt – anyway, why did he care? 'Is your husband coming to join you soon?' The words bumbled out before Johnny could stop them. Then again, he'd always had a masochistic streak.

Paige's head shot up and her eyes met his. They were cold; the golden flecks had all but disappeared. 'He's dead.' She swiped at a stray tear that had leaked onto her cheek. 'A year ago now.'

'I'm sorry.' Johnny fought the urge to reach out and touch her shoulder, to offer comfort. Paige let out a shuddery sigh and waited.

It was almost like he could see the whirl and click of her mind, sense her need to unburden herself.

'And it was my fault,' she continued, her cheeks blanching as she stared at him. 'I've never told anyone that.' She jerked her chin up, looking confused.

He kept his expression blank. 'I told you. Sometimes it's easier to talk to a stranger.' He shrugged. 'Perhaps because it doesn't matter what we think?'

'I don't like talking about it.' She swallowed. 'I saw a counsellor for a couple of months after, but…' She shook her head. 'I thought it would just be easier to forget. But it's not, is it?' Her dark eyes darted back to his. 'You don't know what I'm talking about.'

'I might.' Johnny took a deep breath. 'But that's not important. I'm happy to listen if you need to talk now.'

'You said the same earlier, bet you wish you hadn't.' Her fixed smile was grim and he could see the tears threatening to fall. Johnny's insides clenched but he didn't move or speak. He wasn't sure why. He didn't avoid pain in others, but he didn't normally invite it either. Yet there was something about Paige… 'I'm leaving soon. I never intended to come for long and I've got a life to get back to. A job. It's important to me.' Something that looked like confusion crossed her face and disappeared.

'I meant it…' Johnny said, gulping. She looked like she wanted to say something else so he waited. He wasn't in a hurry to go anywhere. He'd used up all his hurrying years before. Now his life was about savouring time. If she needed a stranger to talk to, he'd give her that, and not because he was attracted to her. 'Tell me what happened.'

She blew out a breath as if determined to expel her errant emotions. 'It was raining really hard. Carl was driving us home from a party and it was dark.' Paige slowly flexed and unflexed her fingers. 'I said something and he got mad. I tried to change the subject because I was worried he wasn't watching the road properly. He'd insisted on driving.' She shook her head. 'He liked to be in control. It was such a stupid comment, I shouldn't have said it. I'd only started the whole thing because...' She exhaled loudly and looked down. 'That's not important.' Her eyes shot to his. She wore an expression he recognised, although he wasn't sure from where. It signalled a kind of desperation, a need to unburden and confess all. Perhaps she hoped talking with him would somehow alleviate whatever emotions she was finding it difficult to put aside?

'Go on,' Johnny nudged, when it looked like she wasn't going to continue. Paige looked at him for a few moments, her shoulders ramrod straight. The corners of her mouth pulsed and Johnny wondered if she was going to refuse. Then she seemed to deflate, as if the fight had suddenly gone out of her.

'He was distracted and he wasn't looking at the road. Then, when he did, he had to swerve to miss a rabbit of all things. I've no idea why he tried to avoid it; instinct I suppose. He hated rabbits. He hated almost every kind of pet.' She slumped lower on the bench. 'I never used to understand why, but now I think it was because they represented the kind of effort he wasn't prepared to put in. That's not important either, and I'm not talking ill of him. He was a good man, in his own way, and I cared for him, in mine.' She paused and shoved her hands across her face, giving herself a moment. 'He lost control of the car and hit a lamppost. When I woke up, I was in the hospital and he was gone…' Her eyes glistened.

'You feel guilty?' Johnny asked quietly, digging deep for the right thing to ask.

She considered the question. 'I don't know what I feel. I'm devastated he's gone – for Grace, and for the tragic loss of his life. He didn't deserve that.'

'That's tough,' Johnny said softly. 'You miss him?'

She took a bottle of water out of her bag and sipped a little. 'We were married for almost five years, and we began to argue a lot after one. He wasn't faithful.' She pulled a face. 'But our lives were intertwined, especially after I got pregnant. We had Grace and she needed both of us and I felt, *knew*—' She swallowed again. 'I knew I could make it work if I tried. Plus I was doing so well at work, making a name for myself. We worked in the same events company. He took me away from Lockton, showed me the kind of life Grace and I could have. I thought if I gave it time, we'd find a way through.' She stopped, and Johnny wondered if Paige realised she'd just admitted to staying in a marriage because of her career. 'But now he's not here and everything's gone wrong. All the things I've been trying to build – the house, security for Grace, my career.'

'What's wrong with your career?' Johnny asked.

Paige looked down at the ground. 'I've been signed off from work for four weeks. Stress…' She raised her arms and dropped them, letting out a long exhale. 'I still have no idea why I'm telling you this.'

'Signed off with stress?' It was worse than he'd expected.

Paige nodded. 'I collapsed the week before last at an event, ended up in the hospital.' When Johnny opened his mouth, she waved away his words. 'That sounds dramatic. I'd skipped a couple of meals and hadn't been sleeping, forgot to take my pills, that's all. Normal stuff.'

Johnny cleared his throat. 'Depends on what normal means to you.' He knew about that need to push harder and harder, knew all about kidding yourself.

'I plan to go back to the office just as soon as the house I'm buying goes through.' She massaged her temples with her fingertips and frowned.

'Problem?' Johnny probed.

Paige shrugged. 'The owners are stalling and I've got this bad feeling.' She looked at him sharply. 'You won't tell my mam any of this.'

Johnny zipped a finger across his mouth. 'Stranger's honour. Believe it or not, that's a thing.'

Her shoulders relaxed. 'I don't even know what I'm doing here. I should be in London, except I'm homeless and jobless right now. But life doesn't always turn out the way we want, does it? No matter how hard we try.' She sounded so sad.

Johnny leaned forwards, put his elbows on his knees and looked out at the mountains. Even now the colours, the sheer quiet of the moment, took his breath away. 'Sometimes. Perhaps we need to figure out what it is we want before we decide,' he said quietly.

'When you're in your thirties you have to know, or the whole world will overtake you and leave you behind.' Paige let out a long breath.

'What do you want?' Johnny asked, wondering what Paige would say if he told her he was thirty-five and had given up everything.

'I want to be great at my job, I want to be the world's most amazing mother. I want to give Grace a house, security, a perfect life.' Her forehead squeezed. 'I want to be a success, for my family to be proud, I want people to look at me and want what I have.'

'I want to be happy,' Johnny said quietly, still looking at the mountains. 'To have time to enjoy it.'

'If I have all those things, I will be happy,' Paige whispered.

Johnny didn't say anything. He'd been there, done that, felt the same. Until he'd almost died.

Chapter Eight

Johnny grabbed a handful of coriander and added it to the griddle pan where the chicken was frying. In the corner of the kitchen, by the back door, Mack let out a pitiful whine and glanced meaningfully at his empty bowl.

'You just ate – my dinner and yours,' Johnny muttered, feeling surprised and irritated again that the four-legged beast had managed to grab his beef sandwich from the counter in the four seconds he'd had his back turned. He added a few more spices to the pan, hoping Paige would enjoy the sharp splash of heat, remembering their conversation on the bench this afternoon. He wanted to find some small way to soothe her. He only hoped getting her to eat would help. She hadn't been forthcoming about the food she enjoyed, although he'd learned a lot of other things about her. Probably more than he wanted to, since he was cooking for her – drawing himself out of his hiatus after three years. Then again, there was something about that drawn expression he related to, and trying to tempt someone to eat was a long way from his old life.

The charred chicken turned the perfect shade, and he shifted the pan to a board on the kitchen counter as he contemplated the dishes he'd planned over the evening. Fresh guacamole dotted with tomatoes and slices of onion would go down well with the pitta he'd just baked, and would warm first thing in the morning; a fresh salad filled with rocket and baby tomatoes would complement the chicken when it cooled. He'd make the guacamole and salads in the morning and finish it all off by tossing the whole thing in his special dressing which was ready in the fridge. To top it off were his chocolate chip muffins, which had once been described as a 'triumph' by a particularly critical food writer. If those didn't tempt Paige's appetite, nothing would.

The doorbell rang, and Mack let out a bark of delight and went scampering ahead of Johnny, skidding across the kitchen, past his cage and through the large sitting room. The room was furnished with two brown leather sofas that faced a fireplace and a fluffy red rug, along with an assortment of lamps and pictures that belonged to Davey. Johnny knew it was his brother before he opened the door. Call it a sixth sense – they'd always been close. Which was why he knew Davey was coming to grill him. His brother looked shocked as he stepped over the threshold and his nose caught the scent of food.

'You've been experimenting?' He patted Mack's head before marching ahead into the kitchen and peering into the pan. 'Not fish?' He looked disappointed.

'This isn't for Tony Silver.' Johnny shook his head. 'I just felt like making something new.'

'You haven't felt like cooking for three years.' Davey grabbed a knife and fork from a drawer and sliced into the chicken before trying some. 'I'd almost forgotten how good you are. A diet of baked potatoes, tinned soup, chilli and shepherd's pie does that to a man.'

He sniffed. 'Are those muffins?' He eyed the tin on the counter and Johnny placed his palm on the lid.

'If you leave now, I'll let you take one with you.'

'Nice try.' Davey shook his head and pulled out a bar stool, glancing around the kitchen at the pots and pans piled tidily on the wooden counter beside the sink. 'I'm still not used to you living here.' He sighed.

'The place is still yours. I'm only renting it because your last lodger Tom moved out.' He shrugged. 'And because I thought you and Lilith could do with some time alone.' In truth, he'd outgrown living with his brother. Renting from him was the next best thing and meant he could have his own place without the commitment of a mortgage. Plus, back in January he'd wanted to give Lilith and Davey's blossoming relationship a place to grow. Shame it hadn't worked out.

'Yes, well…' Davey grimaced. 'The flat feels empty now I'm alone.' He looked down at Mack who was pawing at his jeans. 'Even when Houdini here visits on one of his seek and destroy missions, it still feels too big.'

'Still missing Lilith?' Johnny asked gently, opening the lid on the tin and handing his brother a plate and one of the muffins, as a wave of sympathy engulfed him. His desserts had made grown men cry. Perhaps this one might finally help his brother open up?

Davey bit into it and let out a low hum of pleasure.

'I saw Lilith at the Jam Club yesterday – apparently her parents have sent a manager to oversee the hotel,' Johnny confided.

Davey shook his head. 'I knew that was a possibility but wasn't sure they'd go through with it. I've no idea why she puts up with them.' He grimaced. 'But I'm not talking about it.'

Johnny rubbed the back of his neck. 'Then I must have lost my touch. Not enough chocolate chips?'

His brother shrugged, licking crumbs from his fingers. 'You've not cooked anything like this for ages. I think perhaps you're rusty. I guess if you practised more – created a new fish dish perhaps – you'd find your mojo again?' He grinned.

Johnny opened his legs wide and leaned against the counter, trying to relax. 'I'm not being obstructive and I don't want to let you down.' He folded his arms across his chest, aware even as he did it that he was feeling defensive. 'I just feel…'

'You don't want to put yourself in the position of being judged again. You're afraid if you do this one thing, it'll open up a whole can of worms and suddenly you'll be working day and night trying to build an empire, treading on anyone who gets in your way – leaving a trail of souls in your wake?' Davey smiled sweetly and took the last bite of muffin, before wiping crumbs from his chin.

'Not exactly – and that's an exaggeration – but…' Johnny shook his head as his mind drifted to Paige. 'It's taken me a long time to find myself, to understand what it takes to make me happy. I enjoy my life – the pace, the fact that I can do what I want when I want without anyone judging me or expecting anything. It's so much easier not to care. I just…'

'Sometimes feel like it's not enough?' Davey asked. 'Like perhaps something is missing?' He snatched the tin and grabbed another muffin, and Johnny resigned himself to the fact that he'd have to bake another batch.

'I think this twin connection is getting tired. If you could just step out of my head for a moment,' he snapped, feeling grumpy.

Davey shook his head. 'I'm only saying I understand why you want to take things easy, to have time to smell the roses. You were only thirty-two when you nearly died.'

'Twice.' Johnny took another muffin from the tin and bit into it. Okay, now it was official – he hadn't lost his touch. The realisation made him happier than he'd expected. 'From a heart attack partly brought on by stress.'

Davey pursed his lips. 'I think the undetected heart defect might have had something to do with it.' He pointed a finger at Johnny's chest. 'That's fixed now. But I do get it.' He shrugged. 'I've watched Lilith struggle with a similar thing. That pathological need to succeed, no matter who or what gets hurt or left behind. Including me, unfortunately. That's not something I want to be a part of all over again. Being a spectator sucks.' He took in a deep breath and let it out. 'Which still doesn't mean I want to talk about her,' he added, when Johnny started to ask. 'But the thing is, you can still cook and make a name for yourself without driving yourself so hard. I'd be there with you. We could build an extension onto the pub, open a restaurant – employ a team if we do well. I know we've had this conversation a hundred times, but I want you to think about it. You're not yourself, John. You were never a person to sit back and let life pass you by. Even when we were kids. You wanted to tear down walls, build new ones. To make the world a better place – one chocolate dessert at a time.' He eyed the last muffin in the tin with a twinkle in his eye.

Johnny shook his head. 'And look where that got me. I lost everything.' He winced. 'My restaurant, my fiancée. Because I cared so much about succeeding – about being the best – it almost killed me. I think some people are just built like that.' Paige was. He'd recognised her as a kindred spirit the instant they'd met. Perhaps that was why he felt so drawn to her? 'I don't want to risk getting caught up again.' Mack put his paws against Johnny's knees, perhaps sensing the emotion in his words, and he stroked the Retriever's head, feeling instantly calmer. 'Life's easier if I don't let myself care about anything too much…'

Davey let out a long sigh and shook his head. 'You're wrong. When you realise that, I'm hoping you'll change your mind.' His eyes shone when Johnny backed away. 'At least think about the fish dish – if you can make muffins like these, you can handle a paltry change of menu.' He held up a hand when Johnny frowned. 'I'm just asking you to think about it. But you need to be all in, or we won't do it at all.' He shrugged. 'That's not my choice, but I'm not here to make you unhappy.'

'Fine.' Johnny sighed. 'I'll see what I can do. I don't want to let you down. I want the pub to be a success, but…'

'You don't want to be dragged down a path you're not willing to travel?' Davey smiled. 'We're twins – believe me, I get it. I don't want to see you almost killing yourself again either. But you've got to let yourself care about something, John. Otherwise, what is life about?'

'Sunsets, sunrises, long walks, taking time to savour every moment,' Johnny said wistfully.

'Alone.' Davey frowned at Mack, who was now chewing the edge of the doormat by the back door. 'Unattached and uninvolved, aside from a wayward dog who was forced on you. That's not much of a life.' He sighed.

'It's the only one I want,' Johnny replied, knowing he was lying to himself.

Chapter Nine

Paige's head ached, she hadn't slept well again and her entire body was aching, but she held her head up as she strolled past Meg's Christmas shop. There was a bark and she turned to see Johnny waving from a few metres behind her, not far from the entrance to Buttermead Farm. He was wearing a navy T-shirt with the words 'Live More, Worry Less' in white lettering across the front. He held a large bag and the fluffy Golden Retriever trotted at his heels. At least today the dog was on a lead. She glanced left then right, hoping to find somewhere to hide or duck into, feeling a lead weight in her belly as she realised there was nowhere to run. After her confessions yesterday afternoon, she'd been hoping Johnny wouldn't turn up to the library, suspecting he'd make an excuse. An emotional meltdown was enough to scare most people off; Carl would have run a mile. She steeled herself as he approached, stepping back when the dog tried to leap up and put its paws on her thighs.

'Mack.' Johnny pulled at the lead. 'Sit.' The mutt ignored him, choosing instead to attack his shoelaces as its tail flipped back and forth like a flag in a tornado. 'We're still working on that elusive concept "obedience", but I've a secret ace up my sleeve involving Agnes Stuart.' Johnny tapped a finger against his nose, as his sharp blue eyes moved up to take in Paige's face, resulting in an almost instant flood of heat to her cheeks and a million other places. 'I popped into the farm before going to the pub to see if she was around, but she's out with Fergus. You're up early.'

Paige nodded. 'I'm heading for the library, thought I'd better get started since we only have five days until we open. Besides, I could say the same of you.' In truth, she was surprised. Johnny hadn't struck her as the type of man to rise with the sun. Carl hadn't usually wanted to surface until after noon. Which had been a strain after Grace was born.

He gave her a wry smile. 'My body clock's faulty. I've been working on it since I moved to Lockton, but come rain or shine I wake at five without fail. A curse for a man whose mission in life is to take it easy.' He glared at the dog, who was still chewing his shoelaces. 'Although it was probably a good thing this morning, because Houdini here had escaped from his cage again and managed to find his way into my kitchen bin and the compost.' He shuddered.

'Yuck,' Paige murmured.

'Let's just say the whole house needed a bath, and leave it at that.' He scraped a hand across his head, and Paige could see his hair was wet at the ends.

She glanced down the high street in the direction of the library, feeling her cheeks burn as she remembered her confession from yesterday. If she'd left home about ten minutes earlier, he'd never have caught up to her. 'Um… I probably should get going.' Once she got to The Book Barn she'd shut herself away in the office, or find some other way to avoid him. Johnny had seen inside her head now. He knew more about her than any other living soul and that made her feel vulnerable.

'Or we could pretend we've never met?' Johnny said quietly. 'I can see you're feeling awkward, and I'm guessing it's because of what you told me yesterday. There's no need, but the heart isn't always logical, is it? I find it's best to just work with that.' He offered her his palm. 'I'm Johnny, I work in Apple Cross Inn as a cook most days, but at the moment I'm helping to decorate the library. I like hiking, daydreaming, chocolate muffins, and I've been known to forget entire conversations overnight.' He looked serious. 'This is Mack.' He pointed down to the dog, who was now tangling with its tail. 'He's ornery, and has an unhealthy attraction to beef sandwiches, bra straps and used tea bags. And you are?'

Paige stared at him for a few moments before taking his hand and shaking it slowly.

'I'm a little confused,' she said quietly, feeling slightly off balance, surprised at how easily he'd read her. She was even more surprised that she could feel herself starting to relax, despite the promises she'd made to herself moments earlier.

'Interesting name,' Johnny said, his eyes sparkling as she mustered a tiny and unexpected laugh. 'Shall we walk?' He moved to stand beside her and pointed along the pavement. 'I believe we're going in the same direction. And since we've only just met, we'll chalk that up to a lucky guess.'

Paige smirked, but fell into step beside him.

'I'm going to Apple Cross Inn,' he continued. 'I've got to help prepare lunch before I head to the library. I don't want to be late – the woman who helps out there will skin me alive if I am.'

Paige snorted, looking at the pavement.

'I've got some library books in here, and I made lunch for later – there's far too much for one. I know we've never met, but perhaps you'd like to share? I have it on good authority my chocolate muffins are to die for.' He held up the huge bag, and Paige found herself noticing the way his T-shirt stretched across his lean, muscular chest. Something shot through her, that glimmer of attraction she'd felt yesterday, and she instantly tamped it down, peering into the bag. It was filled with an assortment of tins and tubs, the red picnic rug from yesterday, and a flask of what she hoped was coffee.

'If you eat that much every day, your T-shirt's not going to fit soon.' She glanced at the hamper, realising she was halfway to flirting with him. It had been a long time since she'd been so at ease in a stranger's company. Was it because he reminded her of Carl? Or because she'd unburdened herself to him so completely?

'I hoped I might share it with a stranger – you never know when you might bump into one.' They walked in silence for a few moments. Mack seemed happy on the lead. He bounded ahead, sniffing the grass poking out from between the paving slabs and random hedges, before stopping and looking back.

'So… what days do you work in the pub?' Paige asked.

'Every day except for Thursday,' Johnny said. 'Apple Cross Inn belongs to my brother, Davey. I came here soon after he bought it. We used to share the flat above the pub, but earlier this year I moved into a house, just outside the village.'

'You enjoy cooking?' Paige asked, determined to keep the attention on him. He had a dangerous effect on her, and if she wasn't careful she'd probably lose her head again – then her mouth would open and the confessions might pour out. She'd probably tell him she hadn't had sex in almost twenty-five months because her marriage had been dead for years; that she couldn't sleep because she was so terrified of failing and not giving her daughter the security and life she deserved. Or that she was lost without her daily routine, despite the fact that she was starting to feel less ill the longer she stayed in Lockton.

'It passes the time,' Johnny said quietly. 'Tell me about your job. I have the impression it's important to you. Call it a hunch,' he added with a wink.

'I work for an events company – putting on conferences, lectures, parties, you name it. I've been working there for almost six years. I enjoy it, it keeps me busy, and I'm good at what I do.' She knew her voice had changed, grown more animated, but at the same time, her stomach felt like it had filled with rocks. 'I work long hours, in between caring for Grace.'

'It's stressful?' Johnny asked, just as they reached the entrance to Apple Cross Inn and stopped. They'd be parting in a moment, and she couldn't tell if the feeling in her chest was disappointment or relief.

'No more than anyone else's job.' Her voice was deliberately light.

Johnny paused and turned to her. His eyes were so blue they made Paige think of the sky above the mountains. How peaceful they seemed, how easy to lose yourself in. 'This is my stop.' He swept an arm towards the pub. Mack was straining at the lead, no doubt excited about finding another place to wreck. 'It was nice to meet you, Paige Dougall. I'll look forward to meeting you again. I'm guessing it might be sooner than we think.'

'Sure,' she said, feeling uncomfortable.

The edges of his eyes crinkled as he looked at her. He opened his mouth and then closed it, opened it once more as his forehead furrowed. 'Can I give you a piece of advice – stranger to stranger? Then we can pretend it never happened when I see you next?'

Paige frowned. 'Okay…'

He took a deep breath. 'Take a walk further up the road before you head into the library. Find some time to smell the flowers. There are begonias at the end of the high street.' He pointed a finger upwards. 'Look at the sky. I'll tell you from experience, you might regret it one day if you don't, or wonder what was so important that you never found the time. Remember, if you're ever looking to have another conversation with a stranger who's prone to bouts of amnesia, you know where I am.'

'In the library?' Paige asked, smiling despite herself. 'Or here?' She nodded towards the window where she could see the pub's bar.

He smiled. 'Or sleeping by the lochan, wrestling with a mischievous dog, maybe even hiking near one of those.' He pointed to the horizon where a set of mountains hugged the sky. 'I make a point of doing something I love at least once a day. Just in case.' Mack tugged at the lead again, his body alert as he faced the entrance to Apple Cross Inn. 'I'm not sure why he's so excited. Davey told me he'd fixed the cage.' He snorted and nodded to Paige, before turning and sauntering through the door.

Paige watched him for a few moments, transfixed by his easy movements. He was so relaxed she was almost jealous. Then again, he didn't have a daughter to support, a busy job to get back to, or a load of things to prove to himself. For a brief moment, she wished her life could be a little less complicated, before she thought about all the things she needed to achieve, and wiped the idea from her head.

Chapter Ten

The library was quiet when Paige opened up. She'd taken five short minutes to walk as far as the end of the road before taking a deep breath and tapping her foot as she looked up. But instead of the peace and clarity Johnny had promised, Paige's mind had filled with Carl and the failures of her marriage – so she'd turned and headed back.

The library smelled of fresh paint and the ladder was still set up where Johnny had finished painting the back wall the day before. There was still a full wall and the office and entrance to complete, which would take another three days – not to mention fifty bookshelves to erect. Paige had worked late into the evening and had built two more, but she'd given up when she'd started to nod off. Her da had driven over to collect her, insisting she come home to eat. But she'd foregone her mam's pork chops and bathed Grace instead, falling asleep in the chair beside her bed where she'd been reading *The Great Gatsby*. She'd been here nine days now, and it was her third novel.

There were two books sitting on the reception desk and Paige went to turn them over. *Best Pubs* again – she frowned at the pile of guides in the corner where she'd placed a copy the evening before. Next to it was a small red hardback called *The Power of Small Moments*. Paige looked back at the entrance, wondering if someone had sneaked in and returned them overnight; or perhaps Morag had dropped them on her way to the post office? It didn't take a genius to work out what the culprit was trying to say. But she didn't have time for small moments – not when she had so many big responsibilities to worry about.

She picked up the red hardback and turned it over. Aileen had often left books out for Paige when she'd helped at The Book Barn. She still remembered so many of them. The first few had been classics, 'an essential part of her education,' Aileen had said; they were followed by some gripping murder mysteries; then there was non-fiction, history, science, philosophy, followed by self-help guides. Aileen had left out a few steamy romances just as Paige had turned eighteen. She'd loved the books, devoured them in her spare time – reading had both relaxed and inspired her. She'd wanted to be a librarian then, to take over when Aileen retired. But she'd met Carl and left Lockton in search of adventures outside fiction; joined the big wild world, leaving behind her cosy life. It had been years since she'd read anything other than emails or let herself get lost in a fantasy world. Paige had forgotten how much she missed it.

She placed the books carefully onto one of the non-fiction piles. There were a lot of books missing, if Paige's inventory was correct. She planned to recommend a book amnesty to the new librarian – an event to encourage members to return books they still had at home without fear of fines. Her features tightened as she imagined someone taking her place. Paige quickly shelved a couple more of the paperbacks, adding them to her inventory. Then she set to work on building the next shelf.

'Hello, stranger.' Johnny arrived when she'd finished putting it up. He swept in with the large bag and placed it onto the counter, then tied up Mack before admiring her work. Something twisted in Paige's gut when he turned to look at her. She felt wrung out this morning and wasn't in the mood for any more confidences. But he smiled as if nothing had been said. 'I'd better get on with the painting. You did a lot yesterday, after I left.' Paige had arranged some of the rustic shelves into position and had pushed more piles of books into their correct locations. It would take at least four more days to shelve them in the right places. Her neck ached, and she rubbed it as Johnny went to put on the overalls before standing at the bottom of the ladder, holding the roller and tray of paint. 'I'll finish this wall, then we should take a break.'

'You've only just arrived.' Paige scowled.

He grinned down at her. 'I know it's early but I mentioned I'd made muffins, didn't I? There's coffee in that bag as well.'

'I'm not—'

'Hungry? I'll bet you didn't eat breakfast?' She felt her cheeks redden. 'You challenged me, remember; I dare you not to finish a whole muffin after one bite.' His eyes dropped to her waist. Paige had put on her favourite jeans this morning and the belt had gone down another notch. She knew she'd lost weight, but didn't need anyone drawing attention to that. She was saved from snapping at him by Morag sweeping through the entrance, closely followed by her da who was wearing his policeman's uniform and holding a red canvas shopping bag.

'Ach, you're doing well.' Morag smiled and tapped her cane on the floor as she took time to look around. 'You've still got some painting to do, laddie.' She pointed to one of the beige walls. 'Are you taking a break already?'

'I was about to start.' Johnny smiled, climbing a couple of rungs of the ladder. 'I was just negotiating a muffin break with the boss.'

'Muffins?' Morag licked her lips. 'Will you be ready to open on Thursday, lass? That's just five more days. That woman, Ms J. Martin from Creative Scotland, just called to confirm she's visiting then.' She turned to Paige before slowly examining the walls that still needed painting, and the shelves that still had to be built.

'Sure.' Paige pulled out her pad, where she'd listed all the chores to be completed when she'd woken in the twilight hours. 'Johnny will finish decorating in the next three days… I'm sure I can get all the bookshelves built by then.' Paige tapped her pencil on the list. 'The books will need to be shelved into the correct locations. Then the computers have to be set up, and after that it's finishing touches – posters, rugs, beanbags, that kind of thing.' She swept an arm towards the counter. 'We're definitely on track.'

'You do good work, lass.' Morag smiled, making Paige feel about a hundred feet tall. 'I'm impressed.' She looked at Johnny and grinned. 'You're quite the team.'

'Did you put an ad in the *Morridon Post* for the new librarian?' Paige asked, checking the next item off her list, ignoring the quick pinch in her chest.

'Ach, I knew I'd forgotten something.' Morag tapped her fingertips against her forehead. 'I'll make sure that's done later. But they'll need to be at least half as good as you.'

Her da held out the bag he was holding before checking his watch. 'I forgot to give these to you last night and again this morning – you left early, lass, and your mam said you didn't sleep.' He gave Paige a quick kiss on the cheek. 'They've been on the bookshelf at home since Aileen passed, some of my favourite Charlie Adaire novels.' Paige pulled the paperbacks out of the bag and placed them on the counter.

Morag glared at the pile. 'I read one of those once.' She shuddered. 'Couldn't bear the detective. She spent far too much of her time poking her nose into other people's business. Completely unrealistic.' She shook her head as Marcus gave Paige an amused wink.

Paige placed the books on the fiction pile, adding them to her inventory. She watched Morag pace the room, slamming her cane onto the floor a few times, looking irritated. 'You okay?' Paige asked, as the older woman looked back at the thrillers.

'Ach, I'm fine, don't mind me. Just thinking about some eejit who came into the post office yesterday. Which reminds me.' Morag glanced at her watch. 'I'd better get back. I'm expecting a delivery – I left a note saying I'd only be a few minutes. I wanted to see how you were getting on.'

'Fancy a muffin, Morag?' Johnny asked, climbing down from the ladder so he could grab a tin from the bag on the counter. He took off the lid and the scent of chocolate wafted through the room, making Paige's stomach growl. Morag took one and bit into it then let out a low hum of pleasure.

'Looks like there's a lot you're hiding under that bushel, Johnny Becker. I'll definitely be expecting something more ambitious from you at the Jampionships this year. And I heard something about *Best Pubs* visiting Apple Cross Inn – I hope you have a few recipes like this up your sleeve? I'm sure you wouldn't want to let your brother down.' Paige saw Johnny's smile drop. 'I've got to go…' As Morag passed Paige, she patted her arm. 'You do good work, lassie, but you look tired and a little drawn. I know your mam and da are concerned.' She signalled to Paige's da, who was reading the back cover of a book he'd picked up from a pile of thrillers Paige had left out. 'Take a break, try one of these.' Morag held up the half-eaten muffin and her eyes shot to Johnny, who had pulled a thermos and three hardback books from his bag and put them on the counter beside the Charlie Adaire novels. He picked up the roller again and returned to the ladder. 'If there's ever a man worth taking a break with, he's it. Remember, sometimes there's a lot more to a person than meets the eye.' She waved her muffin between them before heading for the door.

Marcus placed the thriller back on the pile of books with a disappointed sigh and walked up to give Paige another quick hug. Then he took a muffin from the tin before tucking it into the pocket of his uniform. 'A snack for later, I already ate all your mam's doughnuts. Got to go, lass, someone's been building fences around a field just outside Morridon. They've blocked a public footpath.' He shook his head. 'I'm not sure whether it's to keep people in or out, but I promised I'd take a wee look and talk to the owner. I'll see you tonight. I hope you'll be back in time for dinner.' He looked her square in the eye. 'Perhaps we can take one of our walks again after, have another chat?'

Paige swept a shaky palm over her forehead. She wasn't about to confide in another man this millennium, especially not her da.

He'd never liked Carl; imagine what he'd say if he knew the full story of their marriage? How ashamed he'd be of the mess she'd made of her life. 'Sounds good,' she lied. 'Although I'm not sure what time I'll finish here.'

Twenty minutes after her da left, Johnny climbed down from the ladder so he could pour coffee into two mugs. He handed Paige one before standing back to admire his handiwork. 'Another one done.' He grinned at the white wall. 'It'll need another coat but the next one won't take as long.' The new colour made the room seem even brighter, helping to pick out the red carpet and piles of colourful books. 'Let me put the rollers in water and we'll take a break – perhaps you'll try a bite of muffin?' He beamed.

'I suppose a bite wouldn't hurt,' she murmured, wondering if that was true.

After cleaning up, Johnny put some of the tubs he'd pulled out of the bag into the small fridge in the office. Then he laid the red rug out on the carpet and quickly fed Mack, who'd managed to decapitate another chew toy while they'd been working. He handed a muffin to Paige, but when she tried to turn back to the pile of books, he shook his head.

'Just ten minutes. I think these muffins deserve at least that.' He leaned on the counter as Mack looked up from his chew toy, spotted the muffin and whined. 'Not for you, boy,' Johnny murmured, grabbing a treat from the pocket of his jeans and chucking it over to the dog, who caught it in his teeth and quickly chomped it down. 'I found some books at home last night when I was looking at recipes.

Library books I'd forgotten I'd borrowed.' He reached behind him and picked up the three hardbacks – one on celebration cakes, one on birthday cakes and another on icing, and handed them to Paige, coming to sit beside her on the rug.

'You bake?' Paige opened the top one and thumbed through the pages. 'Of course you do, you made muffins.'

'Not that often. I'd forgotten how much I enjoy it.' Light danced in his eyes. 'But I always make a cake for Davey on his birthday – it's a tradition.' He shrugged. 'I was looking for ideas last year.'

'I thought you were twins. Don't you share?' Paige asked, pausing on a page with a pink castle cake on it, thinking of Grace.

'Nope. My mother insisted on letting us make our own choices. Being born on the same day doesn't have to mean we like the same things.' Johnny shuddered. 'I prefer cheesecake – pretty much any flavour. Davey's partial to chocolate – as much of it as he can get. He likes his cakes to be decorated with as much icing as I can load on, and he gets a kick out of different shapes. It's a joke between us – you know, how silly can we be?' Paige watched a tinge of red climb Johnny's cheeks. The fact that he was embarrassed made something inside her start to thaw. 'I made him one in the outline of a dog last year,' he continued. 'I'm pretty sure that's what gave him the idea for Mack.' He sighed, glancing over at the dog, who was staring at the tin with his tongue hanging out. 'This year I'm thinking of making a cake in the shape of a Porsche.'

Paige let out a loud and involuntary hoot of laughter, and turned the page.

'Are you going to try some?' Johnny pointed to her muffin.

'Sure, fine.' Paige bit into it and almost hummed. The flavour and texture were incredible and she found herself nibbling a little more. 'Did you really make these yourself?' She looked back at the tin. Johnny nodded and picked out a muffin so he could take a bite. Paige watched as he chewed – he had a solid jaw, a steep nose in the exact perfect proportion to the rest of his face. There was the hint of a dimple in the centre of his right cheek; he really was a handsome man. But Carl had been handsome too, and so charming at first… She sighed. 'I made Grace a princess cake for her last birthday. I hired a tin.' Paige pulled a face; it had taken hours. She'd made it one evening, iced it the next, and hadn't finished until three a.m. She'd been so tired that she'd almost fallen asleep the next day. Even now she couldn't understand why it had been so important for her to get it flawless – she only knew how long it had taken her to complete. But Grace hadn't cared that the shape wasn't perfect, or that the icing was the wrong shade of pink. She'd shrieked with delight and dived in. Paige put the book on top of the others. 'I may have to borrow that one – it's Grace's fourth birthday soon. I know Mam could knock one up in minutes, but I'd like to try to make it, perhaps surprise them both…'

'I'll help if you want,' Johnny offered. 'There's a castle cake in that book I've been wanting to try. I thought about making it for Davey, but I've already got a house.' He grinned again and Paige couldn't stop another bark of laughter from spilling out. She bit into the muffin before she realised she'd almost finished half of it. She hadn't laughed or eaten so much in a while…

'This is really good,' she said, holding up what was left of her muffin.

'You sound surprised?' Paige took another bite and Johnny gave her a satisfied smile. 'I'll chalk them up as a success. I've made something for lunch; I hope you'll take another break and sit with me later. We can have another talk?'

She frowned. 'What about?'

He chuckled. 'We can talk about safe subjects if you'd like? Stranger to stranger. I'm partial to conversations about the weather, or the merits of a good lettuce – we could agree our conversation topics upfront?'

Paige eyed the remainder of the muffin as her taste-buds watered. 'I vote we go through our to-do list.' She found herself grinning when he groaned, then checked her watch. 'That's ten minutes.' She stood and brushed her jeans before picking up the three cookery books. 'There's still a lot to do.' Johnny stared at her and she sighed. 'Finish another wall, and we'll take a break after that?' She walked to the office, wondering why for the first time in a few years, her shoulders felt so light.

Chapter Eleven

Johnny sank onto the beach and closed his eyes, listening to the water in the lochan below Buttermead Farm lapping against the pebbly shore. The morning sun was high and it warmed his cheeks. There was the sound of stones scattering in the distance, and he lifted an eyelid just as Mack tapped a paw into the lochan before flinching away and then trying again, his golden fur bright against the greens and greys of his surroundings. Johnny had changed into a pair of dark swimming trunks when he'd arrived at the lochan, but after taking a short dip in the clear blue lake while Mack had watched, he'd got dressed again and decided a short sit-down might be in order. He couldn't be too long – it was his day off from the pub, but he wanted to make sure he arrived at the library just after it opened so he could support Paige on the first day.

He settled back, keeping an ear out for the errant Retriever who he knew would get into mischief if left alone for long. Not that there was much damage he could do to himself around here. 'Stay,' he murmured softly, as he took a deep breath and smelled blossoming heather, fresh water and pure air, remembering how just a few years ago his nostrils would have been filled with the aroma of sizzling onion and garlic, or the scent of fresh fish, game or meat cooking on the grill. His mind conjured some of the extravagant plates he'd served in his restaurant, mulling the excitement he'd felt, the overwhelming feeling of pride at his creations, before he shut the memory down.

There was a splash and Johnny sat up slowly, concern prickling across the back of his neck as he realised Mack had entered the lochan, and was now paddling in the direction of a grey and white seagull floating in the centre.

'Mack, what the hell are you doing? Come back!' Johnny shouted, standing and walking towards the shore, his pulse ratcheting up a notch as he realised the dog wasn't listening. Instead, Mack continued in the same direction, kicking his legs with childlike determination as he got deeper. The gull took one last lazy look as the dog approached, blinked and then took off, soaring up towards the high sides of the grey peaks lined with trees that framed the lochan. Mack looked surprised, and he turned his small head, darting his attention this way and that as if he'd just realised exactly where he was. He spluttered as his mouth ducked under the water suddenly, suggesting he was getting tired.

'Mack, heel,' Johnny shouted again, knowing it was useless – the dog hadn't followed a command since Johnny had adopted him; why would he start now? The pup tried to turn himself round, paddling faster now, his eyes wide and filled with fear. 'Wait, dammit!' Johnny's palms began to sweat as he pulled off his T-shirt, trainers and jeans and threw them onto the beach, moving faster than he had in years. He cursed under his breath as he saw Mack bob under the surface for a moment before reappearing with a surprised choke. A few seconds later he followed the dog in. 'Jeez!' The water was freezing and took his breath away. Johnny looked down into the clear depths where pebbles twinkled in the sunlight. The joyful sight was at odds with the fear now gripping his throat. He'd been in for ten minutes earlier, but for some reason the water felt frigid now. He puffed out a breath, trying to steady himself as he watched Mack go under once more. How many times could the dog get himself back up before the water claimed him for its own? Ignoring the heavy hammering in his chest, the blood pumping wildly through his veins as he fought down panic, Johnny put his head into the water and began to front crawl, moving quickly. His life might be far slower and stress-free now, but he made a point of keeping himself in shape. Another life lesson he'd decided not to forget.

Mack looked delighted to see him. He was still paddling, his head barely above the lip of the water, looking this way and that, spluttering and panting hard. 'You eejit,' Johnny murmured gently. Feeling every cell of his body relax as he scooped the young dog under one arm, he rolled onto his back with Mack on his chest and did a slow backstroke until they reached the shore. All the while Mack nipped at his jaw, probably his way of saying thanks, but the bites were sharp. As soon as they reached dry land, Mack instantly forgot his earlier predicament and clambered up and over Johnny, flying out of the water to shake himself – soaking the jeans, trainers and T-shirt still scattered across the pebbles. Johnny sighed and shook each of them in turn, before pulling them on over his wet body and boxers, just as Agnes Stuart sauntered up and over the hill that separated Bonnie Lochan from Buttermead Farm. She wore a dark pair of trousers with a pink T-shirt, and a chocolate-brown Labrador – almost the exact same size as Mack – walked carefully by her heels. The moment the two dogs spotted each other, they came to an abrupt halt and barked before poising to charge – their hunched positions and eager expressions reminding Johnny of desperate lovers who'd been parted for years.

'Mack, heel!' Johnny yelled, knowing it was futile even as Agnes let out a loud shout and her dog instantly stood down, sitting on her haunches and tipping her head upwards, her expression a picture of adoration and delight. Agnes knelt and produced a treat from her pocket, patting the dog on its head, while it grinned, its teeth bright white. 'Mack, come back now!' Johnny tried again, feeling a little embarrassed as the mutt bounded towards them up the pathway, scattering pebbles and stones this way and that.

He put his fingers in his mouth and tried a low whistle he'd seen on a YouTube training video, hoping by some miracle the dog would respond. He winced as Mack crashed into Agnes's heels, instantly jumping up at her, before hooking his paws onto the bottom of her trousers, scraping her legs before leaning down to nip at her heels. She bent and tapped him gently on the nose, whispering something Johnny couldn't hear before standing. Then Johnny's jaw dropped as Mack suddenly quietened and both dogs fell into line, following Agnes slowly down the path. She looked like the Pied Piper, calm and in control, but as she approached, Johnny could see a hint of fire in her green eyes.

'Davey told me you'd be coming to visit,' she murmured, frowning at Mack as he peeled away from her heels and began to jump up, trying to grab onto the bottom of Johnny's jeans. 'He mentioned you were both in need of some training. Stop!' she said firmly, making Johnny and Mack jolt. 'Looks like you arrived not a moment too soon. It's good my granddaughter Evie took her pygmy goat to live with her last month. Miss Daisy enjoyed a ramble down here. I dinnae know what would have happened with a dog like that loose.' She scrutinized Johnny's wet hair and damp T-shirt. '"Perfectly Imperfect".' She read the slogan on the dark blue material and raised an eyebrow. 'You got some of that right, laddie. You been for a swim?'

'A couple.' Johnny sighed and looked out over the clear blue lochan as Mack began to bark. 'The tearaway decided to go bird hunting and tried to drown himself. I called him back but…' He puffed out his cheeks as the memory made his heart thump hard in his chest. He'd grown fond of Mack over the last few weeks, fonder than he'd realised. Which, for a man who'd decided to keep his attachments to a minimum and his life stress-free, was an uncomfortable realisation. 'I guess he couldn't hear.'

'You have treats?' Agnes asked, frowning at Mack as he began to bite Johnny's shoelaces.

Johnny shrugged. 'I did, but he stole the rest from my pocket when I went for a swim.' Agnes wrinkled her nose. 'In truth, the training's not been going that well.' He pulled a face. 'I came today to see if you could help. I can't stay long as I want to go and see Paige at the library. I wasn't keen on giving Mack a rigid routine. We've agreed on a few commands, and I hoped if we took it slowly he'd get the gist.'

Agnes raised an eyebrow as she assessed Johnny, her heart-shaped face bemused. 'That's bampot talk. You wouldn't trust a pilot who'd just got the gist of flying, or a dentist who had a rough idea of how to take your wisdom teeth out.'

'That's not quite—' Johnny started, then stopped when Agnes deliberately shook her head.

'Dogs need boundaries, repetition and a proper master,' she said firmly. 'Without it, they'll be miserable.' She glared at the lochan. 'Or in this case, drown. I know Davey gave you the wee dog as a gift, which you decided to share, so perhaps you're not all in. But you either need to take care of him properly or give him up.' Her expression was firm.

Johnny tried not to bristle. 'I'm planning on keeping him. He's good company, most of the time. I just…' He looked back at the lochan, remembered the painful thump in his chest when Mack had gone under. He'd worked hard over the last few years not to get himself worked up over anything. But somehow the dog had sneaked into his heart. 'Perhaps I haven't been taking the training seriously enough. The videos I've been following haven't worked.' He sighed. If Mack learned to follow orders, it'd make life easier all round.

'Then the first lesson is to keep your eyes open and snacks to hand if you've any chance of getting that wee rascal to do as he's told. I'm not an expert, but I've trained enough pups in my time to know that.' She glanced down at her Lab, who was staring up at her with melting eyes.

'Watch.' Agnes held a treat above her dog's head, encouraging her to put her bottom onto the grass. A butterfly fluttered past Mack's head and Johnny quickly snapped the lead onto his collar as he strained against it, watching the insect fly off.

'You're about to have a lesson in how to behave – you need to focus,' he murmured, smiling despite himself.

'Now you try!' Agnes said, handing Johnny a snack. 'Come on, just a few minutes, Mack won't be able to learn for much longer – he's an attention span to rival a teen's. Hold the treat in your hand, just like I did. Now bend in front of Mack and let him smell it.' Johnny did as he was told, while Mack's large brown eyes widened and he sniffed at the food, his jaw opening into a grin. 'Raise it above his head, quickly before the wee laddie eats it. Now!' she commanded, reminding Johnny of the first chef he'd worked under. The man had dominated everyone in the kitchen with just a word, and Johnny had ended up managing his kitchen much the same – as if fear and stress were the powerhouse of success. His team had been terrified of him; it embarrassed him to remember those days now.

He watched confusion flash across Mack's face. 'I'm really not sure he understands.' Then the dog lifted his head and tried to grab the treat – as he did, his bottom lowered to the ground. 'Wow.'

'Stroke him, tell him he's a good laddie and give him the treat.' Agnes stood back, beaming as Johnny followed her instructions feeling ridiculously proud. 'Now you'll want to practise that and keep it up between our sessions. He's a bright dog with lots of potential. He just needs guidance from you. Let's go back to the farm for a wee blather so we can work out a schedule. I'm thinking we'll need to have a talk about what I expect from you and the cutie. I'll cook one of my omelettes and these kids can catch up. This is Angel.' She knelt and smiled at her dog, who immediately held up a paw. 'She's a bright lass. Learned this trick all on her own.'

Johnny looked down at Mack, who was once again chewing his shoelaces. 'I'm wondering if it would just be easier if we swapped for a few weeks?' he joked, half serious, as Agnes turned and headed back towards Buttermead Farm.

The farmhouse kitchen was large with wooden beams that lined the ceiling and bright yellow paintwork. There was a large blue Aga on the left of the room, gnarled rustic cabinets, and a massive dresser which filled the opposite wall. A white butler sink sat underneath an open window which had pretty views of the garden and rolling green fields scattered with sheep. The middle of the room was taken up by a square oak table with a jug of yellow and white flowers in the centre, surrounded by eight chairs. Above it a chandelier sparkled as sunlight shone in from outside. 'Take a seat.' Agnes waved towards the table as Johnny followed her in. Angel instantly trotted over to a fluffy brown dog bed in the corner of the kitchen and picked up a chew toy. Mack followed, seeking out a small piece of rope. Johnny passed the dresser and stopped to pick up a book titled *A Ninja's Guide to Playing Cupid*. He shook his head as he browsed the pages, noticing a few sections had been marked with Post-it notes. Agnes had a reputation in the village for matchmaking, but so far he'd managed to stay out of her line of sight. He quickly put the book down, hoping she hadn't spotted him reading it.

'Ach, that's due to go back to the library. I still need to make some notes, then perhaps you can take it for me when you come for our next lesson?' Agnes asked as she put the kettle on. 'Aileen ordered it in for me especially – an act of kindness for all the local singletons, she told me. I've read it cover to cover; there's a lot of good ideas for helping out lads and lassies who find themselves alone.' She gave him a piercing look and grinned.

'Hot toddy!' There was a squawk from the corner of the room, and Johnny turned to see Agnes's grey and red African parrot pluck at a tail feather before twirling on the top of her cage.

'Indeed, cutie.' Agnes laughed, turning back to take a couple of mugs out of one of the cupboards.

Johnny cleared his throat. 'I appreciate the compliment, Tiki,' he murmured, pulling out a chair. He watched as Agnes got out a large frying pan before grabbing cheese, an onion, and an array of vegetables and fresh herbs from the fridge. 'You want help?' he asked, standing as Agnes nodded and pointed to the chopping board.

'I'll make coffee. I've fresh bread in the oven, you get on with that.' She eyed him as he picked up the knife and began to chop briskly. 'I've always admired people who can do that without cutting themselves.'

'Took me years to learn how,' Johnny said, remembering the hours he'd spent in the kitchen perfecting his craft and the wounded fingers he'd earned as a result. Those were the days when cooking had been a fun affair, before ambition had stripped away any joy. It took just a few minutes to create the small piles of perfectly shaped ingredients, before he picked up the pan and lifted the lid on the Aga. Then he tossed some butter into the pan and waited while it melted before adding the veg. Agnes finished making the drinks, sliced the fresh bread and put two misshapen blue coffee cups and side plates onto the table, then pulled up a chair so she could watch.

'Davey told me you used to work at a restaurant in New York. I thought it was one of those diner affairs, but now I'm wondering if it was a little fancier than that?' She lifted her mug to her lips, and looked on as he broke the eggs into a bowl and whipped them before adding them to the pan. The movements were fast and efficient; he could have done the whole thing if he were half asleep.

'A little fancier,' he admitted warily. He'd lived in Lockton long enough to know that anything he told Agnes would be shared with Morag and travel around the local population within a few hours. Everyone who visited the post office would get the full lowdown on his life – Chinese whispers Scottish style.

Agnes tapped her nose and smiled. 'I respect a man who knows how to keep a secret, although it makes me wonder why you are.'

'Perhaps I don't want people to expect things from me.' Johnny shrugged, thinking about Paige. The woman almost vibrated with stress from all of the guilt and expectation she'd piled onto her small shoulders. He recognised her pain on an almost visceral level and had no plans to go back down that same path. He only hoped he could help her while she was still in Lockton. He let out a breath as he served up the omelette, sliced it in two and scattered the herbs on top, then carried the plates over to the table, placing one in front of Agnes and taking a seat.

Agnes inhaled deeply. 'That's definitely fancy. I wonder now why you haven't jazzed up the menu in Apple Cross Inn? It's not changed in years. I assumed plain fare was all you could make.' She studied him. Johnny knew she was a canny woman, with a penchant for interfering in people's lives. Many believed the Stuart women hailed from mystic stock in the shape of a long line of witches. Perhaps she could read his mind?

'As I said,' Johnny murmured without smiling. 'All kinds of expectations.'

She sighed. 'Morag and Fergus told me someone from *Best Pubs* is planning on visiting the area soon.'

Johnny took a small bite of the omelette, pleased with the dish. 'A few people have mentioned it.' He frowned, remembering Morag's comment when she'd come into the library. He hadn't changed the menu despite his promise to Davey. Was he letting his brother down? The idea made him uncomfortable. 'I'm sure whoever it is will be impressed with Apple Cross Inn. The real ales will probably earn us a mention.'

'But not the food?' Agnes asked, fixing him with an unreadable expression.

Johnny sighed and put down his knife and fork.

'Spill it!' Tiki squawked from the corner, making him jump.

'You're an enigma.' Agnes pushed her cleared plate aside, put her elbows on the table and linked her fingers, resting her pointed chin onto them. 'Even the parrot can see that. You moved to Lockton after Davey. Handsome, single man who keeps to himself, with no interest as far as I can tell in dating anyone.'

Johnny quirked an eyebrow. Agnes might be the matchmaker of Lockton, but this was the first time she'd set her sights on him. 'I had a fiancée in New York,' he said carefully. 'It didn't work out and I'm not looking for a repeat.'

'A broken heart.' She cocked her head. 'Hard to fix if you don't date.'

Johnny finished his omelette and pushed his plate to one side, sitting a little straighter. 'Actually, I think I broke Tracey's heart.' He sighed, remembering the tears and recriminations, her anger when he'd checked out of the hospital after two weeks and decided to leave the life they'd built together so he could move in with his brother in Scotland. Davey had called him every day while he was recuperating, even offering to fly to New York. Tracey had barely visited because she hated hospitals, and he'd had few friends then. But Johnny had been content alone. The time in hospital had given him time to re-evaluate his life. To see how little he'd been living. He'd asked Tracey to move with him to Lockton but she'd refused. She wanted a different life. So much for the power of love. 'I thought we were here to discuss dog training?'

Agnes let out a light tinkle of laughter. 'Train the owner, train the dog. I believe in a holistic approach. Creating the kind of connection you need with Mack relies on honestly and instinct. Seems to me you're shutting a lot of things out, Johnny Becker, seeking the path of least resistance, refusing to care. But why? Perhaps the dog isn't listening to you because you don't listen to yourself – you lock out your needs because it's safer. You don't connect with him or train him properly because you don't want to risk getting hurt.' He jerked his head at this. 'Perhaps your lack of dog training is just the tip of the iceberg. If you don't move past the things holding you back, can you truly change the way you are with Mack?'

'There's nothing holding me back and nothing I'm looking to change.' Johnny shuffled in his seat as the dog dropped the chew toy and came to stand by his feet, perhaps sensing he was uncomfortable. Johnny frowned and leaned down to scratch the top of Mack's head. He'd not let anyone aside from his brother get close to him in years, but somehow this four-legged demon had got to him.

'You love that cutie, any eejit can see that,' Agnes said softly.

'I do,' Johnny admitted, more to himself than Agnes, feeling a sliver of uncertainty trickle down his spine. 'I don't know what I would have done if he'd drowned.'

'Then you need to start working on that training straight away,' she said gently. 'I know you're a man of few words. I know you like to keep to yourself and live a life that's as slow and uncomplicated as possible. Whether it's because you're running from something, or trying not to repeat mistakes from the past, I haven't figured out… yet.'

He brought his head up, and their eyes collided.

'You think because you keep yourself to yourself that Morag, Cora and the rest of the people in the village don't talk, or notice the way you live?' she asked. 'I've had my eye on you for a while.' Johnny felt his cheeks heat. 'As I said, you're a mystery. That makes you more interesting than most.'

Johnny laughed, but it had an awkward edge to it. 'I'm fairly sure I'm boring. That's kind of my life's purpose now.'

'But why?' Agnes pressed.

'Why, why, why?' Tiki repeated, as Mack let out a loud bark.

'Um, I'm…' Johnny trailed off as Agnes chuckled.

'You'll tell me when you're ready. It's all part of the training. I have a feeling a lot of things in your life are about to change.'

'That's not part of my plan.' Johnny stood suddenly. 'I need to go, Paige will be waiting.' He pushed his chair back and picked up the two plates, placing them into the sink as Agnes stood by looking amused.

'Take some treats,' she said softly, grabbing a small blue packet out of one of the cupboards and handing it to him. 'Let's have our first proper lesson tomorrow morning, down by Bonnie Lochan. You can make lunch when we've finished. We'll be working on Mack staying in one place – and perhaps we can have a chat about why you gave up New York.' She grinned as he paled.

'Okay,' he said roughly, as he put the lead on Mack and headed out of the kitchen, wondering if his life was about to change whether he liked it or not.

Chapter Twelve

The sun was shining as Paige approached The Book Barn and opened up. She walked into the entrance and took a moment to admire the room. Would all the hard work be worth it? They hadn't advertised the opening yet; Paige had thought it would be a nice touch to leave it for the new librarian to organise. Now she wondered if that had been a mistake. What if no one came? She felt a renewed connection with the place, a stirring inside her as she looked around at the bright white walls, the posters, leather chairs, lamps, and the inviting long brown sofa someone had donated years before. The library was important to her. She rushed around to get a closer look. All the shelves were set up now and she'd spent hours the evening before organising the final touches, putting out the last books.

To the left of the entrance, a couple of oak tables had been set up, complete with computers and chairs. Johnny had stayed late as well to finish those, refusing to leave until Mack had begun to whine and he'd been forced to go. To the right of the entrance was the children's corner. Paige was particularly proud of that. Her mam had promised to bring Grace over later and she couldn't wait to see what her daughter made of the huge beanbags, posters, colouring pads and pretty displays of picture books. She'd missed too many story times over the last few years – today she'd like to start to rectify that.

'You are open?' There was a shout from the entrance.

'Yes, we're open. We're doing a soft launch today. Once a permanent librarian has been hired, I expect they'll follow up with some kind of grand event. Please do come in.' Paige put her bag behind the counter and smiled.

'*Sì.*' Lilith walked into the library and took a moment to look around. 'It looks good.' She pointed towards the corner where Johnny had set up the tables and computers. Paige had taped passwords onto the screens so it would be easy for people to pop in and log on whenever they wanted. 'I can use the computer now?'

'Sure,' Paige said.

Lilith pulled out a chair and put her bag on the table before glancing around. 'Johnny is not here?'

'Not today. He's finished the painting.' Paige felt a flutter of disappointment in her belly. 'He might pop in later if you want to catch up?' Johnny had threatened to visit, but Paige hadn't believed him. Now he was free to do as he pleased, it seemed unlikely he'd take time out to be with her. He'd have a hundred more interesting things to be getting on with. Men as charming as that rarely had the attention span to follow through on their promises. She'd learned the hard way that it was best to keep your expectations low.

She watched Lilith key the password into the computer before typing 'chef' into the search box of a jobs website which covered Morridon and the local area. Then she opened another tab and began to search for vacancies in and around Rome. Paige realised she was staring and took a step back, moving around the table when she noticed that a book had fallen over on the shelf directly opposite where Lilith was seated. She picked it up so she could read the cover: *The Courage to Go Your Own Way.* 'It's funny how every time I come into the library I spot something new. Which is crazy, considering I put all the books out myself.' Paige held the paperback up to show Lilith. 'I'm sure I've never seen this one before.' It was labelled correctly and in the right place, so she started to slot it back on the shelf.

'I'd like to see.' Lilith's lips pinched into a white slash, and she wriggled her fingers until Paige gave her the book. The Italian rifled through the pages before glaring. 'This is a joke – you know about the hotel?'

Paige's eyes widened as Lilith's all but spat fire. 'I'm sorry. What about the hotel? The book fell over on the shelf, I just picked it up. You watched me.' She jerked her head. 'Just now.'

Lilith blinked a few times, then her shoulders slumped. '*Sì.* Excuse me, I'm…' She exhaled. 'People gossip in this village. Sometimes I feel like everyone is talking about my failures.' She pointed to the paperback. 'My papa would probably call that fate. Or perhaps you have the same gift as Aileen for finding the right read at the right time? She was always so kind.'

'I really don't,' Paige protested.

Lilith stared at her for a beat, considering. 'I will borrow it. Perhaps it will give me courage for the changes I need to make.' She put the book to one side before turning back to the computer. Paige noticed she'd opened another browser window and started to make notes on a pad just as a man walked through the entrance. He looked familiar and it took Paige a moment to understand why. He was skinny, with a wiry build, but he had the same colour hair as Johnny and the same blue eyes – even from here she could tell they were related. She saw his attention dart to the table where Lilith was sitting. Then the easy smile dulled and the similarities disappeared.

'You must be Paige,' he said. His voice was smooth, even as his focus shot back to the corner of the library and he frowned. 'I'm Johnny's brother, Davey Becker. I came to borrow a book on cooking fish… but…' His eyes met Lilith's just as she looked up, and the room fell silent as they both stared at each other.

'I'm, um…' Paige pointed to where the cookery books were shelved, but Davey had already gone to join Lilith.

'Hello.' His voice was low. Paige busied herself at the desk, trying not to listen, but the acoustics in the barn made it difficult not to hear. 'I… I heard your parents sent a manager to help at the hotel.'

'*Sì.*' Lilith went crimson. 'So you were right,' she snapped. 'Perhaps business before pleasure was not such a good idea after all.' Her shoulders stiffened, and even from where she was standing, Paige could see she was upset.

'I…' Davey said. 'I'm not here to gloat, I—'

'You made your feelings perfectly clear when we broke up in February,' she grumbled. 'When you wanted me to move in with you and I said not yet.' She gulped as pain streaked across her face. 'You, or my job and family: that was your ultimatum, I believe.'

'What I said,' Davey said patiently, leaning closer, 'was that I wanted you to make room in your life for something other than work and your father – to put *us* first for a change.'

'But when I wanted to discuss it, you wouldn't talk.' Lilith's cheeks were almost fluorescent.

There was a noise at the entrance, and both Lilith and Davey jerked back. Morag walked in before looking around. 'Ach lassie, you've done well.' She pointed to the walls. 'The lad did a decent job of decorating too. Your mam said she'd bring your wee girl in later. I saw them stop by the Christmas shop to see Meg not long ago.' She scanned the room. 'The lady from Creative Scotland said she'd pop in some time soon. I wish we were busier.' She waddled up to Lilith and Davey, using her cane. 'You two making up?'

'No,' Lilith snapped.

Davey flushed and turned away. 'I forgot I need to do something at the pub.' He nodded vaguely at Paige and Morag, then frowned at Lilith before heading out.

Morag turned to Lilith. 'Ach lass, you two need your heads knocking together.' She let out a long sigh. 'Have you anyone in your hotel who might like to visit the library today?'

Lilith logged off the computer and grabbed her things, looking flustered. 'I'll ask when I get back.' She handed Paige *The Courage to Go Your Own Way*, and fumbled in her bag before producing a library card. 'I'll come back another time. The manager Papa sent wants to know what my plans are for tomorrow's evening meal. I've no idea why, since he'll change the menu whatever I decide.' She pulled a face as Paige scanned the book and handed it over.

As Lilith left the library, a cool wind blew in through the entrance and a woman dressed in a fitted green suit strode in, closely followed by Jason Beckett. Paige backed away from Morag as the older woman let out a low hiss.

'Jeannie Martin.' The woman was pale and slim with dark hair that reached her shoulders. She had a bag slung over her shoulder, which she reached into, before pulling out a pad. 'Sorry to turn up unannounced. Jason…' She reddened. 'Mr Beckett wanted to come, and he's got an event at his library in Morridon this afternoon. I thought it would be nice if we all met up.' She broke eye contact so she could look around. 'I'm impressed you've got so much done and managed to open in such a short time. I love the sofa area, what a brilliant idea.' She pointed to the corner.

Jason perused the area with a frown. 'I would have put the children's section further from the door,' he murmured. 'They've got far too much space – try to focus on the adults, they pay all the fines.'

'It's lovely to meet you, lass. I'm Morag Dooley.' Morag ignored Jason and held out a hand. 'I think you'll agree the place is looking bonnie – exactly as agreed.'

'It is.' Jeannie walked away, making notes on her pad as Jason followed.

'Just wait for the eejit to find something else he doesn't like,' Morag whispered, as Paige scoured the shelves to make sure everything was perfect. She watched Jason pluck a paperback off one of the units.

'*The Enemy Within*.' He waved it in the air as Morag barked out a laugh.

'Couldn't have picked a better book for him myself,' she whispered to Paige.

'I've got a copy in Morridon,' Jason said, his voice light. 'It's rarely in the library, we have a huge waiting list.' He looked around the quiet room, his meaning clear, and placed the book ceremoniously back on the shelf.

'How many visitors are you expecting on an average day?' Jeannie asked Morag.

'It's our first full day of being open.' Morag scratched her head. 'So it's difficult to predict. Most of the village will be sure to pop in later. I've been promoting it in the post office and we've leaflets in most of the shops. It's still early but' – her eyes slid to Paige – 'our former librarian Aileen used to have a gift for choosing the right book for the right person. She told me once that Paige here was cut from similar cloth.' She shrugged. 'Even her name is perfect; it's like she was born to work here.' Paige opened her mouth to disagree and was silenced by a sharp look from Morag. 'I'm sure as word spreads our membership will increase.'

Jason huffed. 'I heard stories about Aileen, but I never believed them. You think you have a gift?' he asked Paige, his tone sharp.

Paige gaped as Morag shot her a beseeching look. 'Yes?' The word came out as a question and Jason's lips curled into a sneer.

'Show me.' He twirled a finger in the air, taking in the library.

'What?' Paige squeaked.

'Choose me a book. It shouldn't be hard with a talent like yours.' His plump lips pursed, and Paige blew out a breath as her eyes lurched around the room. When in doubt, Aileen had usually recommended a non-fiction book. She walked across to the relevant shelves, sensing in this instance that the old librarian would have been right.

'History,' she whispered, as her pulse quickened. She let her fingers trace the various spines, drawn to the colours and textures until she found herself wanting to stop at one. She supressed a giggle as she pulled it out.

'*The Man Who Knew Everything*.' Jeannie read the cover aloud and Morag let out a hoot, which quickly transformed into a spluttering cough. 'Aren't you reading that at the moment, Jason?'

He pouted and jerked his head, throwing an irritated glare in Paige's direction. 'Lucky guess,' he grumbled.

'A brilliant skill for any librarian – you clearly have a flair.' Jeannie smiled at Paige, then turned back to Morag after scribbling something in her pad. 'What events have you scheduled? Have you set up a regular story time? School visits? Any authors coming to speak?' Morag's gaze slid back to Paige.

'I have a regular programme,' Jason interrupted. 'It's a good way of getting the community involved. It's important to create relationships with local celebrities. Isn't there a musician turned decorator living around here?'

'Tom Riley-Clark's not interested in doing events,' Morag growled. 'But he'll definitely be supporting The Book Barn.' Her forehead crunched. 'I'll guarantee there won't be a person in Lockton without a library card by next week.'

'I launched the Morridon library with a huge fanfare.' Jason's voice was crisp. 'You'd be unlikely to attract our quantity of visitors. We had over sixty people attend.'

'What did you do, Jason?' Jeannie asked softly, beaming at him.

'A local historian came to speak. He'd uncovered some treasure buried on a farm close to where he lived, further into the Highlands, and had written a book about it. We did a treasure hunt, it was a huge success. If you need my help with the launch, my door is always open. I've already put together some ideas in case you needed the benefit of my experience? It's in PowerPoint.'

'That's a good idea,' Jeannie murmured, scribbling something else in her pad. 'Perhaps you two should meet up.'

Jason smiled and he turned to Morag. Her back stiffened and Paige got a bad feeling in the pit of her stomach. 'No need. The lass has already sorted that out.' Morag waved a finger at Paige. 'She works in the business and has hundreds of connections. We've a mystery author booked to speak in just under two weeks. I'll warrant that'll see your sixty visitors and raise them a few more. Cora has started making posters already and we'll be providing refreshments from the local pub.' Paige gulped as she heard Jason's sharp intake of breath. 'The press are coming, and we expect to attract visitors from far and wide. I don't think we need any help. Unless you want to advertise our launch in *your* library, of course?'

'That sounds brilliant!' Jeannie clapped.

'I haven't heard about an event.' Jason gave Paige a dark glare.

'We were waiting to open the library before anything got announced,' Morag lied. 'The author is very well known and we've been concerned about attracting too large a crowd if we publicised it too early.'

Jeannie blinked and scrawled something onto her pad. 'If you can tell me the date before I leave, I'll make sure I come along.'

'So will I,' Jason said, giving Morag a suspicious glower.

'Ach, I'm sorry, lassie,' Morag said again, after Jeannie and Jason had left the library in a flutter of promises and offers of help. She tapped her cane onto the floor as she paced. 'The man's an eejit. If I didn't say we had something planned, that woman would have handed the whole thing over to Jason.'

'I saw,' Paige said softly, trying to ignore the new tension across her shoulders as she looked around. 'But a launch event… It won't be difficult to organise the logistics, but we need to find an author – someone who'll be happy to attend, someone well known or interesting enough to draw a big crowd.'

'Aye.' Morag frowned. 'I'll ask my customers in the post office. I wish I could think of someone…' Her voice sounded a little off pitch and Paige turned to ask if something was wrong. Before she could, there was a loud clatter from the entrance and Mack came bounding inside. He was on a lead today and he strained forwards, aiming for Paige. Johnny followed, carrying the same bag from the weekend.

'What's wrong?' he asked, reading their faces.

'Jason Beckett,' Morag snapped. 'We need to find an author for a big launch event for The Book Barn in two weeks.' She shook her head, her face crumpling.

Paige grimaced. 'Even if someone was willing, it's unlikely they'd be available. I've booked big authors for events before – most of them need to be contacted months in advance.'

'Isn't that man from *Best Pubs* around the Highlands at the moment?' Morag's face lit up as she looked at Johnny. 'He writes books – think you could ask?'

'We're not supposed to know he's coming, Morag, so we can't.' Johnny looked at Paige and he pulled a face. 'I don't think that's your answer, sorry.'

'It's okay.' Paige patted Morag on the shoulder when her mouth sagged. 'I'll find someone. Even if I have to call every author and publisher in Scotland.'

'That's a lot of work for one, lass,' Morag murmured, glancing at Johnny. 'Perhaps you can muster some help.'

He looked like he was about to respond but Grace came running in through the entrance clutching a bag, closely followed by Cora, who was out of breath. 'Mummy!' she shouted, as she spotted Paige and ran up to cuddle her legs. 'Meg gave me these.' She opened the bag to reveal an array of silver and gold baubles as Mack let out a loud bark. Then she dropped to her knees and put the bag carefully on the floor so she was the same level as the dog.

Paige was about to tell her to back off, but Johnny knelt beside Mack, pulling him back a little. 'You like dogs?' he asked gently.

Grace looked at him, her eyes like saucers. 'Doggy.'

'You can pet him. He's friendly, sometimes a little too much. He's called Mack. What's your name?' His face had softened and Paige felt a melting sensation in her chest. Grace grinned at him; she was normally so shy around strangers.

'Grace.' She shuffled forwards a little more, her curls shining like gold in the sun. 'Can I stroke?' she asked.

'Yes,' Johnny said, and Paige watched as Grace patted Mack on the head. Instead of jumping up, which she expected, the dog stayed put and bent his head lower, giving Grace better access.

'How's the training?' Morag asked, leaning on her cane.

'Better,' Johnny said. 'Although I've never seen him this calm.' He looked thoughtful. 'I've a lesson with Agnes tomorrow morning.' He turned to Paige. 'Will you come? My intentions are purely selfish.'

He looked pointedly at Grace, who was stroking Mack's head while the dog whimpered with pleasure.

'I'm not sure,' Paige said.

'Aye, lass, you should. Grace would love a trip to Buttermead Farm. Besides, you've been stuck here for the last week getting this place ready to open, you've barely seen her,' Cora said, walking up to join them. 'I'll mind The Book Barn for an hour or two in the morning if you like? It's not likely to be busy. You're looking pale – a little fresh air will do you good.'

'I'll mind it,' Morag said sternly. 'I'll shut the post office for a wee while.' She gestured to Paige. 'I've a feeling the lass plans on working into the night, so she'll deserve a break.'

'I'm—'

'Please,' Grace begged.

'Perhaps we can negotiate if it makes you feel better?' Johnny grinned. Was the man ever serious? Then again, something about the joyful glitter in his eyes made her insides perform a series of energetic somersaults. 'Stranger to stranger.' He winked. 'You help with the training – lend me your lucky charm.' He nodded to Grace. 'I'll help with the author. We can chat at the Jam Club tonight. I'm sure if we work together we'll come up with a plan.'

'That's not—' Paige started, as Morag applauded.

'That's settled. The sooner you two put your heads together, the sooner we'll have an author for our launch.'

Chapter Thirteen

Agnes was waiting outside with Angel at her heels when they approached the house at Buttermead Farm the following morning. Johnny was carrying Mack, who'd grown tired on the walk from his house and had eventually sat on the ground and refused to budge. Beside him Paige carried Grace, who'd grown weary at almost the exact same moment, turning so she could raise her arms to her mum. The girl was cute, that wasn't in doubt. With her pretty blue eyes almost the same colour as his own, for a brief moment he wondered what it would be like to have a daughter who looked like him, before he pushed the thought away.

'Morag told me to expect a crowd.' Agnes gave them a broad grin and Mack perked up as they approached, waggling his tail and wriggling until Johnny put him on the ground. 'It's lovely to see you again, lass.' She greeted Paige with a hug, and took a moment to turn to Grace. 'Your nana is so excited to have you home,' she murmured. 'You've come to help train Mack?'

Grace blinked as Paige put her daughter on her feet. Mack bounced up beside her, giving the girl such a look of pure adoration that they might not have seen each other for weeks. The feeling was obviously mutual because Grace patted his head, earning herself a wide doggy grin.

'You have snacks?' Agnes asked.

Johnny pointed to his pocket. 'Millions of them. We practised sitting yesterday afternoon. I can't say he's an expert, but there's a definite improvement.' In truth they'd tried about fifty times, but Mack had only sat twice. He'd been far more interested in gobbling treats.

'I thought we'd go down to Bonnie Lochan again to see if we can get the wee laddie to learn to stay when you ask. It's an easy process – even the bairn could probably get him to respond.' She ruffled Grace's curls and the girl giggled shyly. They joined the gravel pathway that took them past three large white canvas yurts which were set on the outskirts of the main farm. The Stuart family rented them to holidaymakers in the summer months. They were all full at the moment – at least that was what Johnny had heard.

The lochan was empty of people and even though it was morning, the sun was high. It set off a cascade of sparkles across the clear blue water as a gentle breeze flew across the beach. 'We're going to teach Mack to respond to the stay command,' Agnes explained. 'He's young, but if he's mastered "sit", this is the next thing I'd recommend. Let's start with a demonstration.' She looked down at her Labrador, who was gazing at Mack. 'Angel, sit!' The little brown dog immediately plopped her bottom on the ground. 'Come.' Johnny watched Agnes lead the dog in the other direction. When she got to the edge of the shimmering lochan, she bent. 'Stay!' She held up a treat and took a few steps backwards as Angel's chocolaty eyes widened and her body shuddered, but she didn't move. 'Come.' Agnes gifted Angel with a treat when she came trotting up.

'Good doggy,' Grace said quietly.

'You're right there, lassie.' Agnes turned and looked over her shoulder at Johnny. 'Now you try. Let's start with the stay command and work ourselves up to something more complicated.'

'Good luck,' Paige said drily.

'I think I'll need it,' Johnny murmured. 'Don't embarrass me,' he said to Mack, leading the dog away. He grabbed a treat from his pocket and watched Mack's nose follow it. Out of the corner of his eye he could see Agnes, Angel, Paige and Grace, and wondered what the hell he was doing. But he still bent to look into Mack's face, raising an eyebrow to show he was serious. Back in the old days, the same no-nonsense expression had instilled terror into his team – but the dog just widened his jaw and yawned. 'Stay!' Johnny crouched so they were almost eye to eye as he took a small step backwards, but Mack shot up and took one tentative step.

Johnny chuckled. 'You're impossible.'

'If you don't take the training seriously, neither will he,' Agnes warned.

Johnny pointed to the spot Mack had just vacated with another stern nod. 'Sit.' He stroked the dog's head absently as Mack gave him a dose of puppy eyes. 'You don't get a snack until you follow your commands. We're being watched; the aim is to impress. Now stay!' Mack wriggled his bum but stayed put.

'Excellent,' Agnes murmured, and Johnny wondered if she was going to whip out a glittery paddle at the end of the lesson to mark them both out of ten. 'One more step, move away a little more, slower this time.'

Johnny complied, but even as he shifted his body, Mack lifted a paw and began to get up. 'Stay, doggy!' Grace shouted from behind him, and the dog instantly sat his bottom back on the gravel and wagged his tail.

'Did you forget who feeds you?' Johnny grunted, feeling a little embarrassed as he moved away while Mack watched.

'Well done,' Agnes soothed.

'Not sure I had much to do with it.' Johnny glanced at Paige.

'Sorry,' she mouthed, but he dismissed the apology.

'I'm a little out of practice with commands. Grace – if I don't get it right this time, consider yourself hired.' The little girl let out a happy shriek and she came running over to Mack, stooping down to cuddle him around the head as he wrestled this way and that so he could lick her.

Agnes joined them and pointed to Johnny. 'You're either in or you're out. Total investment – there's no in between. The dog can sense your reluctance to commit both to him and the training. That's why he's listening to the lass.' She glanced at Paige. 'Your girl's in love, you should consider getting her a pup.'

Paige's brows drew together. 'I don't have time for a pet.' She looked down at Grace, who was beaming. 'Do you really think it would be a good idea?'

'Only if you can fit one into your life, lass.' They watched as Grace cooed into Mack's ear, patting him on the head while the dog behaved impeccably. A wrinkle appeared in Paige's forehead and Johnny had an unexpected urge to smooth it away.

He shoved his hands in his pockets. 'Let's try it again. Grace.' He walked over to the child and crouched. 'You watch what I do – if I mess up, I'll be expecting you to point it out.' He ruffled her curls and she bounced up onto her toes, making something inside him light up. Then he turned to Mack, who tried to lick his nose. 'Stop!' Johnny used his chef voice again, and Mack looked surprised and backed away. 'Now sit.' Johnny used the same tone and Mack cocked his head, looking confused. He was used to playful teasing, an order here and there, but this was different and he was smart enough to realise something had changed. Johnny grabbed a treat from his pocket, thinking how scared he'd felt when Mack had been in the lochan, how important it was to get him to behave. Perhaps Agnes was right and it was time to take the training seriously. 'I know it's new for both of us. But I mean it. Sit!' He held the treat in the air and watched the dog's nose follow it, before he slowly lowered his backside to the gravel. 'Good boy,' Johnny murmured. 'Now wait.' He moved a few paces and the dog stayed where he was, even though his body was quaking. 'Come!' Johnny commanded, and the dog sprang up and joined him. 'Good boy.' Johnny fed Mack a snack and stroked his head, feeling a strange unfurling in the pit of his belly, a warmth he hadn't felt in a long time. When he stood, everyone clapped, and even Paige was smiling.

'That's enough for today. He'll lose interest if we make him do it again. That was a brilliant start.' Agnes waggled a finger approvingly at Johnny. 'All in from you means a happy pup. You just graduated with flying colours. Perhaps there are other areas of your life which would benefit from "all in" too.' She winked. 'Let's head to the farm.' She squeezed Johnny's shoulder. 'I got some fresh haddock from one of Morag's suppliers earlier and he threw some salmon in too. He drives into Lockton from time to time. I thought you might like to make us lunch. Show off those skills you try so hard to hide.' Her grin was wicked.

'Did my brother put you up to that?' Johnny asked bluntly.

'Not entirely – I don't get the pleasure of a real chef in my kitchen every day. I'd be an eejit not to take advantage.' She winked as Angel and Mack shot ahead.

'Mack!' Johnny shouted, as both dogs disappeared up and over the gravelly pathway which would take them past the yurts towards the farmhouse.

'Ach, they're fine. Angel will take him back to the kitchen, she won't lead him astray. Let them play, they can't go far. Besides, I've a feeling those two are going to be friends. If you can't get up to mischief with a chum from time to time, life's not going to be much fun.' Agnes wiggled her eyebrows as she eyed Paige, then she grabbed Grace's hand. 'Shall we see if we can catch them? Get into mischief too?' After getting permission from her mam, Grace laughed as they headed off, her pretty curls bobbing in the sun.

'Well done,' Paige said, walking up to join Johnny. 'Seriously, you're good with him. I'm sure all the underwear in Lockton will rest easier tonight. I know mine will.'

Johnny chuckled as they fell into step, following Agnes and Grace who were already halfway up the hill. 'I think the life expectancy of my compost bin just doubled too.' Paige laughed and Johnny realised he was hearing more of that sound from her now. The light tinkle… even her shoulders looked less rigid after a morning in the sun. It warmed him to his toes and he realised he'd like to make her laugh again. It had been a while since anyone had triggered that kind of response – wants and needs beyond the day to day had mostly been consigned to his past. He wasn't sure how he felt about it. First Mack, then Grace, now he was responding to Paige – what was happening to his simple life? Then again, his new mantra was go with the flow, so perhaps he ought to follow it, at least for now?

The kitchen at Buttermead Farm was buzzing when Paige and Johnny arrived. The dogs were now lying in a basket together, looking exhausted. Angel chewed on a long rope and Mack lounged beside her, cuddling a pink toy cat. Grace was already at the table, drinking a glass of squash and watching the dogs with a dopey expression. As Johnny and Paige entered the kitchen and passed the dresser, Tiki fixed them with a straw-coloured eye and seemed to nod at Agnes. 'Waterfront!' she squawked.

'Of course, cutie.' Agnes pulled out her mobile so she could connect it to a speaker, and music began to play. 'Tiki's partial to Simple Minds and this track soothes her. Fergus was here earlier trying to get her to choose another song. I'm not sure which of them ended up more frustrated.' She shook her head, her face softening. 'Big eejit can't understand why she won't listen to him – he's just not asking her right.' She sighed and took a huge piece of fish from the fridge, gathering assorted ingredients, then a chopping board, knife and pans. 'Have you ever made salmon kedgeree?'

In Johnny's last restaurant it had been one of his speciality dishes. He'd served it with crème fraîche and a jug of curry sauce which had been spicy, but mouth-wateringly so. People had come from far and wide to taste it, and there had been a four-month waiting list for a table at brunch. Every forkful had been perfect, he'd made sure of it. Sometimes it had felt like he'd given each customer a tiny slice of his soul. He let out a long sigh. 'I can probably figure something out.' He frowned at the bag. 'Morag's friend gave you an entire salmon?'

Agnes's eyes widened with fake surprise. 'Did he? I suppose you'll have to take it home if you have a mind to practise some new dishes, so you can get that mention in *Best Pubs*. No one at the farm likes fish aside from me, and I'm staying with Fergus for the next few nights.' She winked.

Johnny shook his head and grabbed a couple of eggs before adding them to water and putting them on the Aga to boil. Then he grabbed the onion and garlic and began to chop them quickly before forcing himself to slow down. He wasn't in New York now; there weren't a hundred customers sitting at tables outside the kitchen waiting to sample his creations, no restaurant critics scribbling notes onto pads.

'You can sit, lass,' Agnes said to Paige, and Johnny watched her glance around the room uncertainly. 'I'll make us all some coffee while the lad works. Before I forget, there's a pile of books on the dresser there which belong to The Book Barn, if you want to take them when you go?'

'Sure,' Paige said. Johnny stirred the pan again before turning his back on the cooker and leaning against the counter. He could practically do this dish in his sleep and knew he didn't have to hover

over it. He saw Paige grab the books and take them to the table, before pulling up the chair beside Grace. He noticed the book on matchmaking, *A Ninja's Guide to Playing Cupid*, was now empty of Post-it notes.

Paige tapped the other two books on the pile. 'There are a lot of admirers of Charlie Adaire in Lockton.'

'My daughter-in-law Fiona's a huge fan. I used to borrow his books for her all the time,' Agnes agreed. 'It's a shame it's been so long since he published anything.'

Johnny watched Paige play with the cover. 'There are still quite a few of his titles missing from the library, if my inventory's correct. I suppose they'll gradually make their way back as the villagers find out about the reopening.'

'Aye.' Agnes put a cup of coffee on the counter beside where Johnny was working and took two to the table for Paige and herself. 'Don't worry, word's getting out.' She pulled out a wooden chair and sat down. Johnny turned again so he could pick up a pan and add a slab of butter to it before placing it on the Aga. He scraped the onions into the butter and placed a lid on the saucepan so they could sizzle. The whole process felt so natural, like a dance he thought he'd forgotten but somehow he still knew the steps. 'Morag will make sure of it,' Agnes said to Paige. 'She told me about the author event – do you have any ideas?'

Johnny glanced at the women as Paige shook her head. He added spices and herbs to the pan, stirring a stock cube into boiling water because he didn't have time to make his own. It wouldn't taste as good, but he didn't have the ingredients to make anything better.

He felt a prickle of irritation. He'd always been a perfectionist. It was hard sometimes not to give into old habits, despite the fact that he'd tried to leave them behind. He slowly poured the stock into the pan with a frown, replaced the lid and moved so he could watch the women.

'After the Jam Club last night, I did some research into local authors but not much came up. I sent about thirty emails but haven't heard anything back,' Paige said, opening the hardback and flicking to the back so she could read the inside cover.

Johnny cleared his throat. 'I looked too, and there aren't many to choose from. Most publishers don't give specific locations for their writers.' He lifted the lid on the pan again so he could add another dash of water. It looked good, almost as good as when he'd made it in his restaurant. He inhaled. He'd missed this, and the experience had been more enjoyable than stressful. Would it be so awful to cook the same dish in the pub?

He saw Paige's forehead pinch as she read the cover of the book, tracing the words with a fingertip. 'I didn't realise Mr Adaire was originally from Scotland. That didn't come up in my searches. Although this doesn't say where he lives now.'

'Could be anywhere – people move about.' Johnny took the pan off the Aga. He removed the eggs from the other pan and plopped them into cold water, before picking up a roasting tin and placing the rice mixture and salmon inside. 'Food won't be long now.'

'I have a client back in London who works in publishing,' Paige said as Johnny grabbed some salt and pepper and put them on the table. Agnes got up to grab some pretty blue handmade plates in various wonky shapes along with some cutlery. 'I sent an email early this morning to see if she had any ideas. I'll follow up when I get home later.'

'Speaking of later,' Agnes said, putting out some glasses and a jug of water. 'You probably ought to use the rest of that fish up tonight, laddie. It's best served fresh if you want to impress.'

'That's a lot for one.' Johnny pulled the tin from the cooker and grabbed a blue jug from the counter, pouring his sauce into it. Then he plated the kedgeree, adding a boiled egg on top of everyone's portion before presenting the dish with a flourish. It looked almost the same as it had in New York, although the garnish was missing and the plates were a far cry from the sophisticated white bone china he used to use, but in an odd way Johnny preferred it. He half expected Grace to turn her nose up at the food, but she picked up her fork and waited for him to sit.

'Perhaps you ought to invite someone to share it?' Agnes winked at Paige.

'Oh, I'm fine.' She blushed.

Agnes shook her head. 'The lad will need some help. Perhaps you could find Johnny a good cookery book to follow in the library later?' Agnes suggested, as Paige stared at her plate. Johnny was about to tell Agnes he had a million ideas, could come up with his own recipes, had spent a career doing just that. But for some reason he kept his mouth shut.

'I could pop into the library when I walk you back…' He shrugged. 'Perhaps a guinea pig wouldn't hurt either. I've got a lot of ideas, but it's been a while since I cooked for anyone.' He nodded at their plates. 'Not counting today. If I'm going to do this for Davey…' He let out a long sigh. 'A little feedback would be appreciated.' He looked at Paige. 'You're picky about food – I'll need that because if I can impress you, a food critic will be a pushover.'

A flush spread across Paige's cheeks. 'I'm not picky,' she murmured. 'I was going to spend tonight researching authors.'

Johnny shrugged. 'And I promised I'd help with that. We could look together after we eat?'

Agnes smiled as she poured some of Johnny's sauce onto her plate and ate a mouthful of rice and salmon. 'This is delicious. The man has a talent all right.' She winked at Paige. 'You'd be a bampot not to take the laddie up on his offer.'

'It's…' Paige dug in and took a small bite before her eyes met his and widened. 'I… Wow, this is good. It's a wonder you don't do it more.' She ate another bite and the table fell silent. The only sound was the dulcet tones of Simple Minds singing 'Waterfront' in the background and Tiki tapping her claws. Even Grace was eating – small, delicate mouthfuls, but she was clearing her plate. Johnny watched them, feeling oddly content.

'Well, lass,' Agnes said eventually, breaking the silence. 'You going to help young Johnny here work out a new menu for Apple Cross Inn?'

'I'm… well.' Paige blushed again. It was obvious she was reluctant and for a moment Johnny wanted to put her out of her misery, to retract the offer and wipe the concerned look from her face. But for some reason he couldn't bring himself to do it. He wanted to spend the evening with Paige – wanted to feed her and make her laugh. The feelings were a surprise.

'Go on, Mummy.' Grace beamed.

'Okay.' Paige pulled a face. 'Fine, I'll do it. You helped me with the library after all.'

Johnny grinned, wondering why the idea of cooking for Paige, of having her in his house, felt like the best thing that had happened to him in years.

Chapter Fourteen

The Book Barn was quiet when Johnny, Mack and Paige made their way back to it later that afternoon. Paige had dropped Grace in with her mam, promising to meet them at Kindness Cottage in a few hours. The door of the library was partially open, and there was a sign on the front that read, 'Back soon, help yourself and make sure you leave a note if you borrow anything.'

'What was Morag thinking?' Paige shook her head and stepped inside. The building was eerily quiet, but she could see a new stack of books had been left on the counter. There were a couple of romance novels and some car manuals, none of which she recognised from when she'd been doing the inventory. To the side of the pile, face up on the counter, was a book titled *What Have You Got to Lose?* but it had no accompanying note. Paige piled Agnes's returns on top of it and turned to Johnny, who was watching her.

'He's done for.' He grinned, looking down at Mack who'd fallen asleep on top of his trainers. He bent to pick the dog up and cradled him in his arms. The sight was a little disarming and Paige looked away, just as she heard a noise from behind her. Then Fergus McKenzie strode in through the entrance, carrying a pile of books. He frowned at Johnny as he approached the counter.

'Shouldn't you be at the pub coming up with some new recipes? Tony Silver isn't going to be impressed with a tin of soup,' he growled, raising one bushy grey eyebrow as he took in Mack. 'Good to see you back in Lockton, lassie.' He turned to Paige. 'Not sure what took you so long.' He placed the books on the counter. 'These were recommended to me by Aileen. Not sure why the woman thought I'd be interested.' There was a paperback on creating the perfect whisky recipe, another on making jam and one on Scottish witches – no doubt a reference to him dating Agnes. 'I need something else to read – something interesting. Agnes says I need a hobby, but I'm not taking advice from a woman who spends half her life talking to a dafty bird. Morag says you've got the gift.' He pointed to the shelves of books in the corner, then cracked his knuckles in an obvious challenge. 'So show me what you can do.'

Paige twirled a fingertip around a loose piece of hair. 'Um…' She contemplated the bookshelves. She'd been acquainted with Fergus when she'd grown up in Lockton, but barely. She knew he ran a whisky distillery, owned a black and white sheepdog called Tag, and had been dating Agnes Stuart since last year. He had a reputation as a curmudgeon with a soft heart – a fact he liked to keep to himself. 'Any special interests?' Aileen had often kicked off with the same question when someone asked for a recommendation.

Fergus's lips tightened. 'Whisky – and everyone knows that,' he snapped.

Paige exhaled a long puff. What had Aileen advised? *Listen, watch, go with your gut. Books are more than paper; they're an experience, a respite, or a source of knowledge if you're feeling lost. An act of kindness in the form of words. Don't judge a book by its cover and don't judge a person by the way they look.*

Paige stiffened, realising that was exactly what she'd done with Johnny when they'd first met, tarnishing him with the same expectations that she'd had of Carl. But instead, he'd fed her, helped her in the library, and made her laugh. And he'd shown her kindness when she needed it most. Something to think about. She cleared her throat. 'Non-fiction,' she murmured with a certainty she didn't feel, marching over to the correct section. She could feel Johnny watching her and wondered what he was thinking. It was odd how often she found him in her thoughts now. How often when she closed her eyes, it was him she saw, his voice she heard, instead of Carl's. The realisation was confusing.

She ran her fingertips across the book spines, hoping for some divine inspiration like she'd had when she'd chosen a book for Jason. She shook her head. A history book would be wrong; no doubt Fergus would disagree with any of these authors' interpretations. Science? He probably got enough of that at work. Distilling was its own form of experimentation. She dropped down one shelf to books on pets – dog training? She smiled and pulled a paperback out, placing it to one side. *Keeping Rabbits*? She almost laughed, imagining Fergus cleaning out a hutch. Parrots? Paige's finger hovered as she read the title. *Getting Your Bird to Talk*. Hadn't Agnes mentioned something about that earlier? She'd barely been listening, but something made her pull out the book, and give it to Fergus.

He stared at it for a beat, his expression unreadable. Paige's confidence in her choice began to ebb as Carl's gibes about her being useless nibbled at the edges of her brain; then Fergus nodded. 'Aye. Now that's something I can get my teeth into.' A wicked smile spread across his face. 'Teaching Tiki to ask for something other than that damn song, "Waterfront".' He chuckled to himself. 'I'll take it. Aye, that'll give Agnes a surprise, all right – and it'll be an act of kindness for all of us who want to listen to something else.' He turned and marched up to the counter.

'Good job,' Johnny said, once Fergus had left the library. 'I'd never have thought of choosing a book on parrots.'

Paige shoved her hands into her pockets. 'Being here' – she looked around The Book Barn – 'things have started to come back.'

'And you're enjoying it?' Johnny guessed, his expression penetrating and warm.

Paige nodded. 'I love doing something that makes a difference to someone's life. It might just be one small kind act, but Aileen used to say they can have a ripple effect.' She shrugged. 'I'll miss it when I go back to London.' She ignored the way his smile dimmed, turning instead to grab the book she'd just found. 'This made me think of you.' She gave it to him, relishing his loud snort of delight as he read the cover.

'*Taking the Lead. A Guide to Keeping Your Dog in Order.*' Johnny sniggered again. Something inside Paige began to bubble, a feeling of pure pleasure she hadn't been expecting – a reaction to making him laugh.

She shrugged. 'Just in case you forget Agnes's lessons and need a refresher.'

He glanced at Mack, who was still scooped under one arm. 'Shame he can't read.' His eyes met hers.

Paige swallowed hard and took a step back. 'Do you want me to help you choose a book on cooking fish so you can go home?' She knew she was deflecting, but there was something about him, something she was drawn to, that made her a little afraid. She'd made this mistake once with Carl, got involved with a man she barely knew, let herself get swept up. But she was older and wiser now, wasn't she? And she had a child to think about.

Johnny shook his head. 'I've got a million recipes inside my brain. I don't need a cookbook. I'd like to borrow *Best Pubs* though. If I'm going to impress this food critic, I suppose I ought to get an idea of what he likes. Is there anything you enjoy eating?' His voice had deepened, making something inside Paige fizz.

'Chocolate muffins apparently,' she said, and he smiled. 'When I have an appetite, I eat most things. But you really don't have to cook for me. I said yes to Agnes because I knew she'd just keep asking until I did.'

'You're not going to let me eat all that fish on my own?' Johnny nodded at the enormous bag he'd set down on the floor by the counter. 'It's a monster. There were smaller sharks than this salmon in *Jaws*.'

'Well…' A part of Paige wanted to say yes. She let out a breath. It was the exact opposite of what she should do. She watched Johnny shift Mack and grin at the dog again. This man was nothing like Carl. Besides, number forty-two would go through soon, and she'd move back to London. Was it really such a risk? Her whole life was there; nothing was going to change that. 'Sure, fine. I'll come.'

'And we'll have another go at finding an author, together this time.' When Paige started to protest, Johnny added, 'I live in this village – I'm invested in the library doing well.'

'Okay…' Paige watched the puppy yawn and snuggle closer into Johnny's chest, wishing she had someone she could lean on like that. It felt like years since she'd been able to let go, to just accept a small nugget of affection without feeling like she'd lost control.

She led Johnny to the right of the computer tables, where she'd organised the books on food and drink. There were various tomes, as well as a selection of smaller books. Those sat on pedestals with the covers facing outwards to make the display more colourful. She'd done the same across the library, and planned to write reviews and recommendations on white cards, which she would tuck into the front covers for people who needed help making decisions. A few of the food books she'd put out before had been swapped for something different; instead of books on cheese, tomatoes and mushrooms, there was now a guide to whisky, one on Thai food and another on jam making. Good choices, maybe even better than hers. Perhaps Morag had got bored of lounging by the counter and had decided to make her mark? Paige picked out *Best Pubs*. 'Here you go.' She offered it to Johnny, then scanned the rest of the shelf, noticing a book of walks had been squashed in between a book on vegetarian cooking and another on making sushi. 'Where did that come from?' she muttered, turning it over.

'I'm not sure Morag's got the hang of the filing system.' Johnny took *Best Pubs* and went over to the table beside them, pulling out a chair. 'I'll read through while Mack's sleeping. He's too heavy to carry all the way home.' He turned a page and bent over the book, still holding the dog in his arms.

Paige took the book on walks back to the counter. It hadn't been labelled with one of her stickers indicating where it should be shelved, which meant it couldn't have been in the library earlier; unless Morag had found it somewhere, or it had been returned and she'd decided to put it straight on the shelf? She'd have to add it to the inventory. Paige grabbed her notepad from the office and scribbled *Hidden Scottish Walks*, scanning down to the small subtitle at the bottom which read, *Exploring Lockton and Morridon on Foot*.

She turned the book over. The author biography was brief and gave little away. It mentioned that Archie Radiale had moved back to Scotland after relocating to France for a few years, that he'd never married, was passionate about fresh air and exploring the countryside – in particular around the Highlands. There was a line or two on the old, lesser-known walks he'd discovered around Lockton and Morridon – apparently he'd found most of them just by walking out of his house. Interested, she took the book over to Johnny, who was making notes in his phone, with one arm still wrapped around the sleeping puppy.

She put the book onto the table so he could see it. 'This author is local – think he could be interesting in speaking to an audience? I've checked the back cover, but there's not much information about him.' She looked for the name of the publisher, which she didn't recognise. 'Except he lives in Hawthferry. It's a tiny place with only a few houses. I used to walk there with my da.'

'I know of it,' Johnny said.

Paige patted the book. 'He'd probably know a lot about the local area.' She pulled a face. 'We've not got a lot of options and even less time – reckon he could pull a crowd?'

Johnny shrugged. 'If Morag tells people to come, they will.' He used one hand to spread the pages so he could read the introduction and chapter headings. 'I'd be interested in finding out more. I love walking, most of the villagers do… If he can tell us about secret haunts, difficult-to-find paths we might not have stumbled on, he could be exactly what we're looking for.' He shrugged. 'Jason managed an audience of sixty with someone who'd written about buried treasure; it's almost the same thing.' He grinned.

'You're right,' Paige said. 'I can email the publisher tomorrow; any thoughts on how we might find him in the meantime? I'll bet if we catch him face to face, stress the local angle, he'll be more likely to say yes.'

'We could take a stroll, see if we stumble on anything – doesn't the library close early tomorrow? It's a Saturday, after all…?'

'I was planning on staying later.'

'Of course you were.' He smiled. 'Why don't you bring the book to dinner tonight? We can choose our walk?' Paige wanted to say yes, she realised, as something skipped down her spine. Concern, or acceptance? 'You could bring Grace and have an afternoon out – we could take a picnic? I'll knock up some muffins. I'm sure she'd enjoy some time out.' He quirked an eyebrow at Paige as she nibbled her top lip. 'Or you could spend the time here emailing publishers? It would be boring, and Grace would spend a lovely sunny afternoon stuck indoors.'

'Okay,' Paige muttered. 'We'll come. It's important we get an author if we're going to stop Jason Beckett getting involved in the library launch.' She pursed her mouth. 'I don't want to let Morag down.' She contemplated the room, taking in the shelves she'd erected, the soft rugs and snug reading corners she'd lovingly created. 'I want The Book Barn to be a success. It matters to me, I'd forgotten how much.' She'd forgotten a lot of things about Lockton, and now so many of them were coming back.

Mack snorted and his eyes popped open. He started to wriggle and Johnny put him on the floor and stood up. 'I'll borrow these.' He picked up *Best Pubs* and the book on walks. 'Take them to mine – that way you won't be tempted to change your mind.' He winked.

After Johnny had left, Paige pondered whether she should have said yes; if food, wine and music might turn this stranger into something far more dangerous. Yet a part of her knew it was already too late.

Chapter Fifteen

'How about this, lass?' Cora swept into Paige's bedroom in Kindness Cottage holding up a top and waving it back and forth. Her mam had been incandescent with excitement when she'd heard Paige was going to Johnny's for dinner and was determined to help her dress up. 'I bought it for you a few months ago – I've been meaning to post it to London.' The sleeveless silk blouse was dusky pink with sparkles, and it shimmered in the early evening light that shone in from Paige's bedroom window.

'Um, that was kind. I was thinking of something casual, jeans maybe,' Paige murmured, and her mam nodded enthusiastically.

'Then this will be perfect,' she declared, smiling. 'It's been so long since you had a night out, lass.'

'Make-up, Mummy!' Caught up too, Grace came charging in through the bedroom door, carrying Paws and Paige's toiletry bag which she'd left in the main bathroom. Paige opened her mouth to say she barely wore make-up anymore, and closed it when Grace rose up to her toes to give her a noisy kiss.

'I wore something similar when I was first dating your da,' Cora babbled, waving the top again.

'It's not a date, Mam,' Paige said, wondering if she was lying to herself.

Braveheart wandered in and sniffed the air before hopping onto the bed. Grace squealed and jumped on too so she could pet him, as Cora knelt to check Paige's bookshelf. She drew out a hardback on make-up ideas and looked through the pages, stopping on one with a model made up with heavy sparkles. 'Glitter!' She grinned.

'Glitter!' Grace echoed, as she bounced on the bed.

Cora nodded. 'I've got some of the stuff Meg uses on her cheeks and lips. We can dab some on your eyelids too.'

Paige found herself grinning. It had been a long time since she'd dressed up, and while she didn't want to give Johnny the wrong impression, she didn't want to spoil her mam and Grace's fun either. It was wonderful being fussed over; all her mam's little acts of kindness made her feel so at home, so treasured and loved. She just had to be careful not to lose her head this time. She could do that, if she tried. Couldn't she?

Paige wiped her damp palms on her jeans as she approached Johnny's cottage. Her da had wanted to drive her, but she'd felt like a walk. She wanted time to think and perhaps to smell those roses Johnny's T-shirt had mentioned. It was still warm and the sun was high, the light from its long rays sweeping across the trees, flowers and mountains, creating pretty moving shadows and picking out the effervescent colours. Everything seemed so much brighter here, or perhaps she was just noticing her surroundings more than usual. Maybe for the first time since Carl had swept her off her feet, and her life had become a hundred-mile-an-hour dash for the next thing she needed to achieve.

Johnny's house was separated from fields by a hip-level brick wall which framed a small front garden overflowing with wildflowers in a multitude of summer shades. Paige pushed the wrought-iron gate, which squeaked, and headed for the blue front door, taking a deep breath as she knocked.

Johnny opened the door almost immediately and Mack charged up to greet her. Paige knelt to pat the dog's head, taking a deep breath as she looked up. Johnny wore jeans tonight, but instead of the usual jokey T-shirt, he'd put on a crisp blue shirt which seemed to make his eyes dance even more. She rose, and he glanced at the silk shirt and low heels her mam had suggested she put on.

'Pretty. I love the glitter,' Johnny said, and the word made something inside Paige roll over, perhaps acknowledging that despite all her promises to herself, she didn't stand a chance. 'Do you want to come through? Leave your shoes on, I thought we'd sit outside.' He nodded at her bare shoulders. 'I've set up a firepit and I've got blankets if we get cold.'

'I brought a cardigan.' Paige tapped her bag, which also contained a laptop and three notebooks. If she kept tonight professional, it would be easier to ignore the way he seemed to draw her in.

Johnny grinned again and Paige followed him past a sitting room with two sofas and a rectangular red rug. It had an open fireplace and large windows facing the front garden. The kitchen was what Paige's estate agent in London would describe as 'compact', with grey cupboards along the back wall, an integrated cooker, a hob on the wooden countertop, and a large silver fridge to the side.

Something was bubbling on the stove and the oven was on. 'I hope you're hungry,' Johnny said, as he opened the back door and led Paige onto a wide patio. There were a mass of blazing rhododendrons in purples and pinks lining a long narrow lawn which ended in trees; above them Paige could see the tops of mountains. The patio was shaded by a rustic pergola which had been strung with about a million white fairy lights. The effect was almost magical and she gasped. 'I'd like to take the credit,' Johnny said, watching her take it in. 'But this is all down to Tom Riley-Clark. He rented the cottage from Davey and did most of this before he moved into his own place with Meg. Take a seat.'

He pointed to a round grey slate table and two chairs lined with squashy cushions. The table held twelve tea lights in colourful glass jars burning in the centre, and had already been set with cutlery, napkins, small plates and glasses. Beside the table was a long fire pit which hadn't been lit and a pile of fluffy blankets. 'White wine okay? I chose something that would go well with the meal.' When Paige nodded, he disappeared into the kitchen before coming back with a bottle and platter. 'Mozzarella bites with marinara sauce. I wanted something that would go with fish, but I had to use what I already had.' He placed the white dish onto the table, poured the wine and indicated that Paige should take a seat. She put down her bag and slumped into it, feeling awkward. This whole scene was far more intimate and romantic than she'd been expecting.

'Too much?' Johnny read her mind. 'Sorry, I got carried away. I'm not trying to seduce you.' He shrugged. 'Unless you want me to, that is, in which case I am.' He grinned. 'But it's been a long time since I cooked dinner for anyone outside the pub. You're the first since I've been in Lockton, in fact. I let my chef brain take over, and in truth I enjoyed the idea of treating you.'

The comment made Paige's skin prickle. 'It's fine. I was just… surprised.' She picked up the glass of wine and took a long sip. It was crisp and fresh, and as it hit her tongue she could almost feel the tension in her muscles throw up a white flag and surrender. She picked up a cocktail stick and stabbed it into one of the mozzarella balls, dunking it into the sauce before biting. Her stomach grumbled as she ate, and she realised for the first time in months that she was hungry; ravenous in fact. 'Wow. That's good.' She swallowed and reached for another.

'A success.' Johnny grinned and picked up his glass, toasting her in mid-air before sipping. He was always smiling, as if he viewed the whole world through a glass-half-full lens. It was appealing, and for a moment Paige wished she could see it the same way. But living with Carl had irrevocably changed her. 'I'll add them to the menu.'

'You once described yourself as a former chef,' Paige said, glancing at the starter which they'd almost finished. 'I'd say there's nothing former about your skills. I've eaten more since I met you than I have in years.' She frowned as she acknowledged that was true, wondering what it meant.

Johnny let out a long exhale and grimaced. 'I suppose it's my turn to share. Stranger to stranger.' He shrugged and put his wine glass down, and she saw the play of muscles dance along his forearms. 'Three years ago I was a chef, in New York. I had my own restaurant where I was building a name for myself; a good one, the kind you see in magazines.' His voice was toneless. 'I didn't like what it did to me. I put myself and everyone around me under pressure, took those pills you're on to help me get through each day, forgot what was important.' He paused and took a long breath, looking sightlessly into the garden.

'What happened?'

'I gave it up,' he said finally. 'My restaurant, life, everything; and I don't regret it.'

'Why?' Paige asked, surprised. A couple of weeks ago she might have judged him, might have wrinkled her nose because the conversation reminded her so much of Carl. Because he'd walked away from her and Grace; they might have still been married when he'd died, but essentially he'd all but left. But she knew now that Johnny was nothing like Carl. If he'd given up his career, she suspected he'd had a good reason.

'I had a heart attack and almost died.'

'Oh!' Paige let out a small gasp.

'It was a shock, but being in hospital afterwards gave me time to clarify my priorities. Time to figure out how unhappy I was – what an ass I'd become.' Johnny grinned and rubbed his jaw. 'When I left, I sold my restaurant and moved here. I wanted the life I live now. The freedom of no responsibilities or stress.' He stopped as Mack wandered up for a head scratch before trotting into the garden. 'I wanted to have time to enjoy these small moments. I understand how easy it is to get caught up in things that aren't important. At least to me.' He paused, giving Paige time to digest what he'd said, to reflect on it. 'I sense I may have disappointed you.' A slight smile played on his lips but his expression was concerned.

'That's not…' Paige paused. 'Entirely true. We should all live our lives in the way we see fit.' She frowned, thinking about Carl. 'As long as we're not hurting anyone,' she added.

Johnny nodded and stood, picking up their small plates and the empty platter, waving her away when she tried to help. 'I'll get the main course,' he said quietly, and she wondered if she'd upset him. The idea that she had left her feeling oddly unsettled, and she grabbed her cardigan and pulled it on, watching the flickers of the candles as she waited, and the way the breeze tugged at the flowers and trees. It was so peaceful here, so easy just to be.

Johnny returned a few minutes later with two white china plates that were piled with three small but colourful selections. 'I went a bit mad so don't feel like you have to eat it all, but I wanted your opinion on these. They're the types of dishes mentioned in *Best Pubs* so I thought I'd stick to Tony Silver's favourites. There's a salmon and asparagus parcel, pan-fried salmon with watercress salad, and a simple fish pie with a lime twist – these were some of my specialities.' He put the plates down, then poured them more wine, giving her a shy smile as he sat.

Paige picked up her fork and dug in, chewing some of the parcel before nodding. 'You're very talented,' she murmured, scooping up more.

'Thank you.' Johnny dismissed the compliment; he'd probably heard it a thousand times. 'Tell me more about your husband,' he asked, and Paige wondered if he'd been thinking about Carl when he'd been in the kitchen.

He picked up a forkful of the salad. They didn't speak for a few moments and Paige tuned in to the soft whispers of the breeze, the idle chatter from the birds in the trees. Then her mind circled back to Johnny's question. 'Carl was so different from anyone I'd met before. He was handsome and exciting, filled with stories – most of them lies.' She wrinkled her nose. 'I'd lived my whole life in Lockton, loved it here. I worked in the library, was being trained to take it on.' She paused. 'Sometimes that feels like another life. But I must have been longing for something else because he took one look at me and I fell for him, hook, line and sinker. When he asked me to marry him, I didn't look back, didn't see then how wrong we were for each other.' Didn't see that he'd probably never even loved her – just fallen for a pretty, gullible face.

'It's easy to be captivated by the new and shiny,' Johnny said quietly. 'I think the human condition often forces us to seek out whatever we haven't got. Sometimes it's good for us.' He shrugged. 'Sometimes it's not. You want to stay in London though, want to continue with the job and the life you've been leading?'

'Yes,' Paige said firmly. She wouldn't let herself consider anything else.

Johnny pushed at his food. 'Even though it makes you sick?' he asked quietly.

The statement was direct and inappropriate for a stranger, but Paige heard the worry in his words, appreciated them. It had been a long time since anyone outside her family had been concerned about her. 'I'm not ill. The pills…' She shook her head. 'I've stopped taking them. I don't need them now.'

He looked sceptical.

'I've been reading more,' Paige explained, wanting him to understand. 'Aileen always said a good book cures everything.' She squeezed out a smile. 'I needed a break, that's all. I've not had one since Carl died. I let things get on top of me, but I'm feeling so much better now. When the house goes through I'll be able to go back to work, to my life. I'm even eating.' She forked up some of the pie, ignoring the hollow feeling inside.

'That's good.' But Johnny sounded disappointed. 'How's the house progressing?'

Paige sucked in a breath. 'More delays, but the solicitor hopes it'll go through within the next two weeks. It'll be tight, but it has to – I need to get back to my job. I was only signed off for four weeks and I never expected to be gone that long.'

'I'm sorry you're leaving. But at least you'll still be here for the library launch.'

'I have to leave the day after,' Paige murmured.

Johnny smiled at her. He looked a little sad, but there was no judgement in his face, just acceptance. She felt something simmer in her blood, knew enough to recognise the emotion. She cared for him. He was a good man; she'd almost forgotten they existed.

She looked at her plate, and was surprised to find it almost empty. 'I'd say you should put all of this on your new menu,' she said lightly, changing the mood.

He gave her a small smile. 'Thanks, I will. I'll clear the dishes, light the fire and get that book of walks out. We can choose one together.'

Together. The word made Paige's insides fizz. She shot to her feet. 'Why don't I clear up while you light the fire? It'll be quicker.' She headed into the kitchen with the plates, relieved at the brief respite as she tidied the worktop and loaded the dishwasher, fighting to contain the feelings churning in her body. When she returned, the fire was flickering and Johnny had moved the table to the side, with their two chairs set in front of it. He'd refreshed their wine glasses too and was holding the book on walks, but staring into the flames. Paige sat and grabbed a blanket from the pile, pushing it over her knees. 'Have you chosen a walk for us yet?' she asked.

He opened the book, pointing to one. 'This circles the main part of Hawthferry. According to the map, there are some houses around there. It's a pretty walk and easy enough for Grace. There's probably a one in a thousand chance that we'll find Archie Radiale, but we might bump into someone who can help. There are a couple more walks I found, if that doesn't work out.'

'Okay,' Paige said. 'Seems like the best plan. I emailed a few more publishers before I came out, just in case we don't track him down and by some miracle another author is free.' She folded her arms and stared into the fire.

'We make a good team,' Johnny said softly, and Paige's chest thumped. 'I almost forgot, I made something else.' He stood suddenly, disappeared into the kitchen before heading back with a plate of small chocolate squares. 'Beetroot brownies. They didn't take long and I had all the ingredients, but in my top ten of desserts they're close to number one. I'm afraid I have no ice cream though.'

Paige swiped one from the plate and bit into it, letting the flavours swirl around her tongue. 'Ohhhhhh,' she sighed. 'That's just…' She let out an involuntary hum, turning to Johnny. 'Sooo good.'

He was watching her and there was the oddest expression on his face. 'It's truly a delight watching you eat. It's like seeing something bloom. I stopped cooking, lost my joy for it after New York.' His voice was husky. 'But you're helping me get it back.' Paige blinked as something like wonder crossed his face. 'Thank you.' His blue eyes found hers and they both fell silent as their gazes held. There was just the snap and crackle from the fire, a rush of wind through the trees. The sounds were almost erotic, and when Johnny reached up a finger to trace it across Paige's cheek, she found herself leaning in. She ignored all the voices whispering to her that this was just like when she'd fallen for Carl, just like when he'd charmed her – because in this one moment, she didn't care.

Johnny's lips were soft and sweeter than the brownies he'd made for her. He shifted the palm that rested on her cheek, let it run down her neck, trailing the tender skin, which sizzled under his gentle touch. He deepened the kiss as she leaned into him and sighed against his mouth when his hands continued their slow journey, sliding down her arms, which even through the knit of her cashmere cardigan felt like they were sparking with something like fire. She hadn't been touched for so long, had forgotten how it felt to be wanted by someone. It was as tantalising as it was wrong. The kiss continued, slow and easy, before it seemed to ignite suddenly as if someone had thrown tinder onto it, then stood back to watch it explode. Something fizzed and popped in Paige's brain, and fireworks burst across every inch of her skin. Then Johnny's hands stopped their slow slide and his lips softened until the heat cooled to a low simmer. They both leaned back as the kiss ended. Johnny's eyes held hers for a moment. 'It really is a shame you're leaving.' Then he turned back to the fire and Paige twisted so she could stare into it too, feeling off balance and confused.

*

Paige leaned back against the front door of Kindness Cottage after Johnny had walked her home a few hours later. The house was quiet, which suggested her parents and Grace were all asleep, and she closed her eyes, grateful for the peace and time to think. She put the heel of her palm against her chest as she heard the sound of Johnny's footsteps on the gravel drive as he walked away, feeling her heart's slow beat through her silky top. It felt so normal and she wondered why, because her whole world had just tipped on its axis.

She had feelings for Johnny, feelings she didn't want and didn't know what to do with. She took a step forwards, heading for the stairs, wishing she knew what to do next.

Chapter Sixteen

Paige laid her head on the window as Johnny drove them out of Lockton, taking the main road which would lead them through Morridon to who knew where, for the start of their walk. Grace was asleep in the back, tucked into her car seat. Her daughter had woken early from a fitful sleep and had wanted a cuddle, which Paige had gratefully delivered. Mack barked from behind the bars of the cage Johnny had set up in the boot, reminding them he was unhappy about being cooped up.

'We'll stop in a moment,' Johnny murmured, putting the car into third as he took a left onto a bumpy road. Paige tried not to stare at his strong hands, or notice the way his muscles bunched as he handled the car. There was a lot of power there for a man who seemed determined to do so little. A lot of kiss he'd delivered last night in that brush of lips which wasn't supposed to mean that much. But it had left her with a tingling sensation under her skin she hadn't experienced in years, and a potent want.

They took a right onto a road which hugged the base of a mountain. The terrain was lush, green and speckled with multicoloured wildflowers. Further up, on the slopes of the lowest peak, she could just make out the boundary of some ruins.

'Kilcorn Castle.' Paige recognised the large grey stones immediately. 'I used to come here with my da when I was a teen. It's a long way and rocky, but the views are incredible.' She'd visited a few times in her twenties with friends she'd lost touch with now. Perhaps they still lived around Lockton? Maybe she should contact them? It had been a long time since she'd thought about friendships or simple pleasures; there wasn't much time in her life for them now. For a moment Paige thought about her dinner with Johnny, wondering if her life made her happy anymore.

Grace let out a low hum from her car seat, indicating she was waking up. She stretched out an arm to point at the castle. 'Princess cake!' she shouted, and Mack barked in response, bashing his tail against the bars of the cage.

'Cake?' Johnny raised an eyebrow, looking at Paige.

She grimaced. 'Remember, she wants one for her birthday,' she whispered. 'She's four next month.'

'I remember, a castle cake for the princess in the back of my car. Figures. You just shout if you want some help with making that.'

'I'll be fine,' Paige murmured, although the words were more reflex than truth.

Johnny looked disappointed. 'There's a clearing just up from here, with better views of Kilcorn Castle. I suppose you could use it for cake inspiration,' he joked. 'I thought we could stop there before our walk for a snack. I go there sometimes to draw.'

'You draw?' Paige asked, surprised.

'I like drawing,' Grace said, yawning.

'After a fashion.' Johnny shrugged. 'I've enough paper and pencils for the princess here to join me if she wants.'

'Yes!' Grace cheered, and Paige felt her heartbeat skip in response. It was a while since she'd heard such happiness from her daughter – she'd almost forgotten how such simple things could mean so much. Was that what Johnny had been referring to last night?

He pulled the car into a small layby. From here Paige could see a track that led upwards to a grassy clearing. The sun was high and she opened the door and got out, feeling warmth on her legs and shoulders. She'd worn shorts and a light blue T-shirt because she knew it would pick out the golden flecks in her eyes. She'd caught the sun when they'd been by the lochan at Buttermead Farm – she'd looked at herself in the mirror for a few extra moments this morning, surprised that she liked what she saw. Still too thin, but not so pallid. Perhaps it was the time away from work? She'd also eaten more in the last weeks than she had in months, because as well as the meal last night, Johnny had insisted on bringing treats to work, trying to tempt her long-dead appetite. It was a long time since a man had cared about what she ate, longer still since she'd let him. Or taken the time to swipe on lipstick because she thought he might notice. The thought should have made her uncomfortable – but for some reason, it didn't.

She opened the back door and released Grace from the seat, lifting her to the ground. The toddler grabbed Paws and waited patiently as Johnny got Mack out, clipping on his lead and grabbing a rug, tin, flask and large canvas bag with sketchpads poking from the top.

'You were serious?' Paige asked, following as he pointed to the pathway and Grace grabbed his hand. The simple action made her heart stutter.

'There's always time for drawing, just ask the princess,' he said, and Paige gulped and followed, wondering why such a tiny act could make her feel both grateful and scared to death.

'She's a bit fidgety, our model,' Johnny complained half an hour later, pointing his charcoal at Paige as she tapped her foot on the grass and buried her head in the Charlie Adaire novel she'd found in her bag. It hadn't been there this morning, or when she'd gone to the library before Johnny had picked them up. Care of Morag, she guessed. Or perhaps her da, hoping to find something they could talk about later, had squirrelled it in her bag in an effort to help her relax?

After feeding them coffee – milk for Grace – a selection of sandwiches, beetroot brownies and some of his chocolate muffins, Johnny had suggested Paige sit on a large round boulder at the edge of the clearing to read. Big mistake, she'd realised soon after, especially when he'd pulled those large pads from the bag and set himself up to draw.

'Do you understand the meaning of the word still?' Johnny asked softly, his attention fixing on her tapping foot.

'Mummy, still!' Grace said, imitating Johnny as she pointed her pencil to the sky and squinted. She wore an apron that was far too big for her and knelt in front of a sketchpad that had been laid on the grass, her pretty curly hair flowing around her shoulders and down her back. Beside her Johnny held a thick wad of paper and a piece of charcoal which he kept striking across the pad. Mack lay in between them, snoring softly.

'She doesn't know how to relax, your mum.' Johnny winked at Grace as he scribbled, raising an eyebrow when Paige let out a loud huff.

'Relax, Mummy,' Grace said with a beaming smile.

'How much longer?' Paige asked, tapping her foot again before she took a moment to look up from the book and out at the view. It was beautiful and she felt her breath catch in her throat. She pulled her mobile from her pocket and took a quick picture, wishing she had someone to send it to. She eyed Johnny, wondering if he'd notice if she took a snap of him too.

'You keep moving,' he complained, angling his charcoal stick, lining it up against her face.

She sighed. 'We've got a walk to do, remember.' She turned her head to take in the jagged mountain range, which rose out of the horizon, and the cloudless blue sky that framed it. The colours of the landscape were so bright they almost seemed to vibrate. She cleared her throat. 'And an author to find. I want the launch to be a success. The library's important to me.' There was so much history there, so many good memories she'd all but forgotten about.

'All in good time,' Johnny said, brushing wide strokes across the page.

'All in good time,' Grace repeated, earning herself a broad smile. He was so good with her; strange for a man who didn't have children. So different from Carl.

'I suppose today we have time,' Paige said, dismissing the comparison with a sigh, staring back at the horizon. After another ten minutes, during which Paige found herself daydreaming for the first time in years, Johnny stopped so he could peek at Grace's creation.

'You've a talent, princess,' he said and she giggled, making something in Paige's stomach unfurl. When they got back to London, she'd need to make sure she heard that sound a lot more.

She began to read, losing herself in the story. Aileen had loved hiding books in Paige's bag after each shift at the library. 'Life is more than Lockton,' she'd said in her throaty voice, as she'd plied Paige with yet another recommendation. 'Read about it now, and if you get the chance, experience as much as you can. You'll soon learn where your heart belongs – and it won't all be between these pages. But don't forget the power of the right book, or the lessons they can teach you.'

Not in Lockton, Paige thought, as she turned the page and heard her daughter laugh again. She had to get back to work, to the security of the life she was trying to build. A life that relied on no one but her.

'I think we'll need to wrap up soon, princess,' Johnny said about twenty minutes later, just as Paige finished another chapter and turned to the next. 'You finished?' he asked, taking time to examine Grace's drawing and nod. 'A definite talent,' he murmured, nodding again. 'You should show your mum.'

Grace grinned and picked up the pad, then skipped across the grass so she could share her creation. 'Is that me?' Paige asked, pointing to a black scribble with wiry scrawls that looked like arms and a solid black dot which was probably a head.

'Yes,' Grace agreed.

There was a square box beside it. 'What's that?' Paige asked.

'Work,' Grace murmured, making Paige's blood run cold.

Close by was a small squiggle standing alone with a smaller squiggle beside it.

'Me and Paws.' Grace traced a fingertip across them. Then she pointed to a shape in the distance with a long, swishy tail, and another large round squiggle wearing a hat.

'Who's that?' Paige pointed to the pad.

'Johnny – prince. Crown,' Grace said, then gestured to the smaller swirl with the tail. 'Doggy.' She pressed a finger onto the smudge.

'It's brilliant,' Paige said. 'We should take it home.' Grace ran back and folded the paper so she could tuck the drawing into Paws's secret compartment.

'What about yours?' Paige asked, getting up to stretch just as Johnny closed his pad and followed Grace to the bag.

'It's a work in progress.' He grinned. But Paige held out a hand, and he pulled a face before passing it to her. 'I'd recommend you don't expect too much.'

She leafed through the pages and let out a surprised snort.

'I never said I could draw,' he grumbled, as she glanced through a few more. Trees, rocks, people, dogs – the pictures were all lopsided, the shadows were in the wrong places, and there was something amateurish but very endearing about each one. She turned to the picture of her. She was all angles, although he'd got the shape of her head and there was something about the way she was sitting that caught her attention – she was staring into the sky, with the book flopped open beside her. The perspective was way out and she looked far too skinny. 'You don't have to be good at something to enjoy it,' he said, as Paige looked up. His expression was serious and he gestured to the pad.

'I wasn't judging you…' she said softly, worried she'd offended him. 'It's just…' She searched for the right words.

'Most people don't take time for things they have no talent for?' he asked, and she nodded slowly. 'Life doesn't have to be perfect. I told you last night, for me it's about small moments, enjoying the day. Talent, perfection, brings pressure – a need to improve, to push yourself. I enjoy the freedom of being outside, of having the warmth of the sun on my face. I love the quiet, the sounds the pencil makes as it brushes my pad. It's pleasure pure and simple, nothing more.' He shrugged. 'Your daughter understands.' He tipped his head towards Grace who was petting Mack, rubbing his head and giggling – loud belly laughs Paige wasn't sure she'd ever heard before as the puppy practically purred with joy, letting out a series of happy yelps. 'I think it's one of the things kids are so good at – living in the moment, understanding what's important. Finding pleasure isn't about being good or bad at something, it's about taking time to experience it.'

'I suppose.' Paige paused. 'Can I have it?' She pointed to the pad. 'The picture of me,' she added, when he looked confused.

'You're not going to try to sell it on eBay, are you? Because I've got to tell you, I've tried and all I got was advice.' His face morphed from serious to amused, and Paige belly laughed too and shook her head. It wasn't only Grace who was laughing so much more these days, she realised.

'I'd like the reminder – of today.'

Johnny shrugged and opened the book so he could tear the page out to give her. Then he picked up Mack's lead and led them back to the car. Paige trailed after, holding the picture, looking down – thinking that even in this amateur scrawl of a picture, she looked a little sad.

*

'So the walk starts here.' Johnny pointed to some trees on their left as Paige guided Grace along the narrow pathway. 'According to the book, it'll take us almost straight past the author's house. It's not marked on the map, but he mentions starting from the corner of his land, so I'm guessing if we follow the exact path and keep our eyes peeled, we should see it.'

'Carry,' Grace said after toddling a couple of steps, turning and holding up her arms.

'How far?' Paige asked, bending to scoop her up. Paige could smell the strawberries Grace had eaten for breakfast, as the child pressed her nose to her neck.

'Prince,' Grace murmured sleepily.

'Three miles. I'll take the princess.' Johnny adjusted his backpack and opened his arms so they could swap. Grace leaned forwards and fell into his arms; he scooped her up and she wrapped her chubby arms around his neck. He began to walk, and she laid her head on his shoulder and smiled at Paige, who stood staring after them. It was odd to share something so important with someone she'd known for such a short time, and she wasn't sure how she felt about it. Was she risking her daughter's vulnerable emotions by letting her get close to this man? Johnny stopped and turned so he could offer Paige the map. 'It's the blue walk – we pass a lochan and head through woodland. It's fairly flat; I'm guessing it won't take that long.'

'What are we looking for?' Paige asked, peering at the map.

'A big sign with "author lives here" painted across it?' Johnny joked, heading towards an arch of trees which marked the start of the hike. 'In truth, I don't know. This sounded like a better idea when we were discussing it last night. I vote we follow the route and see what we find. If we bump into anyone, we can ask if they know this Archie Radiale – it's a memorable name, so if they live around here they may know him. If we don't have any luck, there's a village a couple of minutes' drive from here – we could always check it out and look for a post office. See what we can find out there.' He waggled his eyebrows and set off again with Grace clamped around his neck. Within a few steps Paige saw her daughter's eyelids droop. She paced after Johnny, trying not to let her gaze drop to his jeans, or to appreciate the way his legs filled them out. There was something about the way he inhabited his clothes, those easy, relaxed movements. Even that dark T-shirt, which stretched across his chest, showcasing today's silly slogan – 'Kindness Always Wins' – and the muscles she'd been pressed against last night. Something inside her – long dormant – stirred again.

After about ten minutes they arrived at a T-junction and Johnny turned to her. 'Which way?' he asked softly. Paige checked the map and traced her finger across the path. 'Right. It's about ten minutes through a wooded area beside a lochan, then there's a kissing gate, and just after that we're going to get close to a house. Apparently there are some rare wildflowers around here, and if we keep an eye out we might see rabbits.'

'Rabbits – hear that, Mack?' Johnny grinned as Mack bounded ahead. The dog was still on the lead but he was starting to look tired and Paige wondered if one of them would be carrying him too before their walk was done. She looked up; the sun was still high and the sky was almost cloudless. She could hear birds in the distance and running water. She took in a breath and let it out slowly, then breathed in again, feeling the air fill her lungs and her pulse slow. She could smell flowers and trees – such a contrast to the stuffy, sweaty odours she was used to at work – could appreciate the way the sun dappled through the treetops, highlighting bark, branches and the earth underfoot; a spotlight drawing attention to all those hidden spaces that were usually forgotten.

'There's a fence.' Johnny came to a stop and Paige almost ran into the back of him. She checked the map again; the metal barrier wasn't marked. It ran across most of the right-hand side of the path, and a sign reading 'PRIVATE' in huge red letters had been attached. Johnny shook his head. 'We can follow the path round, but that fence is going to stop us from going off-piste if we spot a house.'

Paige crossed her arms as she considered their choices. 'Let's keep going, see what we find – there might be an opening.'

It took another twenty minutes and neither of them spoke. Paige let her mind wander until she found herself studying Johnny's back. Grace was fast asleep, her arms heavy across his shoulders. She was usually so shy around strangers; what was it about this man that made her feel safe? 'I can see a building over there,' Johnny said suddenly, pointing through the trees into a thickly wooded area. Paige walked up beside him and pressed her nose to the fence. She could just make out the top of a roof which was partially obscured by branches. 'I was right – that fence is going to stop us from getting any closer.'

'Let's see if there's a gap further up,' Paige said and they walked on, through a kissing gate. Paige held it open so Johnny could walk through and tried not to think about the way his lips had felt last night. But when they tingled, she pressed her fingertips to them. They walked a little further, heading uphill, and at the top they hit a road which was rough with pebbles and rocks instead of tarmac, suggesting anyone who lived close by might not welcome visitors.

'We need to go left here.' Paige ran a fingertip across the map.

'The house is that way though.' Johnny pointed in the opposite direction, along the lumpy road. 'There's that fence, but…' He walked towards it with Mack trotting beside him. 'Is that a post box?'

Just up the road from them in the distance, Paige could see the start of a drive, with a large unwelcoming gate at the end. To its right was a black post box on top of a thick stump of wood. They walked up to check the metal gate, but it was locked and there seemed to be no way of speaking to the inhabitants. There was open woodland to the right of them, but the tall fence made it inaccessible.

'If we knew Archie lived here, it would be worth finding a way to speak to him. That's a big house, bigger than I expected.' Johnny looked up and frowned. 'I know it's unlikely, but I wonder if it's his. A lot of the walks start near here.'

'That house is huge,' Paige murmured. 'The author biography mentioned Archie lived in France for a few years. This might not be his, he could still be living abroad.'

'There's only one way to find out.' Johnny bent so he could examine the post box, pushed a fingertip into the opening and pulled, but it didn't budge. 'There's no name on the outside.' He sighed. 'I suppose it was a bit of a long shot.'

He walked around it a few times as Grace stirred. 'Down, please,' she said as she woke, and Johnny put her on the ground. She trotted over to Mack who was sniffing the earth, perhaps picking up the scent of rabbits. 'Good doggy.' She patted him on the head and he got up and went to sniff the bottom of the post, wagging his tail.

'Back the way we came?' Johnny turned to Paige. 'We can pick up the path over there, I think we're over halfway. We could drive to the village high street. If we're lucky there will be someone working there with Morag's skills, and we can find out who lives here.'

'Sure,' Paige said, as Grace let out a loud laugh.

'Sit, doggy,' she shouted, as Mack jumped up at the wooden post. Grace patted his haunches as he began to sniff the box, then the dog turned so he could nuzzle her neck. But as he did, Grace tripped over the lead Johnny was still holding and tumbled forwards. Paige ran to catch her, but she was too late. She watched with her heart in her throat as Grace fell into Mack and they both landed on the post. Her daughter wasn't heavy, but the combined weight of the dog and toddler were too much for the stump of wood. The whole thing tumbled over and the post box separated from its pole, hitting the ground with a loud clang. The front of the box flew open, and four envelopes and a small parcel tumbled out, spraying everywhere.

Grace gathered herself and began to sniff. Tears rolled down her cheeks as she ran up to Paige. 'Mummy.' The knees of her trousers were dirty and she had mud on her clothes. 'Mummy, I broke it,' she cried, as Mack bounded after her and Johnny tugged him back.

'It's fine,' Paige soothed, scooping her up and cuddling her close. 'I'm sure we can fix it.'

'You okay, princess?' Johnny asked as Grace sobbed into Paige's neck. 'Don't worry, I'll sort it out.' He patted her on the shoulder and went to examine the damage. Then he bent to gather the letters and metal box. As he started to put the mail back inside the box he stopped, his face creasing in surprise.

'What's wrong?' Paige asked, running a palm down Grace's back as she walked up to join him.

Johnny shook his head. 'It doesn't make sense.' He shuffled through the letters again.

'Is it bad?' Paige asked. 'Isn't it Archie's post box?'

'No. It's good.' Johnny turned to look at her, a slow smile illuminating his face. 'You'll never believe it, but it's a hell of a lot better than that.'

Chapter Seventeen

Johnny studied the envelopes and shook his head, wondering if his eyesight was failing. It was only when Paige walked up to join him and he held them out so she could read the name and address scrawled across the front that he knew what he was reading was true.

'Charlie Adaire, the writer of mystery and crime books?' She sounded shocked. 'How's that possible?'

He shrugged. 'That's what it says here. But it gets even stranger – there's a parcel here for Archie Radiale too.' He waved it under her nose. 'That doesn't make sense, unless they both live at the same address?' He squinted at the large gate which all but obscured the house behind them. He could see treetops and there was the top edge of a long roof. 'We came to find one author and instead found two. Think at least one of them would be free to come to the library to do the talk?' He was only partly joking.

Paige pulled a face and walked up to the fence as Grace began to squirm in her arms, struggling to be put back on the ground. She let her go, and the toddler ran up to Mack as Paige peered through the fence. 'I can't see any way in. I suppose I understand these barriers now. An author like Charlie Adaire probably doesn't want a ton of unwanted visitors. I read last night he's a recluse. From what I understand, he's barely been seen since he stopped writing. I suppose that's why no one – not even the magnificent Morag – knows he lives just a few miles down the road.'

'That's odd in itself.' Johnny tapped a fingertip on his chin. 'Morag knows everything. How this escaped her network of spies is anyone's guess. I suppose we could knock on the gate?' he suggested.

'I doubt he'd hear you.' Paige sounded disappointed. 'But we should definitely try.' She marched up to the metal structure, her small body a picture of determination as she hammered on it twice, but nothing stirred. 'We're so close,' Paige said. 'I so want to get an author for the launch. I don't know why I care so much, but I don't want to let Morag down. I want the library to be a success.' Mack tugged at the lead as Grace stroked him again, curling her arms over his collar and around his neck. 'Be careful, sweetie, the dog has to be able to breathe.' Paige frowned and knocked on the gate again before turning around. Johnny could see the whir and click of her brain as she tried to solve their latest dilemma. She was a delight to watch and he felt a small twinge of admiration. The woman never gave up. The realisation gave him a pang of disappointment at himself. 'We could write a note, put it in the post box for Charlie or Archie to find?' she suggested eventually.

Johnny shrugged. 'We'll have to go back to the car. I left my sketchbook in there. If we get it, I can tear a page out and we can leave a message.'

'Short of scaling that fence, there's not much else we can do.'

'I'd better put this back together,' Johnny murmured, looking at the letters and parcel he was still holding. There was something nagging him about the names. 'I'll need to put Mack somewhere first.' He walked up to a nearby tree and looped the leather lead around it as Grace trotted after. The dog licked Johnny on the arm and he grabbed a treat from his pocket. 'Good boy.' He fed him, pausing to pat him on the head. Mack was behaving so much better after Agnes's lessons.

'Hungry, prince,' Grace said, stroking Mack again. Johnny reached into his backpack and pulled out a muffin he'd packed in a small storage box – he'd brought it from the car, just in case one of them got peckish. He held it up to Paige and she nodded.

'Here you go, princess.' He took the muffin out of the box, and Grace grabbed it and took a quick bite. He watched as the toddler devoured half of it. 'Keep an eye on Houdini here while I fix this mess,' he said. He picked up the large wooden post and placed it back in the hole. It was heavy but Johnny could see it hadn't been buried deep – it was a wonder it had stayed upright for so long. He ground it in a little further, leaning all his weight onto it before standing back to make sure it stayed put. Then he picked up the battered post box so he could shove the letters inside. He closed the lid and placed it back on the post. It didn't look stable, and there were dents in the painted black metal which hadn't been there before – but it was the best he could do for now. 'I'll write my details on the letter, offer to pay for any damage.'

'No, doggy!' Johnny turned as Grace let out a loud squeak of alarm. It took him a few seconds to register what was happening. Mack's golden tail was wagging in the air and he was burrowing into a small gap under the metal fence.

'Stop!' Johnny felt a sharp stab of alarm as the mutt squeezed all the way under before popping out on the other side. 'Mack, come back! Sit, stay, dammit.' His chest felt tight as he ran up to the fence. Mack's collar and lead were on the floor by Grace's feet. The collar was undone, but whether that was the dog channelling Houdini again or Grace had taken it upon herself to release him, he didn't know – it hardly mattered now. 'Mack, come!' He pressed his nose to the metal fence as the dog bounded this way and that on the other side, clearly enjoying his burst of freedom. Johnny could see woodland, wildflowers, and in the distance, a long ginger tail flicking this way and that. He knew what that tail belonged to, and knew he only had seconds to persuade Mack to return. He knelt, aiming to get the dog's attention. 'Mack.' He used his firm voice, the one Agnes had taught him, and pulled the treats from his pocket. 'Mack, come!' He took one from the bag and dangled it in front of the fence.

'Come, doggy,' Grace echoed.

'Listen to the princess,' Johnny said, as Mack's large brown eyes blinked with interest and he took a tentative step forwards. But then the undergrowth rustled again, and his ears pricked and he turned his head. That's when Johnny's breath caught. Because out of the vegetation, the owner of the fluffy ginger tail appeared.

'Cat!' Grace squealed in delight, as Mack's body went rigid.

'Dammit, Mack!' Johnny shouted as the dog barked and turned, charging in the other direction. The cat's head jerked up, and quick as a flash it darted left, storming through the layers of wildflowers and bushes in the direction of the house. Johnny shook the fence as Mack bounded after, but it didn't budge. The gap below, which Mack had somehow managed to squeeze himself through, was barely big enough for his foot to ease into. 'Mack!' he shouted again, feeling helpless as the dog followed the cat towards the house and disappeared. What the hell was he going to do? Then they heard a man's shout, a scuffling and a couple of short barks.

'We're going to have to bang on that gate again,' Paige said, grabbing Grace's hand so she could run towards it. 'Let the man know we're out here. Mack's not even got his collar – there's no way anyone will be able to trace him to you.'

They ran to the metal gate and hammered on it with their fists as Johnny felt the beginnings of panic. He couldn't lose the stupid dog; he was just getting used to letting him under his skin. After what felt like hours, the gate opened a crack and Johnny let out a sigh of relief as Mack's brown nose nudged through. The gate opened a little further, and a man with dark hair and an even darker expression followed. He was carrying Mack, holding him firmly by the scruff of his neck. The dog let out an excited bark when he saw them all waiting.

'We're so sorry,' Paige gasped.

'Is this eejit yours?' The man's voice was gruff, with Scottish overtones mixed with shades of something Johnny recognised as European. 'Because it was trespassing and harassing my cat. Barging into my garden and trampling my plants. I was working – for the first time in months – and now I've lost my thread.' He frowned at the three of them, before focusing on Paige. Johnny was about to step in front of her, when she spoke.

'We're really very sorry. Mack got off his lead by accident, it never should have happened.' She reached for the dog but the man stepped back. 'I'm Paige Dougall. We were hoping to speak with you.'

'Why?' The man's eyes were brown, with hints of black. He obviously hadn't shaved in a while and his hair sat on top of his head in untidy tufts. He was wearing a set of creased blue pyjamas. He didn't wait for an answer, and instead shook his head. 'I'm not interested. My double glazing's fine, I don't need a new conservatory, the WiFi out here is great, and I will not give you or any other bampot an autograph.' He looked at Grace, who was still holding the half-eaten muffin. 'So unless you've got a car full of those that you're trying to flog, you can leave.' He shoved Mack through the opening and slammed the gate without ceremony.

'Mr Charlie Adaire?' Paige shouted.

'So what if I am?' the man growled.

'Do you like chocolate muffins?' Johnny hollered, picking up Mack. The dog licked his face, as he looped the collar around his neck and secured the lead. The man didn't answer but it was silent on the other side of the fence, and there were no footsteps on the gravel driveway which suggested he was listening. 'I'll bet you can't get them out here,' Johnny continued. 'I know Hawthferry has no bakery.' He paused. 'I'm a chef. I could bring you some.' He frowned; it was a while since he'd called himself that. Strange how the word seemed to slip so easily off his tongue. He noticed Paige flash a look of surprise in his direction.

'How many?' The man sounded more curious than grumpy.

'Half a dozen? All you have to do is talk. We can even speak here,' Johnny offered.

The man sighed. 'A dozen, and I want them on Monday. Chocolate.'

'Please,' Grace piped up.

'Fine, please,' the man growled.

'Done.' Johnny grinned.

The gate creaked open a crack, and the man's head snaked out. 'What do you want in return? I was serious about the autographs.'

'Mr Adaire.' Paige stepped forwards again. 'I work in The Book Barn.'

'The library in Lockton.' He dipped his head. 'I know of it. Went a few times when I was a wee lad. Aileen Dalhousie ran it before she passed. I thought it had shut?'

'We opened again on Thursday,' Paige explained. 'There's a committee in Lockton who got funding from Creative Scotland, and they've been working to reopen. We've got a launch event planned in two weeks – for various reasons, we haven't secured an author and we badly need one so we can make a real splash.' She talked quickly, as if she suspected her time was short. Judging from the expression on the author's face, he was getting bored. 'We… well, we…' Paige looked behind her. 'Your post box fell and we saw the letters, saw your name – we were here looking for Archie Radiale. Is he a neighbour?'

Charlie frowned. 'Of a sort. He's not keen on company either. He told the publisher not to put so much information about him on that damn walking book. People are always coming around here looking for him.'

Paige sighed. 'It wasn't that easy to work out where to go – and we found the letters in your post box by accident. That fence makes it difficult to get close.'

'The fence is mine – it's supposed to keep eejits from trespassing.' He glared at Mack. 'I had a policeman moaning about it a week ago, but I'm entitled to protect my privacy.'

Paige blushed. 'That might have been my da. He's a big fan of yours. Look.' She held up a hand. 'We're not here to impose. The event wouldn't take long. I could pick you up and drive you there if you're worried about transport.' Charlie's expression didn't change. 'There'd be food, and as many muffins as you can eat. You've hundreds of fans in the village – my da devours everything you write. We'd be very grateful.'

He sniffed. 'I don't usually do events. It's been a while since I published a book.' His eyes narrowed suddenly. 'Who's on this committee of yours?'

Paige looked at Johnny. 'Um, my mam Cora Dougall, and Agnes Stuart.'

'I know of them,' he said.

'And Morag Dooley who runs the post office.'

Charlie let out a sudden bark of disgust. 'Oh, I know Morag Dooley. That woman wants *me*' – his shoulders straightened and he stabbed a finger against his chest – 'to come and talk at your library?'

'Well, she doesn't know it's you exactly, she doesn't have any idea that we've come…' Paige looked surprised. 'We were looking for Archie, but—'

'You can forget about him too.' His frown deepened as fury marched across his face. 'If that woman has anything to do with it, neither of us will be coming within ten miles of your library so you can find yourself another eejit.' He glared at Johnny. 'I'll be expecting those muffins here before noon on Monday.' With that, he slammed the gate.

Chapter Eighteen

Johnny placed Grace into the car seat in the back of his Land Rover and clipped the buckle as Paige persuaded Mack into the cage in the boot. The toddler let out a soft sigh and her head slid to the right. She'd fallen asleep on his shoulder again on the way back to the car and something inside him had unfurled, like a flower sprouting from the earth; another green shoot that he'd been determined to keep in the dark. He slammed the door shut and climbed into the driver's seat, waiting as Paige clambered in next to him. 'Want a muffin?' he asked, trying to distract himself, grabbing the Tupperware container out of his backpack which sat on the floor by her feet. He opened the lid and the scent of chocolate filled the car.

She shook her head. 'You really like feeding people.' She watched as he grabbed a muffin and bit into it.

He swallowed. 'Food helps me think and...' He shrugged, realising she was right; at its most basic, cooking was about giving, fulfilling a need – not a competition or performance, but something much more fundamental. 'Perhaps I do like feeding people. But only if they eat what I cook.' He looked at her empty hands which were clasped in her lap. 'So it looks like we're back to square one with the launch.' He took another bite and stared out of the window at the woods they'd just emerged from. 'Perhaps we'll have to ask Jason for his help after all?'

Paige snorted, then reached across to grab a muffin from the box before taking a small bite. Johnny didn't say anything but he felt a surprising catch of pleasure in his throat when she let out a low hum. The whole thing reminded him of last night, of that kiss he'd been trying to forget. 'You give up too easily,' she said eventually. 'We need to talk to Morag, see what *that*' – she brushed crumbs off her bottom lip, then tipped her head towards the window in the direction they'd just walked – 'is all about. She behaved strangely the other day in the library when I mentioned Charlie Adaire; there's obviously some history there. Perhaps we can do something to fix it?'

Johnny blew out a breath. 'I vote we leave it alone.'

'Take the path of least resistance?' she asked, looking disappointed. Johnny frowned; those were the exact words Agnes had used a couple of days before. 'That's not the way I work.'

'You like to fix things.' He'd seen her at work. He wondered again what made her so determined to put the world right. Was it just a consequence of her bad marriage, or something inherent in the way she was?

'It's worth a conversation. If we can find out a little more, perhaps we can persuade Morag to come here and talk to him.'

'Fine.' Johnny sighed as he finished the muffin and started the engine. 'We'll go and see her when we're back. Might need to drop the princess at your parents' first; I'm thinking she'll be bored and almost certainly hungry for a proper meal soon?'

Paige glanced over her shoulder as Grace let out a sleepy sigh and snuggled her head into the edge of the car seat. 'You keep surprising me. Not many non-parents out there would consider a three-year-old's needs,' she said quietly, sounding impressed. 'You have much experience with kids?'

He clutched the steering wheel tighter, touched by the compliment. 'I used to be one,' he murmured, as he pulled out of the parking space and took the road back to Lockton.

'You never wanted any of your own?'

It took Johnny a few minutes to respond. 'In another life, perhaps. It's a lot of responsibility, a lot to care about. For now I'm content with Mack. Considering the job I'm doing with him, I'd say I'm probably not up to parenting.' The response must have satisfied her because she turned to look out of the window. Although when Johnny glanced at Paige a few seconds later, he could see she had a frown on her face, and for the first time in a long time he felt disappointed in himself, uncomfortable with the way his blasé dismissal had sounded. He pushed the car into fifth and stepped on the accelerator, suddenly keen to get back to Lockton.

A few minutes later, Paige drew out her mobile and tapped the screen. 'No signal,' she huffed, shoving it back in her bag. 'Thought I'd check my emails. There's a lot still to do at the library.'

Wound up in work again, it was as if Paige couldn't let herself relax. She'd looked relaxed last night in his garden when he'd been seducing her with food. He pushed the memory away. 'I want to show you something,' he said, suddenly realising where they were. He took a right five minutes later and pulled into a layby. In front of them was an incredible view of the mountains, one he'd stumbled upon the first year he'd moved into the area. A rollercoaster of peaks and troughs filled the horizon, stretching from left to right.

The colours were incredible – a heady mixture of greens, greys and purples which were offset by the vibrant clear blue of the sky. If he was an artist, this would be the scene he'd want to replicate. As it was, he'd made a few amateur sketches on the days when he'd needed to step away – to take time out of the world. To remember what was important. All those efforts had ended up in the recycling, but he'd enjoyed simply drinking in the view, mimicking what he could see on the page, even if it wasn't any good. Paige didn't say anything for a few moments after he'd stopped, but he saw her slide back in the seat so she could get a better look.

'Pretty, isn't it?' he asked when she remained silent.

'It's beautiful.' Her voice was almost reverent. 'I grew up here, and of course I knew that, but it's weird how it keeps taking my breath away. Like I'd somehow forgotten.' Her forehead furrowed. 'I thought I loved living in London, loved how fast it moves, how no one really knows you. There's such a sense of possibility, like you can be anything and anyone you want. A success at work, in your marriage and relationships, just as easy as that.' She clicked her fingers. 'But it's a pressure too, because if you don't grab onto it, or you fail, you're wasting all that opportunity and somehow that's all your fault.' She let out a long exhale. 'But here… I don't know. Things feel different.'

'How?' he asked, turning so he could look at her. He'd never been able to articulate it, but he felt something similar.

She shrugged her narrow shoulders, drawing attention to her olive skin which almost seemed to sparkle in the sunlight. For such a small woman, she packed a powerful punch and he had to look away as his fingers itched to reach out and touch her. 'It's almost like you don't matter,' she continued, not looking at him. 'Because the world – this' – she pointed to the horizon – 'will carry on whatever you do. It's so much bigger than an individual, isn't it,' she murmured, but Johnny remained silent because he knew she didn't require a response. It was as though she'd forgotten he was even there. 'It was here long before we got here, and it'll be here long after we leave. Which means what we do in this lifetime, well, it's not that important after all.'

He ignored the slow thump of his heart. Paige had just described exactly the way he felt about being in Lockton, exactly what he was looking for when he took his walks in the wilderness. Exactly why he didn't miss a thing about living in New York. Aside perhaps from the way cooking had made him feel.

'I'm not sure what that means though…' she continued.

'Perhaps it means we have a lot less control over life than we think. We're only here for a short time, so what really matters is being happy?' Johnny suggested, his voice quiet. 'Whatever happy means. But I think perhaps we can have some control over that.'

'Do you?' She shuffled in the car seat and he turned to look at her. 'Because from where I'm standing that's the hardest thing to control. No matter how much I try, that elusive happiness you talk about keeps slipping through my fingertips. Perhaps because I don't know what it means anymore. Are you happy?'

Johnny frowned and pressed his hands onto his thighs. The car was getting warm and he opened the window to let in a soft breeze. The question was unexpected and he took a few minutes to consider it. 'I…' A few months ago he'd have said yes, but recently, and definitely since meeting Paige, he'd been feeling restless as each day stretched before him, the same one over and over. There had been this odd feeling that somehow what he was doing was no longer enough. Like he was missing out. 'I'm not unhappy,' he said eventually. 'I'm not sick, or stressed – and I do what I want every day.'

She squinted at him, as if trying to read his face.

'But,' he added, sensing her disapproval, 'I miss…' He didn't know how to put it into words.

'Letting yourself feel?' she asked, reading his mind. His head jerked to hers, and their eyes met. Hers were such an unusual shade of brown, with golden highlights that drew him in – they were old eyes; they'd seen a lot of life, understood more than they were supposed to. 'I get it,' she said softly. 'It's scary.'

'Scary isn't the right word,' he almost snapped. That word made him feel like a coward and he wasn't. He'd always been brave. Moving to Lockton had been fearless, turning his back on everything that mattered to him. Making sure nothing got a hook into his life. Mack shuffled in the back, nudging a nose against the cage and whining, making a mockery of that thought. 'I just, I don't know.' He shook his head. 'I don't want to forget what's important. I had no real friends in New York. I let work take over and there wasn't one person I could turn to when my life went to hell.' He looked down at his lap, wondering what had possessed him to share so much of himself with a stranger. Perhaps there was more power in that than he'd thought. Not just for her, but for him too. 'I've got Davey now, and I know there are people who'll be there for me if I need them.' Not that he'd let them get too close, or let himself care enough about anything to need them.

'I have no proper friends in London.' Paige swiped her forehead, tidying a strand of wayward hair. She didn't look at him. 'All our friends were Carl's – he was the fun one.' She frowned. 'The irresponsible one, if you want the proper word for it, but everyone loved that. Some – women mainly – loved it a little too much, and he in turn loved them.' She took a long breath. 'When he died… I don't know.' Paige shrugged. 'I'm not sure if those friends just couldn't be bothered with me or I pushed them away. I never found time…' She screwed up her face. 'I didn't want to find it. It's not what you get measured by, is it, friendships – that's not the true gauge of success and it's not like I've made a success of much else. Certainly not my marriage. I need my work to feel like I… I don't know,' she said again. 'Like I've succeeded.'

If they'd met three years earlier, Paige could have picked those exact thoughts out of his brain. 'I think we have to find our own way to measure success, to understand what makes us tick,' Johnny said gently, shifting a little more in his seat towards her. She was so beautiful. The sun shone in through the passenger window, picking out reds in her hair which was still swept up and out of her face in a tight knot. He had a sudden urge to pull it out of the rigid clasp, to let the strands fall around her shoulders. She was looking at him now and there was a groove in her forehead between her eyebrows. The same groove he'd seen her make a hundred times before. He found himself reaching up and pressing a fingertip to it, as if he could somehow smooth it out. 'You get this look on your face sometimes,' he said, swiping his fingertip across the skin, which felt so soft underneath the pad of his finger. 'Like you've got the whole world sitting on your shoulders and you're not sure how long you can hold it up.'

She jerked but didn't pull away as he continued to stroke. He could see her breath had quickened by the rapid rise and fall of her chest. 'You mean I don't?' she asked, injecting the barest hint of humour into the question.

He smiled too, continuing to stroke her skin, letting his fingers travel down as if hypnotised, skimming across her cheek. He'd been wanting to touch her all day; he wasn't sure how he'd managed to hold himself back, although he was a master of self-denial. Her smooth olive skin was so vibrant and clear. 'You're carrying a lot,' he said. 'Perhaps you should see if you could let some of it go – unload it for a while, give yourself a break.'

She looked serious. 'What if I don't know how?' The words came out as a whisper, but there was an ache in the tone, an ache of pure longing which told of insecurity and fear.

'That's easy.' He shrugged as his fingertip skimmed the plump skin of her top lip as he continued to explore. He saw a bloom of red spread across her cheeks but she didn't pull away. Her eyes had dilated, and every part of his body seemed to be pulsing in response. 'Stop thinking. Just for a few minutes. Find something else to occupy your mind.'

'That's what you do.' She licked her bottom lip, perhaps unconsciously, or perhaps in response to the atmosphere that had been building in the car. Then, just as Johnny was considering pulling back, just as he started to drop his hand, she leaned forwards, put her palm against the edge of his cheek and stopped. 'I forgot everything last night,' she said before lifting herself up. Their lips met then, slowly, just a feather of a touch, like Paige wasn't really sure she was doing the right thing. Hell, neither was he. This was a big mistake, the biggest he'd made since moving back to Lockton. He could already feel it, feel the way Grace was burrowing into his heart, following the narrow tunnel Mack had already carved out, hacking through his defences, leaving a clear run for his feelings for Paige to bloom. Feelings he was worried were already out of control. He was opening up again, to feelings and expectations, to a world of uncertainty and hurt. But he didn't pull away; instead he kissed her back.

Paige tasted of chocolate, different from last night, but like one of his muffins – and something surged through his blood just as potent as a rush of sugar. His heart was beating harder in his chest as she ran her hand up and over his ear, skimming it through his hair until she set it down on the back of his neck. He'd been pushing his emotions down for years now, controlling them, but there was something about kissing Paige that felt like the start of something. Something he should probably stop before it got out of hand. But just like last night, he couldn't stop himself. Instead he pushed his fingers into her hair, felt for the tortoiseshell clip that held it up onto the back of her neck and popped it open so her soft hair tumbled onto her shoulders. It released a sudden fragrance of strawberries, probably from her shampoo. Johnny deepened the kiss, or she did, he couldn't tell. It was like they were in sync, no longer at odds but moving together, heading to the same place. Two damaged strangers needing something, trying to avoid it, but finding it in each other. Connection, understanding, or just companionship? Johnny wasn't sure. Perhaps it didn't matter. Paige would be leaving Lockton soon, heading back to London. She'd told him that last night. So any dents in his heart, any pathways she was opening, would soon close over again. Which was the only reason he continued to kiss her. The only reason his hand had started to explore, dropping down from the nape of her neck to her shoulders, skimming over her arms until it rested on her waist.

Then his mobile began to buzz in his pocket – like somehow the planets had aligned and delivered a signal at the exact moment he needed a distraction. He tore himself from Paige, taking a moment to register the unhappy surprise on her face, and grabbed it, answering immediately. 'Davey?' Even he could hear the relief in his voice.

'Where are you?' his brother growled.

'I just took Paige to track down an author for The Book Barn launch,' he explained. 'We're near Hawthferry, on our way back now. Everything okay with lunch? I got the soup from Morag, but if you've run out, I can pick up some more.'

'There's plenty of soup.' Davey sounded unimpressed. 'Not many people buying food here today. Perhaps because they've figured they can get the same thing from the post office. Fergus has been in – he's heard from his contact that Tony Silver is visiting the pub a week on Monday, that's just over a week away. If that's true, I'll need Matilda to draw up a new menu, which means you need to decide what you're going to cook. She promised to put something together to impress. How have you been getting on with the dishes?'

'I'm not sure I'm ready.' Johnny pulled a face. Despite the meal he'd cooked last night, he'd wanted more time to work on his recipes. He wasn't sure he was ready to put himself on the line yet.

'John, I know you've been working on it because Agnes told me about the fish she gave you. You're a good enough chef to put something together off the top of your head,' Davey said. 'I'm not asking for perfection, or anything like you used to do. This isn't a performance, it's just an… upgrade of what you'd normally cook. Just work it out, help me do this and I'll hire a chef. You can continue with the lunches and bar food as you are now – these dishes will be on our deluxe menu, nothing to do with you.'

Johnny felt a twinge in his chest. He wasn't sure if it was embarrassment or disappointment. He looked across the car at Paige. She raised an eyebrow and it was clear she'd heard everything. It was quite something to see yourself reflected back in someone else's eyes – especially someone you respected. Someone who never gave up on anything. *Are you a coward?* He could almost hear the question hover between them in the car. He blew out a breath. 'Fine. I've got some ideas. I'll order what we need from Morag.'

'If you need local desserts, my mam makes an amazing fruit tart with raspberries from the garden,' Paige said quietly, almost making Johnny jump. 'She often uses da's honey to make a vanilla honeycomb slice.' She licked her lips as if she'd just tasted some. 'I've not had it for years – Carl hated honey – but it used to be my favourite. It's all local ingredients too. I know she'll make them for you, you just need to say the word.'

Johnny's mind clicked through the menu. 'I think we've got it covered,' he murmured into the phone. 'I'll come to the pub once we've visited the post office and talk to Matilda about the menu as soon as I've worked it out.'

He hung up just as Grace stirred in the back, his face creasing as he turned to Paige. 'Thank you.'

She shrugged and looked out of the window. 'One good turn deserves another. You helped me with the library. Besides – what are friends for?'

'We're friends?' he asked, his voice a little husky. He was surprised and a bit put out by the description.

'Well, we're not strangers, are we? Unless there's such a thing as strangers who kiss.' Her eyes met his, the golden brown darkening despite the sun shining through the windscreen. They were guarded now; perhaps a response to the kiss? Had it affected her as much as it had him?

'Friends,' Johnny murmured, nodding. Wondering if they were both kidding themselves.

Chapter Nineteen

'I made a vanilla honeycomb slice,' Cora chattered, as she led Johnny, Paige and Grace through Kindness Cottage into the kitchen at the back before letting Mack into the garden. Paige had planned to drop Grace off and head straight to the post office, but her mam had insisted they stay for a cup of tea and a piece of cake. She'd wanted to argue but Johnny had accepted before she could. It felt odd being in his presence now, like somehow they'd connected on a different level.

'Princess!' Johnny helped Grace onto one of the stools set around the mottled granite breakfast bar and sat next to her as Paige hopped onto the other side. Cora busied herself making tea and drew the cake out of the fridge, as Paige's da appeared through the door leading from the garden.

'Ach, you're here, lasses. I should have guessed when Mack came to visit.' He bent to peck Grace and Paige on their cheeks. 'How did the author hunt go?'

'We found one,' Paige said, as her mam put a cup of tea with a dash of milk, just the way she liked it, in front of her, then a small slice of cake.

'Not the one we expected.' Johnny grinned as Cora placed a mug and a huge slice in front of him. It was a wonder he kept that perfect body with all the sweet stuff he ate. Paige scanned Johnny's T-shirt, which showcased his perfectly muscled chest, just as he looked up and winked, making her cheeks flame. 'Why don't you explain?' He dug into the dessert and let out a low groan of pleasure.

'We found Charlie Adaire. He lives in Hawthferry,' Paige said.

'Charlie Adaire.' Her da's eyebrows shot up. 'But that's… where?'

'Near the fence people were complaining about. I can show you on a map later. We're hoping to take Morag to see him on Monday, to persuade him to do the talk.' Paige didn't want to go into the details. Ironically, Morag might not want her feud with Charlie broadcast to all and sundry.

'I can't believe he lives so close,' her da murmured. 'I think I might have even spoken to him.'

'This is amazing,' Johnny purred, as he ate another spoonful of dessert.

'Amazing,' Grace echoed, digging into her mini portion.

'Ach, it's an old family recipe. Legend says the original owner of Kindness Cottage used to make something like it for anyone in the village suffering from melancholy. Sadness,' she explained to Grace with a wink. 'She used to deliver it personally, and apparently those little acts of kindness worked. I always think there's something magical about your da's honey.' She grinned.

Marcus's cheeks pinked as Paige took another bite of cake, watching them, feeling something bubble low in her belly. She felt so at home here, even the food tasted different – perhaps because all the love that had been put into creating it had changed it somehow?

She took in a deep breath, realising she was happy, that she felt like she belonged. Then blew it out again, hoping when she returned to London she'd be able to recreate that same feeling for herself.

The post office was busy. Paige and Johnny walked into the red-brick building and straight to the back of the queue of four. Behind the till, Morag rang up a newspaper and a tin of soup and placed them into a white bag on the counter. The shop was dual purpose and supplied the locals with essential daily items, as well as the usual post office fare of stamps, passport forms and car tax. Anyone who needed supplies when it was closed had to travel over fifteen miles to Morridon, so it tended to be filled with customers from dawn to dusk.

Paige glanced around the shop, which was filled with shelves of jams, tins, Dundee cakes, whisky and household items. There was a small fridge crowded with milk, cheese and ham, along with packs of fresh fish, and various meats including sausages. Open baskets of lettuce, tomatoes, spring onions, potatoes, courgettes and cucumbers sat on the floor beside it. Next to the main till was a large glass cubicle with an opening for customers to slide their parcels and paperwork through. Morag used it when she was performing her post office duties, usually between two and four o'clock.

Johnny broke off from the queue, picked up a basket and went to examine the vegetables, picking up a couple of tomatoes and a courgette so he could squeeze them, before his attention was caught by the contents of the fridge. Paige watched as he diligently looked at the packs of fresh fish, picking each one up and examining it closely before making notes on his mobile phone. He was focused and calm, dedicated to his task. Paige hadn't seen him at work before. There was no relaxed gait, no cheeky grin; he was fully focused on his mission. Something prickled in her chest – admiration? Or perhaps concern. This man was far more dangerous than the Johnny she was used to. Especially after they'd kissed. Because this Johnny was well and truly under her skin.

She was surprised when Morag let out a loud cough from behind the till. She looked up to find the queue had disappeared and only the three of them remained. 'Any luck with finding an author?' Morag asked, her forehead creasing as she looked between them both. 'Because I've had that eejit Jason on the phone this morning, offering me the number of his historian again.' She broke off and scoured the shop once more, frowning. 'Where's the wee bairn?'

'At Kindness Cottage – she was tired after our walk.' Paige saw Johnny kneel so he could look more closely at the vegetables.

'Those are fresh from Agnes's allotment on Buttermead Farm,' Morag growled. 'So there's no need for you to manhandle them.'

'They look good, Morag,' Johnny said, making more notes. 'If I make a list of the ingredients I need, can I pick them up next Saturday? I'll want fresh fish for a week on Monday too.'

'Aye, I'm glad you're finally taking Tony Silver's visit seriously,' Morag said. 'Your brother's got his heart set on a mention in that book. I knew you wouldn't let him down.'

'I can't promise to impress,' Johnny said, looking concerned.

'I expect whatever you have planned will be a step up from soup, and Agnes told me about the food you made at the farm. She filled me in on a little of your history.' Her tone was sharp. 'You must have some plans for the pub?'

Johnny shrugged, and Paige felt a sudden urge to protect him from any more questions. 'I've got good news. We went out today and found an author, someone who's bound to pull in a crowd,' she said quickly, aiming to distract Morag.

'But there's a problem.' Johnny wandered up to stand beside Paige, his large body an unexpected source of comfort and support.

Morag's grin dropped. 'What kind of problem?'

The door of the shop opened and Davey walked in, followed by Agnes, who was carrying a shopping basket filled with whisky. 'A delivery from Fergus,' she declared, taking the basket to the counter so she could unload the bottles. 'I thought I'd get out of the farmhouse for a spell. He's spent the morning trying to teach Tiki how to ask for "Auld Lang Syne", but the bird's having none of it.' She turned to Paige. 'He loves that book you loaned him – I've not seen him enjoy himself so much for months. But if he wants Tiki to request a song other than "Waterfront", he's in for a long wait.' She winked and Paige laughed. She was starting to feel like part of the community; everywhere she turned there was someone she'd recommended a book to, an abundance of thank yous and smiles as her small acts of kindness were rewarded. It felt such a long way from her old life.

'I came to see if I could find you,' Davey said to Johnny, smiling when he spotted the basket. 'I have a couple of things to pick up myself.' He patted his brother on the shoulder and winked at Paige before going to look in the fridge.

'Did Fergus mention Tony Silver loves tiramisu?' Morag asked suddenly.

'No.' Davey turned and frowned.

'His contact mentioned it,' Agnes said. 'I thought he might have told you?' She looked surprised.

'No one said anything to me.' Davey looked upset.

'There's nothing about that in *Best Pubs* – I've read the whole thing.' Johnny shook his head. 'I can put something together, but it would never be as good as one of Lilith's.' He stared at his brother. 'You could ask her to make one? She's been cooking them in the hotel restaurant, and she used to make them for you all the time.'

'I remember.' Davey's expression darkened. 'Lilith's far too busy building her empire. It wouldn't be fair to ask.'

Morag let out an irritated snort as Agnes turned to Paige. 'How's the author hunt going?'

'We were about to fill Morag in.' Paige's eyes skimmed both women. 'We came to tell you we tracked down Charlie Adaire.'

Agnes's eyebrows shot up and Morag let out a gasp. 'Where?'

'Just outside Morridon – we were looking for Archie Radiale and it turns out they share the same address.'

'Mr Radiale?' Agnes asked. 'I borrowed one of his walking guides from the library. I heard a rumour he has a big house somewhere around Hawthferry, but we've never located it. Not that we've tried to look. I had no clue Charlie Adaire lived so close to Lockton.' She glanced at Morag and her brow pinched. 'With your contacts, I'm surprised you didn't know.'

Morag cleared her throat. 'Archie sounds like the perfect solution to our author problem – I don't think we need Charlie Adaire. Besides, he's not published anything for years.' She looked annoyed.

'One year,' Paige corrected. 'Most of the village are crazy about him. Charlie would definitely pull in a bigger crowd. If you want to make a splash, he'd be the best bet.'

'Aye, I'd say the entire village would come to the library to see him, not to mention the rest of the Highlands.' Agnes tapped her chin, staring at Morag. 'Imagine how Jason Beckett would feel about him coming to launch The Book Barn? Just think about how many people would turn up. He'd be a bigger draw than even the Jampionships.'

'Aye,' Morag sighed. 'I can imagine the crowds.' She pursed her lips. 'I suppose that would get Jason out of our hair once and for all. But did Mr Adaire agree to do an event? Word is he's pure crabbit if you get him alone.'

'Whose word?' Agnes asked, but Morag ignored her.

'He… well… he wasn't happy.' Johnny paused and Paige took a step forwards.

'We mentioned you were on the library's committee, Morag, and…' Paige grimaced. 'He said if you had anything to do with The Book Barn he wouldn't help. I got the feeling you knew each other?'

'Not anymore,' Morag growled. 'The man's an eejit. Always was. He told you he wouldn't come because of me?' A splash of red climbed up from her throat. With the mass of grey curly hair sprouting from her head, she looked a little terrifying.

'He wasn't keen,' Paige admitted. 'I wondered though, if you went to see him, perhaps you'd be able to talk him into it?'

'You know Charlie Adaire?' Agnes looked shocked and she turned to her friend. 'You never mentioned that, Morag. Not in all the time I've known you – how long is that?' She considered for a moment. 'Over thirty years.'

Morag tossed her head. 'Nothing to talk about. It was a long time ago, before I got married and moved to Lockton. We grew up in the same village, close to Morridon, used to come here together sometimes. Then he moved away from the area. The friendship was a mistake, one I have no intention of revisiting.'

'Not even for the library?' Agnes asked, and they waited as Morag considered the question.

After a moment she sighed. 'Aye. I'd like to see Jason Beckett's face if Charlie Adaire did our launch.'

'So you'll speak to him?' Agnes grinned.

Morag puffed out her cheeks.

'Johnny's taking muffins to his house on Monday morning. We wondered if you'd like to come along?' Paige asked. 'Perhaps you could clear the air, take a peace offering of some kind, apologise for whatever happened. He might be open to talking at the library after that?'

Morag snorted. 'I'll not be apologising to that bampot for anything.'

'You had a falling out?' Agnes asked, still looking surprised.

'Aye.' Morag blew out the breath she'd been holding. 'Just who do you think that eejit woman in the shop who solves all those crimes in his books is based on?' Her fists tightened. 'Not that he got any of his facts straight. She's nosy, annoying, and to top it all off, a lonely lass.' Her expression darkened. 'Does that sound anything like me?'

Both Agnes and Johnny were saved from responding by Lilith walking into the shop. She spotted Davey as he turned and his cheeks instantly went bright pink. Lilith smiled at everyone, ignoring Davey as she stepped forwards. 'I came for my parcel.'

'Your Bellagamba olive oil from the special deli in Italy,' Morag noted. 'Aye, I was expecting you, lass.' Her eyes darted to Davey. 'It's delivered the same day every month – I think the whole village knows that, don't they, lad? Give me a moment, I need to find it.' The room fell silent as Morag disappeared behind the glass counter.

'I heard you are cooking.' Lilith eyed the empty basket on Johnny's arm with interest. 'I also heard Tony Silver was going to be in the area.'

'That's right,' Agnes said. 'He'll be visiting the pub Monday week.' She winked. 'We've just heard he loves tiramisu. Isn't that one of your signature dishes?' Agnes glared at Davey who had clearly lost his ability to speak. He was staring at Lilith, a picture of confusion and longing.

Morag passed Lilith the parcel. 'Same time next month, lass?'

'No.' Lilith grabbed the package and pressed it into her chest. 'This will be the last delivery. I'll be leaving Lockton in just under two weeks.'

Davey's shoulders jerked.

'Aye,' Morag said, looking unhappy. 'I heard about the manager your parents sent to run the hotel. Is that permanent?'

'*Sì*. Papa thinks the business needs new blood. We've not had so many guests as he'd hoped over the last few months.' Lilith shrugged. 'It's seasonal and we're booked up now, but he won't listen. He's been threatening to send someone for a year. Doesn't matter that the hotel is supposed to be mine. You know Papa – business before anything else.' She shook her head.

'I'm sorry, lass,' Morag soothed. 'Do you have another opportunity?'

'My family have offered me a new deli in Rome, close to where they live. I'm exploring my options.' Lilith's focus wandered to Davey again. When he said nothing she sighed, before turning and heading out of the shop.

Morag turned to Davey. 'You're going to let the lassie leave?' She scowled.

Davey's shoulders slumped. 'Leaving is what Lilith wants. Family first – I'm not surprised she's moving back to Italy, I'm only surprised it's taken her so long.'

Paige cleared her throat. 'I probably shouldn't say this. But there's no Hippocratic oath for librarians, at least none that Aileen told me about. Lilith was in the library the other day and I saw her searching for jobs…'

'In Italy,' Davey said, his voice flat.

Paige shook her head. 'That's the thing. I saw a couple in Rome, but some were around Morridon. She wrote a few notes. I'm not sure what that means…'

'Perhaps you should ask her, laddie?' Morag turned back to Davey.

He walked up to the counter and placed a tin of soup onto it. 'I think Lilith and I are all talked out. She made her priorities perfectly clear before we separated back in February. Impressing her father is all she cares about.' His shoulders sagged. 'She most definitely doesn't care that much for me.' He glanced at Paige. 'I'm sorry, but you're mistaken. If Lilith is leaving Lockton, there's only one place she'll be going and that's back to her family, in Rome. I'll see you later, John.' With that he paid and headed out of the post office.

Morag broke the silence as the door closed. 'Ach, that's pride for you.'

Agnes gave her a sharp look. 'Would that be the same pride that's stopping you from visiting Charlie Adaire?'

'It's not the same thing,' Morag snapped.

'Then you're happy to risk Jason Beckett taking over the library opening, which will be just the first step to him getting involved in The Book Barn overall?' Agnes asked.

'I'm not sure if we'll be able to find another author on such short notice,' Paige admitted. 'I can look, and we haven't tracked down Archie yet, but…' She shook her head. 'No one's going to pull in as big a crowd as Charlie. He'll be available too, sounds like he doesn't normally do events – in all honesty he's probably our best, if not only, bet. If we don't pull this off, we're going to have to speak to Jason.'

'Aye.' Morag let out a long sigh. 'You're right, lass. I suppose I'll have to come.' Her lips thinned. 'But the eejit had better not say no – and I'll be bringing a spade so we can bury him somewhere really deep if he does.'

Chapter Twenty

Light streamed in from the skylights as Paige opened up The Book Barn on Monday morning. She'd left Grace at Kindness Cottage with her mam, but Cora had promised to bring her over later. She took a moment to breathe, wondering why the familiar papery scent made her feel so at ease. A hardback edition of *Letting Go of a Bad Life* was on the counter today. Paige ignored it and took her time pacing the large space instead, checking everything was in the right place, feeling relaxed and more than a little content, imagining what it would be like to stay in Lockton.

There was a sound from the entrance and a woman Paige recognised, dressed in jeans and a glittery T-shirt with a snowman in a bikini on the front, sailed in. She was movie-star stunning, with blonde hair which reached her shoulders and glitter on her cheeks that sparkled in the sunlight. 'I saw you at both Jam Club meetings but didn't get a chance to introduce myself,' the woman began. 'I'm Meg Scott. Your mum works in my Christmas shop – you must be Paige. It's brilliant to meet you properly. Cora's so excited to have you home.' She held out a hand which Paige shook. Meg opened her bag and pulled out a couple of books on Norway.

'Aileen suggested I borrow these just before she died.' She pulled a face. 'I like armchair travelling. I'm sorry it's taken me so long to bring them back. I'm trying to think of somewhere to take my fiancé Tom on holiday, but...' She shook her head. 'He's not that keen on the idea of Norway – too similar to here, apparently.' She piled the books onto the counter. 'Got any other suggestions? Evie said you knew each other from school, that you'd recommended a couple of brilliant books to her.'

'Ah, yes,' Paige said. Evie had visited a few days before.

'I've a couple of friends who live just outside Lockton who've been to the library, and they said the same.' Paige felt her cheeks warm. The Book Barn had been busy since opening and she'd recommended a lot of books. It was getting easier now she was familiar with the stock and her mind wasn't filled with schedules, house moves, Carl and work. 'Morag's been telling everyone you're a chip off Aileen's block,' Meg finished.

Paige blushed. 'Thank you. I'm getting the hang of it now. I can show you the travel section if you want to browse.' She walked out from behind the counter and guided Meg to a set of shelves. 'Do you want to visit somewhere cold?'

Meg shook her head. 'Not really. I just know the place will feel right when I find it – you understand?'

Paige smiled. 'That's exactly what Aileen used to say. The right books find you.'

'She had a knack for picking what you were looking for,' Meg murmured. 'Agnes and Evie used to talk about it, but I wasn't convinced until I met her myself.'

'She was kind and very special,' Paige agreed. 'She taught me a lot.' It was only now that she was realising how much. 'These are all the travel guides we have.' Paige checked the shelf. 'The villagers have been bringing books back in dribs and drabs, so if nothing grabs you now, there might be more if you come back in a couple of days. Once Morag hires a new librarian, I'm sure they'll order in more stock.' She considered the book spines; there were so many colours. Strange how she kept being drawn to the guide on Scotland, as if nothing else could keep her attention now. There were so many amazing places to go. So many destinations she'd never visited, hundreds of adventures to take Grace on when she had time. Why was Scotland the place she kept coming back to? She traced a finger along the books and pulled out one of the guides. 'Have you thought about Turkey?' Meg pulled a face and Paige started to put the book back on the shelf.

'No, stop.' Meg slid it from Paige's fingers. 'Did you know St Nicholas was from Turkey?' She cocked her head and her cheeks sparkled. 'I'd forgotten that until just now.' She turned the guide over. 'I'll borrow it. See what Tom thinks. Thanks, Paige. Morag's definitely right.' She patted her arm and headed over to the counter as Paige felt a sudden burst of pride, just as Agnes walked in carrying a shopping bag.

'Ach, you're here. I told Johnny I'd watch The Book Barn so you could go with him and Morag to see Charlie Adaire. Your mam is going to watch the post office with your wee lass.' When Paige started to protest, she held up a hand. 'I'll be fine, lass. I've a feeling it's going to take both of you to get Morag to ask him to do the library talk. There's a history there and it's not a happy one.

Besides, if she does try to murder him, there'll be two of you to stop her before she does!' Her green eyes shone and she turned to take the book from Meg.

The gate to Charlie Adaire's house was open when they arrived. From the car, Paige could see that the wooden pole under the post box had been replaced with a concrete pillar, and the black metal box now sported a huge silver padlock. Paige half expected an armed guard to appear from around the corner and demand to check their fingerprints or passports. Johnny steered into the gravel driveway and parked beside a pretty round turning circle lined with heather. The house was huge, with a double set of windows on either side of the entrance. It had a wide porch and a bright blue front door. There were beds teeming with multicoloured summer flowers bordering the edges and corners of the house. As she opened the doors of the car, the fluffy ginger cat appeared from behind a large plant pot to give them a wide-eyed stare.

'Good call to leave Mack with Davey,' Johnny muttered, reaching into the back seat to grab a tray of muffins as the front door opened and Charlie Adaire strode out. He looked smarter today, and had brushed his hair – it lay flat across his head, making him look both handsome and a little intimidating. His dark eyes slid to Morag and he narrowed them.

'What are you doing here?' He turned and stomped back into the house, leaving the front door wide open. Paige and Johnny glanced at each other.

'The eejit hasn't changed one bit,' Morag hissed, getting out of the car, striding into the porch and through the front door without waiting.

'Think we should leave them to it?' Johnny whispered. 'I'd say they're evenly matched, but I'm pretty sure Morag could take him. She brought her spade, right?'

'We promised to stay.' Paige laughed, starting to follow, but Johnny held her back and took her hand.

'Let's go in together,' he said, dropping it when she looked surprised, leaving her skin tingling. He'd been touching her more since their last kiss, small acts of intimacy she wasn't sure how to respond to. Her heart was telling her to go for it, but her head knew better. She had to stay strong.

They followed the sound of voices to the right, into a large hallway which boasted a chandelier, oak floorboards, and an impressive staircase that was flanked by open doorways leading to either side. Charlie was standing beside a fireplace in a room to their right. The ginger cat who'd followed him waved its tail back and forth against his shins, and Morag stood just inside the door, scowling.

'I'm not sure why you're here,' Charlie snapped. He'd foregone pyjamas today and was dressed in navy slacks and a crisp white shirt, which he'd left unbuttoned at the nape of his neck.

'Aren't you?' Morag raised an eyebrow and went to take a seat on one of the upright royal blue chairs next to the window. 'I'd have thought it was perfectly obvious, and probably what you planned all along when you said you wouldn't do the launch at The Book Barn because of me.' She sniffed and her gaze swept around the large room.

Charlie's attention flipped to Paige and Johnny as they entered and he spotted the muffins. 'You can leave those on the table. My housekeeper is preparing tea with a wee dram if you're partial. You always were.' He looked at Morag again. She'd dressed up in a bright orange dress which Paige hadn't seen before. Her wayward grey curls had been pulled back in a clip – a harsh style, but one which showed off the high cheekbones that were usually hidden.

'I'll take tea,' Johnny said, his movements loose and easy as he walked up to Charlie and offered his hand. The gesture of friendship instantly defused the strange tension in the room.

'You've not changed a bit,' Charlie said, turning to stare at Morag again. 'Do you still frown more than you smile?'

'Do you still leave whenever the whim takes you and expect everyone else to fall into line?' she shot back, getting up and pacing to the window, then leaning on her cane and looking out at the garden.

'Perhaps we should go for a walk, come back in an hour?' Paige suggested. 'If you'd rather catch up in private.' She pressed her fingers onto her hips, eager to escape. This whole thing reminded her of one of her arguments with Carl.

'Take one step out of this room, lassie, and I'll be going for that shovel now,' Morag growled.

'Since the woman wasn't invited, and you're the ones responsible for bringing her to my house, I'd suggest you take a seat,' Charlie said smoothly, looking less angry than his words suggested.

The housekeeper, a young woman dressed in jeans and a pink overall, walked into the room, carrying a tray with a large white teapot and four sets of matching cups and saucers. There was a pile of chocolate biscuits as well as side plates, a milk jug and a small bottle of whisky. 'Sit,' Charlie said, scooting around so he could lay the cups and saucers onto the table. 'I'll serve. Long time.

You look… good.' He took a deep breath as Morag sat again. She scanned the room, until her attention rested on a photo of a large farmhouse on the mantelpiece, and another of the ginger cat.

'Did you marry?' she asked suddenly, as Charlie handed her a cup and saucer filled with tea.

'No.' He poured in milk and a dash of whisky without asking. 'Although I heard you did.'

Morag sniffed the hot liquid and sipped. 'Hemlock?' she asked archly. 'I seem to recall one of your characters being murdered in exactly this way in one of your books. I brought a shovel, but I've no intention of digging a grave for myself.'

'You've read my books?' Charlie's eyebrows shot up but his mouth curved.

'A couple.' Morag flushed. 'Nothing recent – I found the female lead irritating.'

'Why?' Charlie's full lips twitched.

'She's nosy and rude, and spends far too much of her time lamenting the fact that she never travelled. There was some love interest, I believe, someone from her past… although the facts are a little unclear.'

Charlie nodded. He seemed less on edge now, and not as angry as he had been when they'd arrived. Perhaps the unexpected visit from Morag had thrown him off balance, or now they were face to face whatever feelings they may have harboured for each other had resurfaced? Paige had been expecting fireworks, but so far the encounter felt quite civilised. Charlie offered her a cup, nodding at the whisky, but she shook her head. Johnny took his drink and two biscuits, then he dropped one onto the side of Paige's plate and winked. Why was the man so determined to feed her? She picked it up and bit into it, wondering even as she chewed why she had. Perhaps all Johnny's little acts of kindness were just too difficult to resist? After feeling alone for so long, how had this almost-stranger managed to get so far under her skin? And did it matter, or was he just the first rung on her ladder to healing? She could only hope she'd be able to take these feelings back to London with her, to help her on the next steps of her journey.

'What do you mean by unclear?' Charlie coughed.

Morag let out a long breath. 'You mention her ex-lover had left England for Spain after he declared his love for her at the village dance.' She paused, examining her fingernails. 'Which was a very romantic moment in the book, if I recall correctly. After which she promised to join him and never did.' She turned her sharp eyes in his direction, skewering him. 'I thought it was strange that he never contacted her to find out what had happened.'

'I think…' He paused. 'Blair' – he raised an eyebrow at Morag – 'actually told him she'd think about joining him when they were at the dance. Then, my character's lover assumed she would have written to him to say if she was coming or not.' He sighed. 'But she didn't – instead she left him dangling, waiting until he didn't know if he was coming or going. In the end, he assumed she'd never had any intention of following.'

'Or perhaps she wrote?' Morag said, her forehead creasing. 'Perhaps she wrote and he never answered her letter?'

Charlie seemed to consider that for a moment as he bit into a biscuit and chewed. 'If she had, I'd assume he'd have received the letter. Besides, Blair would have called if it was important – she's a canny woman, she wouldn't have left anything to chance. In my books, she simply fell out of love. She's a lonely woman, one who'd rather spend her life in her own company, working all day long and poking her nose into other people's lives.' His face hardened. 'It's what makes her believable and so good at what she does.'

Morag stared at him and Paige saw a pulse beating at the base of her neck – she didn't know if Morag was angry or upset, but her chest heaved in and out a couple of times. 'Perhaps when he didn't contact her, she thought he didn't want her to follow him anymore? Perhaps she waited for him to get in touch, and when he didn't she reluctantly gave up?'

Paige looked at Johnny and he widened his eyes. It was clear the conversation was moving away from fiction and touching on something far more real. Something that explained a lot about the way Charlie and Morag were behaving. Perhaps even more about the way Morag was. Was her inherent nosiness more about the loneliness her da had talked of, the heartbreak she'd clearly experienced, rather than a need to poke into everyone's business?

'But what possible reason could she have had for not coming?' Charlie got up and paced the room, his movements jerky, his voice rough. It was clear he was upset, and Paige looked over at Johnny, who shrugged.

'Should we have more tea, or eat some of my muffins?' he suggested suddenly, injecting warmth into the cold atmosphere. Johnny had a gift for doing that, Paige realised, a gift for adding sunshine to a room. What she'd seen as a fault, a determination to ignore or gloss over a difficult situation, was perhaps one of his strengths. One she'd overlooked because she was always so focused on finding a solution to everything – even those things she couldn't fix. Things like her marriage. 'I have it on good authority chocolate is good for relieving stress…' Johnny continued. 'Isn't it odd that we're talking about dances? Did you know it's the Lockton Scottish Dance this Saturday?' He grinned, but Morag and Charlie ignored him.

'Perhaps her mother was too sick for her to leave and she had to take care of her…' Morag said, sipping her tea slowly. Paige wondered if she was thirsty, or just wanted something to do with her hands. 'Maybe she didn't have time to look for him, or do any more than write – remember, it was winter, and half the time in those days the phone lines were out of action more than they worked.'

Charlie pursed his lips. 'She found time to get married – and that took her less than eight months.'

Morag winced. 'The doctor treating her mother was very kind. He knew how to answer a letter and he didn't go swanning off to Fran—' She stopped abruptly, sparing a quick glance for Johnny and Paige as if she'd just remembered they were there. 'Spain to find himself. Didn't expect her to drop everything and follow him.'

'Yet the marriage didn't last?' Charlie looked more satisfied than angry.

Morag looked down at her cup. 'They had less in common than she first thought. An easy mistake when you marry so quickly. Marry in haste, repent at leisure – isn't that the saying?'

Paige felt herself go cold. How many times had those same words echoed around her head? But she'd tried to fix her marriage, tried and failed. It felt like everything she did now, aside from her work in the library, was a list of the multiple ways she'd botched up her life. She had to make sure she didn't do it again – she had Grace to think about now.

'But I'm not sorry.' Morag jerked up her chin. 'I have a son I love and a good life.'

'So no regrets?' Charlie asked, his whole body stiffening as he stared at her. 'Even after forty years?'

Morag pulled a face. 'Life's too short to spend it worrying about what we did or didn't do. We make our decisions and we live with them. No point in regretting it now.'

Charlie seemed to consider that for a moment. 'And that's your apology?' he asked finally.

'I didn't come to apologise. I came to ask if you'd speak at The Book Barn a week on Wednesday for the launch of our library.' Morag heaved in a breath. 'You said you wouldn't because of me.' She nodded at Paige and Johnny. 'But if you're too busy, or planning on disappearing off on another one of your efforts to find yourself, we'll find another author. I hear someone who writes about walks lives nearby. I've read all of his books and travelled a few of those routes, and enjoyed them very much.' She finished the drink and stood, smoothing her fingertips over her dress, wiping out the creases, which were probably too terrified to stay in place.

'Archie Radiale.' Charlie's smile was sad. 'You could try, although I think you'll find he has a similar schedule to mine. If you take a closer look at his name, I'm sure a woman with a brain like yours will be able to work out why. It's the reason I based Blair on you after all – those excellent powers of deduction.'

Paige let the name tick around her mind. She, Johnny and Morag must have worked it out at almost the exact same moment because they let out a collective sigh. 'Of course. It's an anagram,' Johnny said. 'Of your name. I knew something was bothering me about it.'

'I should have guessed,' Morag groaned.

Charlie shrugged. 'I enjoy indulging my passion for the country-side but I didn't want it to overlap with my crime novels. I'm sure you understand. Besides, the deception makes me smile – very few people have worked it out. I'd have said it was obvious, but perhaps country walks and murder mysteries are just too many worlds apart. I thought you might have guessed when you got into my mailbox on Saturday.' He stared at Johnny.

Paige let out a long breath. They'd just lost their fallback, the one person who might have come to talk at the library other than this man. Without him, they'd probably have to ask Jason Beckett for help. She'd received very little interest from the publishers she'd emailed because the timing was so tight. Her eyes met Johnny's and they both turned to Morag. She must have realised the same thing because she glared at Charlie.

'So what do you want?' Morag's hands were gripped so tightly that Paige could see the tips of her knuckles were white.

He let out a long breath, his forehead creasing. 'I want to refuse.'

Morag let out an irritated huff and glanced at the door, clearly considering her exit.

'If you'd asked me the same thing an hour ago, I would have done exactly that. But now, for some reason, I can't.' He looked surprised by the statement.

'History,' Johnny said quietly, reading the situation with a depth of intuition that surprised Paige.

Charlie glanced over at him and shrugged. 'Or curiosity. I've still got questions to ask, things I want to know. Perhaps things aren't as black and white as I thought. Besides, my writing has been blocked for the last year; I've been devoid of ideas. But just having you here…' He stared at Morag. 'It's as if Blair is sitting in front of me. Suddenly all these possibilities are appearing. I'd forgotten how…' He searched for the words. 'You can fill a room. You always were so full of life.'

Morag snorted. 'You want me to stay – be some kind of muse so you can write another book about your nosy detective?'

Charlie laughed. 'Perhaps.' His eyes circled the room. 'I've been stuck here on my own for too long. I hadn't realised how much it had clogged me.' He gave Morag an odd smile. 'Or how much I needed a dose of inspiration. No matter how cantankerous it is.'

'You were always the curmudgeonly one,' Morag snarled.

'Looks like you both still have lots to catch up on. So come to the dance on Saturday?' Johnny suggested to Charlie with a grin. 'Meet some of the villagers. You've got a number of fans in Lockton. Come and see who you'll be helping by launching the library.'

Charlie started to shake his head.

Morag sniffed and shook her head too. 'That's a terrible idea. The man's already told you he doesn't like going out in public – and if I know anything about Charlie Adaire, it's that once he's made up his mind about something, like moving to France for instance' – she shot him an irritated glare – 'he definitely won't be persuaded otherwise.'

Charlie stared at Morag for a few beats. 'I think you'll find, Morag Dooley, that some things do change.' His cheeks glowed as

he turned to Johnny. 'So I'll come to your dance, laddie, after all.'
He looked back at Morag. 'And I'll be expecting you to keep me
company when I do.'

Morag frowned and then let out a sigh. 'I suppose, in the interests of the library, I can give you one night.' She drew in a breath
and glanced over at Paige and Johnny. 'But we'd better leave now
before I change my mind.'

Chapter Twenty-One

The Lockton Scottish Dance took place every year on the third Saturday in July, in a large marquee that was erected in a field about a twenty-minute walk from Buttermead Farm. Years ago, the mayor had reached an agreement with the events company to allow Lockton to run both the dance and the Jampionships in the same venue, a week apart. The deal had stuck. Paige had been going since she was a child; the whole village attended every year and everyone dressed up. Paige had a new outfit her mam had kindly bought her online. When she'd first arrived in Lockton, the red dress would have hung loosely around her, drawing attention to the sharp angles of her hips and the flat planes of her body. But when she'd twisted to check herself in her bedroom mirror as she'd got dressed earlier, she'd realised shallow curves had begun to emerge. Even her face had filled out, and her eyes seemed to sparkle more than they had in years. Was it being back in Lockton, working in the library and reconnecting with herself, or just time away from London and all that stress? Or was it Johnny's kindness and the feelings he stirred?

As Paige approached the marquee with the tepee-style ceiling and glittering lights dangling from the white canvas, she took a deep breath, gripping Grace's hand as she remembered the moment she'd seen Carl for the first time, six years before. He'd been leaning against the doorway of the large tent, watching her with a twinkle in his eye. He'd looked so handsome. In that instant he'd taken her breath away. How young she'd been then, how full of innocence and optimism; and what a gullible fool. She shook off the memory as she entered and took a deep lungful of air, scanning the interior.

There was a large square dance floor in the centre of the tent – tiles of wood painted white and pink had been laid to create a chequered effect. At the end of this was a small rectangular stage stacked with instruments including a harp, guitar and accordion, along with a couple of mics at the top of long silver poles. There was a low hum of music playing in the background and people around the room were chatting in groups. At the edges of the marquee, tables had been set up and some of the guests were already seated. Her mam and da had left home earlier so they could help with some last-minute setting up, and Cora waved from a large table set in the far corner. Paige held Grace's hand tightly and continued through the marquee, past garlands of fairy lights and blue, green and pink paper lanterns which dangled from the ceiling, giving the place a magical, joyful glow. Grace pointed up as they walked, grinning at the ornaments. Paige smiled back, approving of the vibe the events company had created. As they walked, she scanned the crowd and the people serving at the bar, trying to spot Johnny. She hadn't seen a lot of him this week; she'd talked to him briefly at the Jam Club meeting on Thursday, but aside from that she'd been busy in the library and he'd been working on his recipes. She'd missed him though, more than she should have.

As they passed one of the tables, someone stopped her. 'I wanted to thank you for the book you recommended,' Evie Stuart said, her amber eyes sparkling. She wore traditional Scottish dress and her red hair was tied in a knot on the top of her head. 'I'm already halfway through it – you definitely have Aileen's talent. I'll be back in the library soon to pick up more of your recommendations. Perhaps you can find me one on getting a wee bairn to sleep through?'

Paige nodded. 'There are loads of guides on getting babies to settle; I'll put a few aside.'

'That's kind – you're a gift to this village, Paige.' Evie grinned.

'I want more books too,' Meg piped up. She was sitting opposite Evie, next to a good-looking man with dark brown hair. They were all dressed for the dance and had drinks set in front of them on the table. 'Tom's all for our next holiday being in Turkey.'

'Good choice,' Tom said, smiling. 'I'll be in to experience some of your book magic.'

'I… thank you,' Paige said, a little taken aback by the warmth of their welcome. She shouldn't have been surprised. Everyone had made her feel at home since she'd arrived back in Lockton. The Jam Club, her mam's friends, people she remembered from her childhood who'd wandered into the library to pass the time… It tugged at her emotions, even as she tried to dismiss it, to reject the pull of everyone's kindness, of history and home. She looked around, wondering if she was crazy for wanting to leave.

Tom grinned as louder music began to play, and they turned to the stage just as Davey hopped onto it. Paige scanned the crowd for Johnny again, but there was no sign of him. She squeezed Grace's shoulder as Davey began to talk.

'Welcome to the annual Lockton Scottish Dance,' he said, getting into character and delivering a dazzling grin which reminded Paige of Johnny. 'I hope you're all wearing your dancing shoes, because we've got a real treat for you tonight. The Morridon Folk Band will be providing the music for our event. So clap your hands, then get onto your feet, people, and if you're anywhere near to Callum Ryder, make sure you're wearing armour or steel-capped boots.' He pointed towards Evie's table. 'For anyone who doesn't know him, he's the only man in the whole of Scotland with two size-thirteen left feet.' There was a rumble of laughter and then a burst of clapping from the crowd as the handsome man sitting next to Evie stood and bowed. As Davey jumped down from the stage, Paige continued walking through the marquee, pausing a couple of times as strangers stopped her as she passed, asking her questions about the library and letting her know they were planning to visit for book recommendations soon.

Davey was waiting by Paige's mam and da's table as she approached. There were spaces for her and Grace, and another couple of empty seats. Grace instantly ran to her granda and climbed onto his knee. 'Is Johnny here?' Paige scanned the crowd.

Davey shook his head. 'He's still at Apple Cross Inn practising Monday's menu; he's been working on it all week.' He took in Paige's expression. 'He promised he'd come tonight.' His forehead creased. 'It's not like him to miss out on a party, and it's been a long time since I've seen him this caught up.' He didn't look very happy about the transformation.

'You're looking bonnie, lass,' Agnes commented, as she walked up with Fergus to join them, and gave Paige a quick hug. 'Almost like your old self.' She admired the red dress with a knowing grin. 'Morag and Charlie are on their way now. Morag wanted to make her own way here, but Charlie insisted on giving her a lift. Apparently he was worried she wouldn't make it if left to her own devices.' She looked around the marquee. A few couples had already taken to the dance floor.

'The man's probably right. Morag's always been contrary,' Fergus growled without a hint of irony, sipping from a glass of whisky as his grey eyes scanned the dancers before falling on Davey. 'You all set for Tony Silver coming on Monday?'

Davey nodded. 'Johnny seems happy enough. Matilda made us some menus and we've set up a special dining area in the corner of the pub.' He shook his head. 'I'm not sure why I hadn't thought of doing it before.'

'You got a tiramisu from Lilith?' Agnes asked.

Davey scowled. 'We've plenty of desserts. Cora's coming to the pub tomorrow to make us a couple more, to help Johnny out.' He flashed a smile in Paige's mam's direction. 'I'm sure Lilith has enough to do preparing for her move home.'

'You don't know if the lass is relocating to Italy, you eejit,' Morag rumbled, suddenly appearing from behind a group of dancers. She was dressed in traditional Scottish tartan. Her hair was scrapped back on the top of her head and she had bright red lipstick on. Charlie Adaire stood by her side, gazing at her with an expression Paige could only describe as confused. 'Could be if the right person asked her not to go, she might decide not to move.' Morag pursed her lips.

Davey shook his head. 'I… if Lilith wanted to stay, she knows she only has to ask. I'd give her a job in the pub and she could move in with me if she wanted.'

'We all know how she feels about impressing her da. Perhaps she's too proud or too scared to admit she was wrong?' Agnes suggested.

Davey considered that for a few moments, and his gaze darted around the room before fixing on the woman in question, who was standing near the bar, chatting with a dark-haired man. His expression softened as Lilith turned and their eyes met, then her cheeks reddened before she turned away. Davey scowled and shook his head. 'Lilith isn't afraid of anything. If she wanted me or my help, she'd say.'

'It's hard putting your pride aside after you've been hurt. There's been many a good relationship lost because those involved wouldn't.' Agnes sighed, watching Davey's face, missing a sharp look from Charlie before he turned again to gaze at Morag.

'I wouldn't know what to say,' Davey murmured as he digested Agnes's words. He looked at Lilith again but she had her back to him. Then the music got louder as the band announced they wanted everyone to make their way onto the dance floor.

'You going to dance with me, woman?' Charlie asked Morag. He pointed to her cane. 'If you put that down before we go out there, I'll stop worrying you're going to whack me over the head.'

'Doesn't your detective Blair have a problem with dancing?' Morag's tone was acidic. 'I seem to recall in your last novel she almost broke her arm trying to do hip hop.' She shuddered. 'Hip hop,' she drawled. 'At her age. I told you your characters aren't believable.'

Charlie's lips twitched. 'I thought you hadn't read my latest books, lass.'

Morag's cheeks pinked. 'Someone left it in the post office and I was bored. I used it to line my cat Zora's litter tray after I read it.' She turned away from Charlie to watch the dancing and Paige saw his lips twitch again, then he pulled a pad from his jacket pocket and scribbled something onto it before putting it away.

'I never did have to worry about my ego getting too big when you were around.' Charlie looked amused. 'Are we dancing, woman, or not?' He turned to watch the crowd as another song started up and couples began to skip past. 'I recall you used to be light on your feet – or are you too old and set in your ways to try?'

Morag didn't respond for a beat, then she shoved the cane at Fergus before he could refuse, almost spilling his whisky, and stomped onto the dance floor. Charlie let out a bark of delight and followed, grabbing Morag's arm as they inserted themselves in between the couples.

Agnes leaned in to Paige. 'I've not seen that woman look so happy in years.' Morag's cheeks glowed as they began to skip, and despite the glowers she kept throwing in Charlie's direction, even Paige could see she was enjoying herself. After a few more minutes she laughed. 'That's a match I could see lasting…' Agnes said. 'Funny how sometimes the things we most need are right under our nose.' She shot an adoring look at Fergus. 'I found out the same thing for myself last summer.'

Paige didn't respond, but she watched as Charlie kept darting looks in Morag's direction. He looked amused, and far more alive than he had when they'd discovered him at his house just a week before. Was that what the right kind of chemistry could do? What would happen to her if she let herself fall for Johnny? But could she risk her heart again? Give it to another near-stranger and lose everything she'd built? Worse, could she risk Grace's too?

After the song ended, Charlie and Morag left the dance floor and walked up to join them. Paige watched Charlie pull the black book from his pocket again before scribbling into it.

'What are you doing?' Morag asked Charlie, as Fergus offered her the cane and she leaned onto it. Her cheekbones were dappled with red and despite the frown, her mouth twitched as she watched Charlie pocket the notebook.

'Making notes.' He patted his jacket. 'I think on reflection, Blair might be a dancer. I've just had an idea about a murder at a village ball…'

Morag's forehead crunched. 'I should charge you for all this inspiration. At the very least you should agree to talk at the library on Wednesday. We've been advertising a mystery author all week. If you don't do it, I'll have made a total eejit of myself and Jason Beckett will get his hands on our library after all.' She twirled her cane as the music grew louder and the dance floor thrummed with energy.

'I never told you I wouldn't do it.' Charlie looked amused.

'Which isn't the same as saying you will.' Morag turned to glower at him. Again, Paige could detect a new lightness in her gait, an air of excitement as something fizzled between them. Her mind strayed to her kisses with Johnny before she forced the memory back.

Charlie tapped his pocket. 'Blair wouldn't have put that any better herself. I'll talk at your library,' he said. 'If you promise to go out with me again.'

'Where?' Morag snapped, looking more delighted than annoyed.

Charlie's eyes glinted devilishly. 'There's a stroll I know which finishes in a spooky graveyard just outside Lockton. I've been meaning to visit again. I went a few years ago and thought then it would be the perfect place to set a murder.' He grinned.

'Fine,' Morag grumbled. 'I'll bring my shovel, and we can recreate that murder if you like.' She paused. 'But we'll go *after* your talk at The Book Barn.'

Charlie barked out a laugh. 'Done.' He held out his hand. 'Fancy another whirl?' Morag shoved the cane at Fergus once more and they took off onto the floor.

Paige turned to scan the crowd, looking for Johnny again.

'Perhaps you should check the kitchen at Apple Cross Inn, lass,' Agnes whispered. 'Your mam and da will watch Grace.' She waved in their direction. Grace was chatting happily with Marcus and Cora was fussing, offering her a drink. They looked happy and relaxed. 'They love having their wee grandbaby here. Perhaps it's time you had a break? Must be hard raising a lass all on your own. Might be nice for you to take some time out for yourself.'

Paige nodded, thinking perhaps the time had come for her to do exactly that.

Chapter Twenty-Two

Apple Cross Inn was quiet when Paige walked into the pub. The bar area was small and painted dark green, with oak beams and a low ceiling that she imagined would have anyone the height of Johnny ducking under it most of the time. There were a couple of people sitting to the right of the oak counter, but the rest of the pub looked empty. Matilda glanced up when Paige entered and beamed. She was a pretty woman, with a curvy figure and a mass of curly red hair which she'd plaited down her back.

'He's in the kitchen, but watch out, he's in a terrible mood,' she said as soon as Paige approached, grinning and pointing to a door next to the bar which led to the back. Paige opened it and walked through into a hallway. To the right was an open door and to the left a set of stairs, which probably led up to Davey's flat. The hallway was dark and painted the same green as the pub, with warm oak floorboards. Paige followed them into a bright kitchen with metal cupboards and a huge professional countertop that took up most of the centre of the space. The kitchen was tidy and nothing looked out of place; every surface shone with an almost unnatural sparkle. Paige stood by the door, watching Johnny work. He wore a white apron and his strong arms flexed as he piped something onto a lined baking tray. His face was all business, his mouth set flat as he squeezed the mixture with a determination she hadn't thought he possessed. There wasn't even music playing; all semblance of fun had been wiped from the kitchen. To the right of the shiny hob sat a pie which was obviously cooling. A small tub of vegetables sat beside it; perhaps Johnny had already prepared some, ready for when he served the pie?

She cleared her throat and he looked up, his features lighting immediately, making something deep inside her respond.

'You look pretty,' he said, his voice a little husky as he took in the red dress. Paige had put a cardigan on as she'd left the dance. It was still warm outside but the air had cooled, and even though the kitchen was hot she felt goosebumps rise on the surface of her skin. 'Where's the princess?' Johnny asked, leaning to search behind her, looking concerned when he realised she was alone.

'At the dance.' Paige coughed, feeling awkward suddenly. 'With my mam and da, they said they'd watch her. I was sent to look for you. Are you still preparing for Monday?'

'It's not that late, is it?' Johnny frowned. 'I thought I'd try out macaroons – I made them all the time in my restaurant, but these just won't work.' He pointed to a baking sheet which he'd tossed to one side, where an array of multicoloured macaroons sat abandoned. Paige walked over to examine them.

'What's the matter? They look perfect.' She bent to peer at them more closely.

'They haven't developed feet; the insides have holes. I'm not sure if it's because I'm out of practice, or because the oven's all wrong.' Johnny glared at the tall silver cooker at the edge of the kitchen as if he planned to challenge it to a duel. 'This never happened to me once in New York,' he growled, turning back to his piping. He squeezed out more of the mixture and then cursed when one of his creations came out more oval than circular. He scowled, then scooped it up with a palate knife and dropped it unceremoniously into the bin.

'Do you want help?' Paige asked, fascinated by the transformation. He looked tense and frustrated, and suddenly, inexplicably, she wanted the old Johnny back. The man who made her laugh, and realise the world wasn't so serious, that there was room for imperfections, room for things to go wrong. But most of all, the man who reminded her life was for living and laughing – not for getting lost in ambition and work. He let out a loud huff but didn't respond to her offer. 'Is it that important that they're perfect?' she asked, folding her arms. Johnny's blue eyes flicked up to meet hers. They were icy, devoid of humour, and his lips thinned as if he were priming them to snap out a sharp retort. His eyes held hers for a few seconds more, before his shoulders relaxed and the tension at the corners of his mouth eased.

'I'm being ridiculous, aren't I?' He straightened and shook his head, rolling his shoulders. 'I've been working so hard for the last few days. I started cooking again.' He looked around the immaculate kitchen, coming to his senses. 'I was enjoying it at first, but then I wanted to push and push – because suddenly impressing Tony Silver was all I could think about.' He looked up at the ceiling. 'Mack's still upstairs waiting for me; I totally forgot about him. Let's call that a walk into the dark side I don't wish to repeat. Thank you for saving me.' He held her gaze for a moment, then his forehead bunched as he checked his watch. 'Has the dance started already?'

'About an hour ago.'

Johnny pulled a face. 'I'm sorry. I believe I promised you and the princess a dance, yet here I am making a fool of myself.' He looked around the kitchen, shaking his head. 'I don't know what got into me.' He gave her a wry smile. 'I think perhaps I was trying to impress you.'

Paige's stomach fluttered and she found herself smiling. 'I was hoping you'd do that on the dance floor. There's still plenty of time if you hurry. Shall I help?' She pointed to the counter.

He sighed, then shrugged. 'You're right. There are far more important things to do tonight – dancing, for one. If you wash your hands and put on an apron and a hair net, I'll show you how to finish these. Macaroons aren't even on the menu, and we've got plenty of desserts planned so I'm not sure what I was thinking. I suppose we could finish them, take some to the library on Monday. Besides, I'm still on my mission to get you to eat more.' His eyes travelled over her dress, dropping to her hips, before he must have realised the slow scrutiny was rude and jerked his head up. He waited while Paige did as he'd asked, tracking her movements around the kitchen in a way that made her heart race. When she came to join him, he passed her the piping bag and stood back. His expression was so different now. The old Johnny was well and truly back.

'What – no tutorial?' she asked, her lips curving.

He shrugged as his mouth mirrored hers, then folded his arms. The light dusting of hair across his forearms glittered gold underneath the kitchen lights. 'See what you can do first. I'll watch and tell you where you can improve.'

Paige leaned over the baking sheet and picked up the piping bag. She pressed the edge of it, slowly squeezing the mixture until it abruptly squirted out, landing in a wonky pink blob. 'I really can't cook.' She shook her head, feeling a sudden urge to berate herself. 'I didn't get any of my mam's genes in that regard. Even a sandwich can be challenging.' Carl had often sneered at her lack of skills in the kitchen.

'And that matters because?' Johnny snorted and moved so that he was closer. His body was warm against the back of her dress, and even though they weren't touching Paige was more than a little aware of him. 'May I?' he asked, his breath hot against the edge of her neck, and she nodded as tingles danced across her skin. He leaned forwards and wrapped his arms around her, placing his hands over hers on the piping bag. With Johnny's mouth right next to her ear, her whole body seemed to come alive, waking from the hiatus it had been forced into. Not just because of Carl's death, but because of his indifference to her for the last years of their marriage. The affairs and dents to her confidence had left her feeling like a total failure. Only since meeting Johnny had something awoken. Something deep inside her was returning to life – she just wasn't sure she was ready to acknowledge or trust it.

'You do it like this,' Johnny murmured against her ear, squeezing her hands, pushing the mixture slowly out of the piping bag until it dripped onto the baking parchment in a perfect globe. 'You're a natural.' He laughed as he eased their hands to the left, squeezing again until another perfect circle appeared next to it.

Paige cleared her throat. She was so aware of Johnny now, of the taut muscular planes of his chest against her back, of the way his arms encircled her, making her feel warm and coveted. He smelled good too – something citrusy, perhaps lime, which complemented all the sweet fragrances filling the kitchen. Then there was the sudden clatter of loud footsteps, and Johnny eased back and dropped his arms as Matilda came skidding into the kitchen. Paige felt her cheeks burn as the barmaid raised an eyebrow before grabbing a couple of lemons from the fridge and leaning against the countertop, as Johnny backed further away. He picked up a couple of stray cooking utensils so he could pack them into the dishwasher.

'Evie told me about your book recommendations.' Matilda surveyed them both before she smiled at Paige. 'I wondered, if I came to the library on Monday, could you find me something to read?' She pulled a face. 'I've been struggling to sleep and I've not been able to concentrate on anything. I thought a book might help.'

Paige shrugged. 'I can try.'

'She'll do better than that,' Johnny said, his voice proud. 'The woman's a veritable genius when it comes to the art of choosing the right read.' He walked up beside her and pointed to the baking tray, just the slightest brush of his arm against hers making her stomach perform a series of acrobatic leaps. 'She cooks too,' he joked.

Matilda grinned. 'Then leave a few of those out for me. I've got a ton of books to bring back to the library. Some on art and a couple of paperbacks – I'll pop in.' She looked pointedly at Johnny. 'You should head to the dance.' She gestured to the exit with the lemons in hand before disappearing back to the bar.

'I think you could finish the rest,' Johnny said lightly as the room fell silent. Paige concentrated hard as she squeezed out the rest of the mixture, creating a varied mix of shapes, none of which were remotely globe-like or circular. After filling the dishwasher, Johnny put the food he'd prepared into the fridge before coming to check on her creations. He shook his head as the edge of his mouth quirked.

Paige smiled. 'I thought we weren't aiming for perfection.' She scanned the tray of mis-shapes. 'This has confirmed what I always knew – I'm not cut out to be a chef.'

Johnny scooped up the tray and put it in the oven. 'We'll see what the visitors to the library think. I need to get Mack from upstairs. We could head to the dance for an hour or so – I think he'll be able to behave if we don't stay too long. I'll dance with the princess and perhaps we can dance too?'

Johnny held her eyes for a moment before he turned and walked into the hallway, leaving Paige wondering what all the feelings bubbling inside her meant.

Chapter Twenty-Three

The marquee was buzzing when Paige and Johnny arrived half an hour later. Music played loudly and the floor was filled with dancing couples. Grace jumped off her granda's knee the instant she saw them. She was beaming, and she opened her arms wide as she ran up.

'Mummy, prince – doggy!' She knelt and scratched Mack as he tried to lick her face, clearly as delighted by her appearance as she was with his. 'Will you dance?' she asked Johnny shyly as she rose.

'Wouldn't miss it, princess.' He beamed before giving her a mock gasp. 'Wow, you look beautiful, is that a new dress?' Grace giggled and turned a becoming shade of pink.

'I'll watch Mack,' Paige murmured, a little disarmed by the shot of pure delight that lit up her daughter's face. Then again, Johnny was charming, she'd always known that. Cora came to join them as Johnny scooped up the toddler and put her on his hip, whisking her into the middle of the throng.

'The lass has a crush,' Cora said, as they watched Johnny and Grace's heads bob when they joined the dance.

'Yes, prince!' Grace shrieked with excitement.

Paige frowned. 'She's not normally so good with strangers, but Johnny's great with her. I suppose they've developed a connection through their mutual love of drawing and Mack.'

'Aye. She'll miss him when you leave.' Cora sounded sad. 'And the wee dog.' She patted Mack, who was sitting quietly watching the dancers. There'd been such a big change in him since the training at Buttermead Farm; clearly Johnny was keeping up with the lessons. Another surprise.

Paige took an unsteady breath. 'Grace will forget about them as soon as we're in London. Once she's with her childminder and life returns to normal.' Whatever normal meant. Although whatever happened, Paige knew she'd have to find time to be kind to herself and to have fun. If she'd learned anything since being in Lockton, she'd learned that. The idea of going back to her old life made something inside her freeze but she dismissed it, watching the dancers instead. The music slowed and the couples broke off into small groups. Grace had her head on Johnny's shoulder and he'd slowed his movements to a gentle rocking. Paige watched Grace sigh as her eyes fluttered, then shut. It was then that Johnny looked over and winked. They looked so perfect together, exactly the picture Paige had always imagined when Carl had been alive. But the man had never had time for his daughter. In two years, he hadn't so much as lifted her out of her cot; the only good thing was that Grace hadn't been old enough to recognise the rejection. She waved as something caught in her throat, then watched Grace's arms tighten around Johnny's neck and her body grow slack as she fell asleep. After a few more minutes, Johnny walked slowly off the dance floor. Paige went to take Grace, but her mam stepped in.

'Let us take her. Your da's had enough excitement after meeting his favourite author; he wants to go home. I'll ask Fergus to watch

Mack so you two can dance.' Cora winked at Paige, before opening her arms and gently taking Grace into them. Paige leaned over to kiss her daughter's blonde curls as her mam whispered, 'Don't rush back – you deserve some time to relax and the wee lass will be fine with us.' Then Cora gently kissed Paige's head before sweeping both Grace and Marcus away.

Paige stood for a few moments, looking after them. 'You want to dance?' Johnny asked softly. 'I know I put Grace to sleep, but if you start to drop off I promise to tread on your feet.'

'Fine.' Paige laughed, relaxing as he led her onto the dance floor. The music was still quiet and couples were swaying together. Johnny pulled Paige to him, circling her with his arms, and she let herself lean into him, let her head press against his shoulder as she breathed in his scent. Chocolate again; limes too. It had been so long since anyone had held her. Her body started to respond to the press of Johnny's palm against the small of her back, and tingles travelled outwards, making her skin heat. He moved them slowly around the dance floor and Paige relished the feel of his body, listening to the patter of his heart. Was it her imagination or had that steady beat quickened? She pulled away and looked up into Johnny's face – he was staring at her, his blue eyes dark. There was a question in them and Paige swallowed. 'Shall we walk Mack home?' she asked, her voice husky. She was taking a chance, she knew that, complicating things at the exact wrong moment because she was leaving Lockton in less than a week. But in this moment, she wasn't sure she could stop herself.

*

It was almost nine by the time Paige and Johnny arrived at his cottage, and the sun was starting to lower in the sky. Paige pulled her cardigan tighter as she waited on the doorstep while he unlocked the door, watching as Mack bounded inside, heading for the kitchen before skidding to a stop and charging back. Johnny fed him, then went to the fridge and withdrew a bottle of white wine before tipping it in Paige's direction. 'Okay with you?'

She nodded, watching as he filled two glasses.

'I've got something to show you,' he said suddenly. When she raised an eyebrow, he chuckled and headed into a large pantry to his right before walking out with a plastic cake carrier. He put it on the counter and lifted the lid. Inside was a round cake with three tiers. The top wasn't finished, but Paige could already tell by the shape that it was going to be a castle.

'Um… I wasn't expecting…' She pressed a fingertip to her stomach, as if a mere touch could stop the butterflies.

'I've just been playing with ideas, practising really.' Johnny looked embarrassed when she stared. 'I used to enjoy making cakes and I felt like baking. I'm no expert when it comes to decorating, but I thought if I put some edges here and a huge flag on the top…' He used his large hands to outline his plans and his cheeks coloured. 'Maybe decorate it white with purple and pink flowers – it might work. What do you think? For Grace?' He looked worried when Paige didn't respond. 'Too much?'

'I…' She couldn't find words. The fact that he'd thought about Grace both touched and confused her.

Johnny frowned. 'If you hate the idea or want to make the cake yourself, that's okay. This is a prototype; it's too early for the real thing and Mack's got his eye on it already. I know you'll be back in London by Grace's birthday, but… I thought maybe we could celebrate before you left? It's not every day a girl turns four.' He put the lid back on the carrier when Paige stayed silent and began to return it to the pantry, but she shook her head, making him stop.

'I'm… a little lost for words. I'm sorry. It's just…' She let out a slow breath.

Johnny shrugged. 'I was curious – honestly, it was more for my own entertainment. And the princess, well, she's a cute kid.' He avoided her eyes.

Paige moved closer and put a finger to his lips when he opened them, no doubt getting ready to give her a new excuse. His skin was soft and she let herself lean forwards. 'Thank you,' she said huskily. 'For thinking of Grace and for saving me from a few days of torture as I tried to make something that wouldn't resemble that.'

His shoulders relaxed. 'After seeing you cook earlier, I'm not going to argue.'

Paige barked out a laugh but didn't move away. She could smell Johnny again, that hint of chocolate and limes mixed with something earthier. Their eyes met and held. She could read his intention, and nodded.

'I'm not good at relationships – it's been years since I wanted to be close to anyone,' he said softly.

'Neither am I,' Paige choked, waving her bare ring finger at him. 'Failed marriage, remember, a woman who had a husband who thought I wasn't enough. If you're looking for a relationship, you should run a mile. But that's not what I'm here for. I'm going back to London in five days, I was signed off for four weeks and the time's almost gone.' Just saying the words made her want to wrap her arms around herself.

'Then what's this?' Johnny asked, moving closer.

Paige could feel the heat from his body as she stepped towards him. 'Friends… kissing friends?' She searched for the right words. 'I don't know, do we need to define it?'

Johnny sighed. 'I'd like to say we don't. But I've a feeling you might.'

Paige could tell he was torn. It wasn't that he didn't want to touch her, she could see he did, but he was obviously concerned. Then again, so was she – but that wasn't going to stop her. 'It's been a long time for me. A long time since a man made me feel special. Can we just say I'd like to feel that again and leave it at that?'

'Two friends offering comfort?' He didn't look convinced.

She bit her lip. 'I haven't been with anyone since Carl. The last person who touched me… like that.' She paused, wondering if she could even remember the encounter. 'Was him. I'm pretty sure now that he'd just been with someone else.' Her forehead scrunched. 'He was never that good at hiding it. That's a bad memory for me. It left me feeling so…' She searched for the word. 'Unworthy. Like such a failure. I want to move on.' She looked into his blue eyes. 'To create a new memory with someone who cares…'

'So you want to forget, to scratch out the past?' Johnny asked, looking surprised, and Paige wondered if she was kidding herself. But she nodded anyway. He reached out then, stroked a hand down her cheek and picked up a strand of hair, playing with it between his fingers as they drifted closer. Mack yawned loudly. 'Think we're boring him?'

'I'm sure we can do something about that.' Paige blinked, then smelled limes again. She wanted to touch him, but she wasn't going to make the first move. That was all Johnny's. She needed someone to want her; needed not to be someone's second, third or fourth choice.

'Will this change anything?' Johnny's brow furrowed. He was still playing with her hair, smoothing it with his fingertips, slowly massaging each strand as if it were precious. The movements set off a low buzz in the centre of her body, an ache she hadn't felt in years.

Paige swallowed. 'No. We'll still be friends – we're already kissing friends.' She lifted her face. 'Now we'll be friends who've seen each other's underwear. You've seen it on my mam's drive, now you get to see it on me.' A burst of warmth bloomed across her skin.

He grinned. 'I'll be seeing a lot more than that.' Mack made a sudden snuffling sound and he grimaced. 'And so will he. We already know Mack's feelings on your underwear.'

He dropped the strand of hair and stepped back, and Paige's stomach lurched. Johnny was moving away now, and she knew with a certainty that pierced her chest that he was going to say no. That he was going to grab his shoes and walk her home. Because she was asking too much. But instead Johnny headed to a cupboard and grabbed a handful of dog biscuits, then he knelt and waved them under Mack's nose. The dog's eyes instantly popped open, and he jumped up as his master led him out of the kitchen into the sitting room. Paige stayed where she was. She heard the cage door open and then close, heard a happy bark from Mack, a thunder of feet on the stairs as someone ran up and down, returning in what felt like seconds. Then Johnny wandered back into the kitchen and closed the door.

He stood looking at her, his expression contemplative and a little vulnerable. 'You really sure?' he asked again, and hope bloomed in Paige's chest. She couldn't speak so nodded, waiting as he stalked across the kitchen until he was in front of her. She traced his face before noticing the fluttering pulse at the base of his neck. She could see the rapid beat, the only indication that she was affecting him. The spot looked tender and she wanted, with a tug she hadn't been expecting, to press her lips to it, to drag her tongue over the salty skin so she could find out how he tasted. The fantasy was unexpected and gave her a jolt.

'Where?' She cleared the catch out of her throat as a smile spread slowly across Johnny's face.

'I do my best work in the kitchen. Ironically, it's where I feel most at home.' He scanned the space before focusing on the rustic oak table positioned under the window to their left. 'Perfect.' He took her hand and slowly linked their fingers in an erotic coupling that set Paige's heartbeat skidding up a notch, then he walked across the kitchen to the table.

She followed, almost tripping over her feet. Because she didn't want to wait, didn't want to change her mind. Then Johnny turned and eased her back until her legs were pressing against the side of the table – until she was almost sitting. Even the sensation of the hard wood against her skin felt good. Then in a quick lift she was on the surface. Johnny eased her legs open so he could step in between. He reached into his pocket and placed two condoms on the table. 'I had some upstairs. I guess it pays to be prepared.'

'You knew this would happen?' She didn't know if she was disappointed or shocked.

Johnny brushed his thumbs across her cheekbones, making every cell thrum. 'Nope. I'm as surprised as you. In case you're wondering, I'm making this up as I go along.' He bent his head so he could nibble her neck. The light dusting of stubble on his jaw played havoc with the skin across her collarbone. 'There's no recipe for this, no perfect steps. None I've discovered, anyway.'

'I'll take a look in the library.' Paige attempted a joke as Johnny began to feather light kisses across the front of her chest, easing her cardigan over her arms, effectively trapping them so he could get to her shoulders. She moaned as his mouth drifted across her skin. Carl had never made her feel like this, even in the early days of their relationship – like every millimetre of her skin was precious; like she had to be savoured; like she wasn't just one in a very long line. She'd been too inexperienced to realise it when they'd met, but now she knew better. 'I don't think you need a book, and those aren't words you often hear from a librarian. You're doing fine, great actually.' The words came out on a long sigh.

Johnny chuckled against her skin, a quick bump as his kisses grew deeper, then he tugged the cardigan off her arms, throwing it over his head so it landed behind him with a soft thud. Now she was free, Paige wrapped her arms around his neck, pulling him closer, easing herself forwards on the table. She let her fingers explore his hair, trailing them over his ears and neck, tracing his chest until they rested on the bottom of his T-shirt. She hesitated before pushing up the soft material. His skin was as smooth as she'd expected, and she spread her fingers, taking her time, letting them lower to his waistband. She savoured his sharp intake of breath as her fingers nuzzled deeper, the involuntary jerk he couldn't control. The scent of limes filled her nostrils and she dipped her head, breaking their kiss so she could skim her lips across the surface of his chest. She pushed the T-shirt over Johnny's head, catching his look of confusion as she chucked it over his shoulder. Perhaps he was as surprised by this urgency to connect as she was? She dismissed the thought, the desire to examine it. Instead, she set her attention to the button and zip on his jeans, felt him slide the straps of her red dress down her arms. His fingers were fiddling with her bra strap and then that went too, along with her shoes. The silk of her dress bunched around her waist and Johnny pushed up the folds of her skirt, traced a fingertip up each side of her leg.

Then their kisses slowed, became deeper. The feelings Paige had been holding in, the belief that they could do this and nothing would change between them, began to fracture. But she ignored it, pushed away the stab of concern. She'd ignored a lot worse in her life. And she'd emerged stronger.

Then Johnny put a hand against the top of her shoulder and began to edge her slowly down until she was lying on the table. The wood felt smooth against her back. She gazed up, watching him slowly scan her naked body, feeling a wave of heat sweep her skin. His eyes slid to her face and he smiled. 'You're quite something,' he murmured. 'I've never had anything on my table I've wanted so much.' Then he was leaning over her, taking her mouth in his, and she was moving forwards as they locked together. He began to move, put a hand under her head, ran a careful fingertip over her cheek as they kissed. Blood was thundering through her veins, and she could almost hear the echo from his. Inside her things were stirring, connecting – like a myriad of ingredients merging to become something else, something more. Was it too much? Paige pushed the thoughts down, the feelings that felt too similar to the ones she'd felt years before. She didn't want that – she wasn't naive now. This would change nothing. She wouldn't let it.

Then she stopped thinking as they continued to climb, as the tension built and the world blurred.

Chapter Twenty-Four

The Book Barn was peaceful when Paige opened up on Monday morning and paused on the doorstep as she took in the bright room. Noticing the ordered shelves neatly filled with multicoloured spines that she'd spent hours carefully arranging over the last couple of weeks. She strode in, swinging her bag, taking in a deep breath and inhaling the aroma of books, feeling her chest fill with emotion. Then she stopped abruptly beside the front counter, when she noticed that the book called *Letting Go of a Bad Life* had disappeared from the spot where she'd left it. Now a paperback titled *Home Is Where the Heart Is* sat face up in the same space beside the till. Paige turned it over and glared at the sunny skylights.

'Aileen, what are you trying to tell me? I listened to my heart six years ago, remember, and just look how that turned out,' she shouted into the empty space, feeling a little desperate – then the emotion morphed into embarrassment as not so much as a floorboard squeaked. 'Not you then,' she murmured, feeling disappointed when the old librarian's apparition didn't appear. She put the book to one side, ignoring the message someone had obviously sneaked in to leave; had it been Morag, Agnes – or her own mam? It was no secret they wanted her to stay and now they had another reason. Lockton was a small place and most of the village would be aware she'd gone to Johnny's house on Saturday night; perhaps a couple had guessed just how far their relationship had progressed. But she had a job to get back to in London, a life she was missing. Wasn't she?

Paige scratched her cheek as she walked around the library, checking more shelves and taking another moment to breathe in the gorgeous scent. There was the sound of footsteps by the entrance at the exact moment she heard her mobile buzz in her bag. She pulled it out and checked the screen to find the estate agent was calling. Maybe he had news of a further delay, or perhaps the house was finally going through? Her fingers reluctantly hovered over it before she put the ringing phone back in her bag. By the time she turned, Davey was waiting by the counter.

'Everything okay?' she asked, taking in the strain around his mouth.

'Yep.' His attention darted to the computer table where Lilith had been sitting when he'd visited the week before last. 'I was wondering.' He blushed as he looked at her. 'You don't know me well, but I've heard on the grapevine you have a gift for finding people the right book.' He tried to smile. 'That your choices have brought happiness into people's lives. Some say you learned how to tune in to what people need from Aileen. She was always so kind, so determined to help people. Agnes Stuart told me she thinks you've been passed the mantle by her ghostly spirit.'

Paige laughed. 'Perhaps I've just made a few lucky guesses?'

'Or you have good instincts.' He shrugged. 'A gift is a gift, doesn't really matter where it came from. I was wondering if you could tell me something.' Davey folded his arms across his chest, looking awkward. 'I know Lilith has been searching for jobs here.'

'I can't tell you much more,' Paige said. 'She's not been back to the library and I already told you everything I saw.'

Davey shuffled his feet. 'I don't want her to leave Lockton,' he blurted, looking a little desperate. 'I've no idea how we got into this position, and I've no idea how to get us out of it. I want to know, did she borrow anything?' He looked unhappy. 'I feel like I'm asking you to give away her secrets, like for some reason I want to tell you mine.'

'Hey, no Hippocratic oath for librarians, remember, and if you need to unload, feel free.' Paige had watched Lockton's various residents do the same with Aileen. She'd always assumed there was something about a person who surrounded themselves with books – all that creativity – that made people feel they were a lot wiser than they were. Or perhaps it was just the air of kindness that had surrounded the older woman?

Davey scratched his head. 'Lilith doesn't get on with her family. But what they think of her is important. She's spent a lot of her life trying to live up to something. So perhaps this move is just another step to her doing that.' He sounded like he was clutching at straws. 'We already know her father has offered her a new business – a deli in Rome – given her a new dream to live up to. He probably decided she'd benefit from a change of scene. But I don't know if she's planning on going for it.'

'Have you tried asking?' Paige asked gently.

Davey let out a long exhale. 'Sounds simple when you say it.' He stared at the floor. 'But I've never been good at talking.' His eyes met hers; they were so like Johnny's. Why did everything seem to remind her of him? 'So, did she borrow anything?' he asked again. 'Because it might give me a clue as to what she's planning.'

Paige gazed at him for a moment, considering. 'She took out a book called *The Courage to Go Your Own Way*.'

'Really?' A grin lit up Davey's face before it dimmed. 'But what does that mean?'

'You'll have to ask her.' Paige cocked her head, suddenly overwhelmed by a desire to help. 'Do you need to borrow a book on communicating?'

Davey blushed, then nodded slowly. 'You have a gift,' he murmured. 'Agnes was right.'

An hour later, Paige pulled up a chair and slumped into it. She'd been rushed off her feet as various Lockton residents visited to get library cards, return books, or request new ones. It was getting busier every day; after the grand opening on Wednesday and all the new members they were likely to pick up, they'd probably need more than one librarian. Not that Morag had got around to hiring the first one yet. Paige was leaving at the end of the week and there was still no one to take over. As she tried to relax, she remembered the phone call from earlier and pulled her mobile from her bag, dialling to pick up the message that had been left.

'Ms Dougall.' Paige recognised the plummy voice of the estate agent immediately. 'I'm sorry to be the bearer of bad news, but I decided to call as soon as I heard. I'm afraid Mr and Mrs Easton at number forty-two have decided to take their house off the market.'

She stared at the phone as the estate agent continued. 'They're not going to Dubai. It seems they've fallen pregnant.' Paige sat immobile, wondering why she didn't feel upset. 'It was unexpected – they delayed the sale because they wanted to get to twelve weeks to be sure. Now they are… well, the house is perfect for raising a family – which is of course one of the reasons why it appealed to you. They asked me to tell you they're very sorry to have wasted your time.' He paused for breath. 'I've got another lovely property that's just come up a few doors along. It's a similar price, and I've emailed over the details – just call when you want to arrange a viewing.' When the message ended, Paige deleted it before looking around. She should have been devastated. She'd lost a fortune on conveyancing fees and surveys, and the house had been everything she'd wanted – a place to nest, security for her and Grace, proof she could take care of her daughter with no one's help. But instead of disappointment, something that felt a lot like excitement bounced across her chest.

'Mummy!' Grace arrived with Paige's mam a few minutes later and skipped up to the counter. She wore trousers and a pink T-shirt with a sparkly pony decorating the front. 'Nana told me we could get a new book. She said she'd watch the desk so you could read to me.' She held out a chubby hand.

'Aye, lass,' said Cora. 'I've got an hour or so before I have to be back at Meg's. Grace and I finished off the library opening posters this morning.' She laid an array of colourful sheets on the counter. 'I'll put a few up while you read to the bairn. There are leaflets to give to anyone who comes in. Meg's agreed to put some in her shop, and I just bumped into Davey and he said we could do the same in Apple Cross Inn. Although word spread quickly after

Morag announced at the dance that Charlie was coming to do the talk – according to her, we've already attracted more visitors than we need.' She opened a drawer and picked up some Blu Tack as Grace tugged Paige's sleeve, then led her to the children's area.

There were four squashy red beanbags on the floor next to a red rug. Grace placed Paws into one and then sank beside him before pointing at the beanbag next to her; 'Sit, Mummy,' she said. Paige did as she was told and smiled. In almost four years she'd never been able to spend time with her daughter in the middle of a work day. Grace handed Paige the book and leaned over so she could see.

'That's beautiful.' Paige pointed to the first page. The castle reminded her of the cake Johnny had made.

'Pretty,' Grace agreed.

'You always wanted to live in a castle.' Paige ruffled Grace's blonde curls as the toddler gazed at the picture. Her skin had tanned in the last few weeks, and she looked happy; she was chattering and giggling more too.

Grace got up from the beanbag, grabbed Paws and sank into Paige's lap, before turning to cuddle her. 'I love you, Mummy,' she whispered.

Touched, Paige rubbed her nose in Grace's hair and took a breath. 'I love you too, my beautiful baby.'

'I'm not a baby!' Grace wriggled. The corner of the picture book jabbed into Paige's side, but she couldn't bring herself to let go. Instead, she hugged even tighter. 'I'm four soon,' Grace murmured.

Paige chuckled. 'Of course. Tell me what you want for your birthday, my big girl. I'll buy it when we go home,' she whispered. Grace tugged back so she could look up into Paige's face. Her expression was serious, and Paige guessed she was about to say something important. 'Tell me...'

Grace sucked in a breath. 'I want a princess cake,' she said, then her forehead knotted. 'And I want to live in Lockton. I don't want to go home...'

Chapter Twenty-Five

Johnny took a few moments to look around the kitchen at Apple Cross Inn. Monday had finally arrived, and he was as ready as he'd ever be. The worktops and floor were spotless and everything had been prepared. There were pies, fishcakes, sliced vegetables, soup and desserts made by Cora. Matilda had designed new menus and Davey had created a special dining area in the corner of the pub, and another in the small garden at the back. Now they just had to see if Tony Silver from *Best Pubs* turned up.

He bustled around the kitchen and found himself grinning when he spotted the pile of perfect macaroons waiting to be iced, remembering his evening with Paige, the rush of feelings he hadn't been expecting. He'd thought about her all day yesterday, wondering what those feelings meant, why he wasn't desperate to make his escape; to go walking in the mountains with Mack, or to while away an hour or four sketching. For the first time in three years he wanted to run towards something, rather than away.

'All set?' Davey wandered in, holding a paperback as he assessed the kitchen and smiled.

'*Start Talking*.' Johnny read the title and frowned. 'I wasn't aware you'd stopped.'

Davey tucked the book under one arm, hiding the cover and spine. 'I went to the library this morning and saw Paige. She recommended it. I thought I might need help with my communication skills.'

Johnny's pulse leapt at the mention of Paige. 'She okay?'

'She's glowing – I believe you might have something to do with that.' Johnny turned to open the fridge and peered inside as something bloomed in his chest. He was afraid his brother might read his expression before he'd had a chance to come to terms with the feelings himself. 'The food looks amazing.' Davey came to look into the fridge too. 'If Tony Silver isn't impressed, I don't want to be in his guide. This feels like old times, when I visited you in New York.' He turned and folded his arms, staring at Johnny. 'I'm sorry I forced you into it.'

'You didn't force me.' Johnny shrugged. 'All the preparation, the cooking, was more fun than I expected.' He ruffled his hair, realising he was telling the truth. 'I've been enjoying cooking for Paige; this was a natural next step. Perhaps all this worrying about getting too caught up was a mistake.' He went to wash his hands in the sink. 'Maybe we could add the odd fish pie onto the menu.' He wasn't sure he was ready to change anything else.

Davey regarded him for a moment. 'This is the first time we've talked about changing anything in your life and you haven't run for the mountains.'

Johnny shrugged. 'I've been living a half-life here. I know you've told me that a million times but it's taken Paige, Grace, even Mack for me to realise you were right.'

'You like Paige?' Davey raised an eyebrow.

'I do. The kid's cute too.' Johnny let out a long exhale. 'I'm thinking about asking if they'll stay in Lockton.' A few weeks ago, just the idea of letting someone into his life would have had him sprinting for the door.

'Big move.' Davey's eyebrows locked.

There was a loud knock and they spun around to see Lilith entering the kitchen. She wore a figure-hugging navy dress, and her dark hair tumbled around her shoulders and neck. She looked at them silently before placing a cake carrier on the table.

'W-what are y-you doing?' Davey stuttered. Just before Christmas, Davey hadn't been able to speak to Lilith without stumbling over his words, but he'd got over that in the few weeks they'd been dating. But now his cheeks were red and his eyes signalled pure surprise, with more than a hint of longing.

Lilith's neck coloured as she studied them both. 'I brought you this.' She pointed to the container and straightened her shoulders. 'I wish you luck with Tony Silver.' She scoured the kitchen. 'I don't think you'll need it, but I wish it anyway.' The room fell silent and Lilith cleared her throat. '*Arrivederci.*' She spun on her heel and headed for the door.

'Thank you, Lilith,' Johnny said, frowning at Davey, who was immobile. 'I heard you were leaving Lockton?'

Lilith turned back and the bow on her top lip wobbled. '*Sì.* I'd have thought Morag would have filled in the whole village after I told her this morning.' She looked directly at Davey. 'I have a job in Edinburgh. I'm moving on Thursday.'

'With your family?' Johnny asked, when Davey flinched in surprise.

'No, I am…' Lilith paused. 'Going my own way. It is time to leave the hotel. The new manager' – she hissed out a breath – 'is an imbecile. I can't stand by and watch him work in my hotel any longer. Papa is furious.' She cleared her throat. 'Then again, business always did come before anything else with him. It took me a long time to realise that…'

'I'm sorry,' Johnny said.

'I'm…' Davey opened his mouth, as the book slipped out from under his arm and hit the floor with a loud thud.

'*Start Talking*?' Lilith read. She stared at the cover for a beat before gazing at him. Davey cleared his throat and the silence stretched, until Lilith nodded. 'Well, it seems you haven't read it. A little advice: perhaps you should.' Then she tossed her hair and left the room.

Johnny shook his head, opened the cake carrier and smelled coffee. 'It's a tiramisu.' The creamy dessert was sprinkled with a perfect layer of chocolate and looked delicious. 'I think this is a message for you. Aren't you going to go after her?' He turned to Davey.

'I've no idea what to say.' His brother's voice was strained. 'She dumped me and turned her back on our whole relationship.' The corners of his eyes crinkled as he screwed up his face. 'Things were going so well and she finished it just like that.' The click of his fingers echoed around the kitchen. 'How can I trust her not to do the same again?'

'She seems to have learned her lesson. She's not moving to Italy, she brought you this…' He pointed to the dessert. 'We all make mistakes. You have to admit, we've both made plenty of our own.'

'But what if Lilith hasn't learned? What if in a few months she decides to take up her father's offer of a deli in Rome?' Davey blew out a long breath. 'I'm not sure I can go through losing her again. I loved her.' His voice held an ache.

'You're afraid?' Johnny asked, wondering how he'd missed how deeply his brother still felt.

'Terrified.' Davey bent and picked up the book before twisting it in his fingers.

'You could talk to her?' Johnny said.

Davey's lips thinned. 'I've no idea what I'd say. What words could I use to tell her how I feel? To make her understand how much she hurt me? How do you build trust with someone who walked away that easily?'

Johnny pointed a finger at the book. 'If you read that, you might be able to figure out the answer to those questions for yourself.'

Tony Silver, the man with grey hair that matched his name, glanced up as Johnny approached the small table in the corner of Apple Cross Inn. Davey and Matilda had arranged a few in the quiet nook and added white tablecloths and wine glasses to give it a professional touch. The small plate in front of the man was scraped clean and his silver cutlery sat at a neat ninety-degree angle. Just twenty minutes ago the plate had been filled with a crispy fishcake and a side of freshly cooked vegetables, perfectly complemented by the crisp glass of white that Johnny had recommended to accompany it. He felt a sliver of pleasure, a hint of pride he hadn't felt in a while. Not since Paige had first eaten one of his muffins, to be exact. The man smiled when he saw Johnny.

'I wanted to meet you, to compliment you on the food.' He picked up the starched napkin Davey had ironed earlier and ran it across his mouth as his lively eyes crinkled at the corners. 'The fishcake was delicious. It's rare I find a chef who can get the flavours and texture so right.' He scanned Johnny's face. 'You look familiar – have we met?'

Johnny shook his head. 'You might be mixing me up with my twin Davey; he owns the pub.'

Tony Silver nodded. 'That's it, he greeted me when I arrived – you have the same mannerisms. That's a very impressive dessert selection.' He pointed to the menu which Matilda had painted and embellished with tiny sketches of grapes, cheese, fish and vegetables. 'I'm pleased to see tiramisu – my mother is Italian and it's my all-time favourite dessert, so it's got a lot to live up to.' He raised a bushy eyebrow.

Johnny smiled. 'I don't think it'll disappoint – the person who made it used an old family recipe. I have to admit, it's not mine.'

'I admire a chef who's happy to work with others,' Tony said. 'We all have our own speciality, and the macaroons? Another favourite, I have to confess.' He patted his belly and smiled, his teeth a bright contrast against his tanned skin.

'Those are all mine,' Johnny admitted, feeling the silver of pride grow.

The critic tapped the menu. 'Then I'll have a serving of both. You have a rare talent. You've managed to impress me, Mr Becker. There aren't many chefs I meet in this job who can do that.' He sat back in his chair and folded his arms.

He was wearing a starched white shirt and reminded Johnny of some of the older chefs he'd worked with when he'd been training;

men and women he'd respected. How would they feel about the life he led now? About the way he'd turned his back on his talents? 'Thank you,' he murmured.

'Where did you train?'

'London and Paris. I had my own restaurant in New York.' There was no point in hiding the information and Johnny expected Tony would be impressed.

'Brave decision to go from all that to this.' The critic scanned the pub but he looked more curious than disdainful.

'Life change,' Johnny confessed.

Tony nodded. 'I did a similar thing when I was younger. Gave up a big job in the city to become a journalist. It was risky and hard work. I had a few lean years, but it was the best decision I ever made. I followed my passion.' His eyes gleamed. 'I think it's hard to be happy if you don't do that. Lots of people aren't courageous enough to follow the life they were born to.'

Johnny jerked his chin up. There was that tingling under his skin again, the uncomfortable sense of disappointment in himself. He was having that more these days, ever since he'd met Paige.

'Do you have plans to expand the pub? I notice there's room at the back to build on, and your brother mentioned something when he showed me to my table.' Tony glanced around the space. 'A restaurant would work well, and I imagine you'd have a lot of customers judging by the quality of the food and the fact that this place is busy.' The pub was emptying now, but when Tony had first arrived every table had been full. News of the new menu had travelled fast.

'I…' It was the plan Davey had suggested and Johnny kept turning down. 'My brother would like that.'

Tony's gaze grew sharper. 'But you wouldn't?'

Johnny let out a sigh. 'I'm not sure.' Why was he was sharing so much; was it because Tony was a stranger, the power of an unknown ear working its magic again?

'Pity,' Tony said. 'I meet a lot of people in this job, and only a very few chefs make it into *Best Pubs*. If your desserts are anything like the main course, I can tell you you'll be one of them. It's an opportunity. Then again, I'm the last person who should encourage anyone to go in a direction they don't want to go in. Is cooking not your passion?'

Johnny opened his mouth and closed it. 'It is,' he admitted. 'I'm…' He swallowed, looking around the pub again as he realised how much he loved working here, had loved cooking for Paige, creating all the food for today in the kitchen. 'Perhaps adding a restaurant might be a good idea,' he murmured, waiting for the feeling of panic, the hard thump in his chest that told him he was making the wrong decision. 'I'll get your desserts.' He turned away and walked slowly back to the kitchen as his mind whirred.

Davey was reading *Start Talking* when Johnny entered the kitchen. It looked like he was already halfway through, but he slammed the book shut and rose. 'How did it go?'

Johnny quickly plated a new order, then sliced the tiramisu and piled a few of the colourful macaroons onto a small dish before giving them to Matilda, who'd come to pick them up. 'We're going to be in *Best Pubs*. Tony thinks we should open a restaurant, add to the back of the pub.'

Davey folded his arms. 'And you haven't run a mile?' He scrutinised him.

'Actually' – Johnny gulped – 'I think he might be right.' The words flooded out, but he knew they were right, knew it was time to move forwards.

'You do?' Davey croaked. 'But we'd need a full-time chef.'

'Or two?' Johnny suggested, turning to face him. 'We need a partner. Someone to share the burden, to give me time to do the things I enjoy. I don't want to live the life I lived in New York, but I've realised recently that I'm ready for more.' He was ready to let himself live. To go all in, as Agnes had suggested.

'But who?' Davey asked.

'Lilith.' Johnny watched as a flare of colour travelled up his brother's face. 'She knows how to run a hotel and a restaurant. She's a great chef; that tiramisu is a triumph. Perhaps with the right encouragement she could be persuaded not to move to Edinburgh after all. Maybe if the right person asked her to stay in Lockton and take a different job…? A job here, with us.' He winked. 'She would.'

Davey glanced at the book on the counter, then slowly smiled. 'Perhaps she would,' he murmured.

Chapter Twenty-Six

Paige bounced from foot to foot with excitement as she looked around The Book Barn, taking in the community of people scattered around the room. Her mam had arrived early to help hang colourful banners at the entrance of the library to announce the official opening later this morning. Fergus, Morag and her da had been moving furniture to make space, and had just finished laying out rows of chairs for the audience. Agnes was double-checking all the shelves. She'd already turned Charlie Adaire's books so they faced outwards and put piles of his backlist on tables. Davey had come to help out too, and was on the other side of the room spreading a red tablecloth onto a long trestle table they'd borrowed from the Jam Club. It had space for cakes and a large urn ready for hot drinks. Johnny had promised to bring freshly baked chocolate muffins, and Paige expected him to arrive soon. She'd barely seen him since Monday. It was her fault – she'd been caught up in preparations and had put him off. He'd wanted to talk, but she'd avoided being alone with him; there was this look on his face after the weekend which both delighted and terrified her. A look she wasn't ready to confront.

'Think anyone will turn up?' Paige joined her mam, who was arranging library packs onto a table, filled with leaflets and forms for new visitors to sign up.

'Of course, lass,' Cora soothed, as Grace came to grab Paige's arm. She'd been by her side for most of the morning, trailing after her with Paws. Her daughter spotted the paper and crayons in the children's area that Cora had put out and gave a delighted roar, tugging away and charging over. Paige watched as she knelt to scribble, in a world of her own. Her life felt on track at long last – would she lose this feeling of contentment when she returned to London? Had losing number forty-two been an omen? Should she go back at all? Grace didn't want to, but the toddler wasn't old enough to know what was best. The decision loomed and Paige wasn't sure she was ready to make it. She had too many fears whirring around her brain. Could she give up everything she'd built in London; her career, security and independence? And what would happen with Johnny if she stayed?

'There's a queue outside.' Morag walked up to join her and winked. 'I'll warrant there'll be standing room only in a few minutes. Do you want to do the honours, lass, and let them in?'

'Okay.' Paige began to head for the entrance but Morag clutched her arm. 'I know you're supposed to be leaving tomorrow, but there's a job here if you want. I've not advertised for a librarian. Your mam, Agnes and me will run the library for the time being if you decide to go. After the Jampionships finish this weekend, we'll all have more time. But I've got to say, it's obvious to anyone that this is where you're supposed to be. You fit, lass.' Her brown eyes twinkled. 'Aileen always said when you'd had enough of your adventures, you'd return.' She winked.

'I...' Paige hesitated.

'Don't make a decision right away. You've got another day and I know you'll make the right one,' Morag said.

Paige trembled as she walked to the entrance, her insides a jumble of emotions. She drew in a breath when she spotted the large crowd outside, then opened the door. Lilith was first in the queue. She held a cake carrier which she lifted when she spotted Paige.

'I made mini tiramisus.' She looked awkward. 'I'm leaving Lockton tomorrow; I had ingredients to use up.'

'Aye, that's good of you.' Agnes came to join them. 'Why don't you take it to the refreshment stand?' She pointed to the corner where Davey was laying out mugs. Lilith nodded before marching in his direction. 'You've done well, lass,' Agnes whispered to Paige. 'You get back in there too, make sure Lilith finds Davey.' She shooed her in their direction. 'I'll welcome our new visitors and tell them where to sit.'

Paige approached the refreshment stand, but stopped before she got too close. The couple were gazing at each other and neither of them spoke. Lilith broke first and put the carrier on the table. 'I heard you made it into *Best Pubs*.'

Davey shoved his hands in the pockets of his jeans. 'Your tiramisu clinched it.' He gulped. 'I came to the hotel on Monday, and again yesterday afternoon, but they said you were out.'

Lilith looked surprised. 'No one told me. I've been taking walks. Saying my goodbyes.' She jerked her chin up. 'Why did you visit?'

'I want to talk…' Davey said softly.

Lilith snorted, but her expression turned hopeful. 'So, you finished the book?'

'Twice.' He stepped forwards. There were people around – some were watching – but neither of them seemed to care. 'I learned a few things.' He licked his lips anxiously. 'I know I said a lot of things in February. Some I regret.' He grimaced. 'But you put your father's demands before me and that hurt.'

'*Sì.*' Lilith's chin dipped. 'It was a mistake. I've been trying to impress my papa for years, but I've realised I never will. I wanted to tell you, but…'

'You were scared?' Davey asked gently.

Lilith gulped.

'It's not easy, is it?' He took another step towards her, until they were toe to toe. 'I've been afraid too. I didn't want to put my heart on the line again, to tell you how I felt. I didn't want to ask you to stay in case you refused. But if I don't ask, you'll go anyway. The book Paige loaned me showed me that.'

Lilith looked wary. 'You want me to stay?'

Davey put a hand to her cheek. 'We're going to build a restaurant on the back of Apple Cross Inn. We want another partner, someone who can cook.'

Lilith blinked. 'Me?' The word was a whisper.

'*Sì*,' Davey said, his voice husky. 'But I want more. I want you to move in, I want us to build a future together. I'm not asking you to turn your back on your parents, but I am asking you to put *us* first.'

Lilith looked torn. 'I have a new job in Edinburgh.'

'Tell them you're not coming. Tell them you've found someone who needs you more. I'm not your father, Lilith – for me you'll always be enough.' Paige saw Lilith shiver, watched her lift her hand and place it over Davey's.

'*Sì*,' she murmured. 'So are you.' Then she pressed her lips to his.

Twenty minutes later, there was a gasp from the audience as Charlie Adaire arrived, looking handsome in a pair of dark trousers and a powder-blue shirt. He only had eyes for Morag as he strode up to join her and Paige. 'You're late,' Morag snapped, though her chest puffed out like she was a bird trying to impress its mate.

Charlie checked his watch. 'By four minutes. Jeez, I was writing, woman,' he growled, as a spark lit his eyes. 'Since I met you, my head has been filled with ideas. I never thought a muse would be bossy or cantankerous – aren't they meant to be pliable and serene?'

'That's not the kind of musing you'll get from me.' Morag snorted and blushed scarlet, then waved at the audience, some of whom were looking on with interest. 'I hope you found time to put together your talk. You're on in less than ten minutes and there are still people due to arrive, including Jason Beckett and Jeannie Martin.' She sucked in her cheeks. 'You'd better not let me down.'

Charlie chuckled. 'That's for me to know and you to find out.' He winked at Paige. 'Where are my chocolate muffins? I'll not be saying a word until I've had at least one.'

'Johnny's bringing them.' Paige turned just as he strode through the entrance with Mack, carrying a large box. He wore jeans and a navy T-shirt with 'When in Doubt, Say Yes' printed across the front. Something inside her flowered. Joy – she recognised it at last, the slow thump of her heart and the way her body warmed.

'Prince!' Grace ran up to Johnny, carrying Paws.

'Princess!' Johnny said, grinning, and his eyes caught Paige's and held. Grace clutched his legs before dropping to the ground to do the same to Mack, who was standing patiently beside his master. The dog glanced up at Johnny, who nodded, then hurled himself at Grace. 'Are you okay to watch him?' he asked, and the toddler grinned. Johnny looped the lead around the bottom of one of the bookshelves, securing Mack.

'You can put the muffins on the table,' Morag ordered. 'Let's go and get you one now.' She glared at Charlie, and they followed Johnny as he greeted Davey and Lilith before laying out muffins and macaroons next to her mini tiramisus.

Paige deliberately stayed where she was, watching Grace play with Mack. Paws was on the floor now, the zip on his stomach partially open and a piece of paper poking out. It was probably Grace's most recent artwork. She smiled. 'Wow, it's busy,' Jeannie declared as she strode up to join them, glancing around the room as Jason trailed after her. 'I heard about Charlie Adaire.' She patted her green handbag. 'I brought one of his books – think he'll give me an autograph?'

'I'm sure he will,' Morag rumbled as she joined them, leaving Charlie at the refreshment table chatting with Johnny. 'I told you we had a surprise.'

Jason scanned the crowd and his mouth went taught. 'I hope you've considered all the health and safety aspects of this event. I could have advised on the things you need to look out for—'

Morag shook her head. 'We've got it covered, laddie, no need for any help.'

Jason pouted. 'I hope you've at least got someone keeping an eye on the toddlers.' He eyed Grace who was still playing with Mack. 'There are crayons on the tables! It's really irresponsible, you're asking for—'

'I'm impressed,' Jeannie interrupted, and Jason's jaw dropped. 'There are at least a hundred people here, and a queue outside with more. I think, Jason, you and Morag should liaise. Perhaps The Book Barn's team could give you some advice on getting a few bigger names to talk at Morridon.' She raised an eyebrow as Jason's cheeks puffed.

Morag's lip curled. 'Mr Adaire's a special friend of The Book Barn; he's already agreed to do regular talks.' Paige knew he'd done no such thing, but guessed he soon would – especially if he wanted to keep his muse. There was a buzz from the crowd and they turned as Charlie made his way to the front of the audience. 'The talk's about to start,' Morag whispered. 'If you'll excuse me, I promised I'd do the introductions to kick it off.'

Paige went over to the counter as Morag took to the small stage and the crowd hushed. She leaned onto the smooth wood, watching as Grace continued to play with Mack, ignoring *Home Is Where the Heart Is*, which had been placed face up on the counter again. She watched Johnny turn away from Davey and spot her, felt something clutch at her throat as he weaved his way slowly through the crowd.

'I'd call this a success,' he whispered as he approached.

Paige swallowed and nodded.

'I wanted to talk to you.' Johnny walked behind the counter and leaned next to Paige. His shoulder pressed against hers, making something fizz in her belly. He took a long breath and she knew what he was about to ask. 'I want to know if you'd consider staying in Lockton?' He turned and Paige felt an equal mix of fear and joy battling inside her. She opened her mouth, even though she had no clue how she was going to respond. *No!* her head screamed, but her heart was yelling, *Yes, yes, yes.* She knew she was skittish, after all those years with Carl feeling like she wasn't enough. But was she ready to take another chance?

Then Mack let out a quick yip and Paige jerked her head, looking over at Grace as the dog somehow shed his lead and grabbed the paper poking from Paws's stomach. Grace toddled after him, giggling as he charged towards Johnny. The crowd were still focused on the stage as Charlie talked on, but Paige shot out from behind the counter, desperate to stop the dog's antics from ruining the event. Johnny got to Mack first. He leaned down to grab him and plucked the paper from his jaws as Grace came running up, clutching the lead and Paws. Johnny gave the drawing back to Grace as he clipped the lead onto Mack's collar again, muttering something about Houdini and extra training.

'No – for you!' Grace pressed the paper back into Johnny's hands as he stood. She beamed as he grinned and unwrapped it. It was a scribbled sketch, this time with the stick figure of a man, a golden dog and a woman with long brown hair; between them was a small blob with golden curls and they were all holding hands. Above them, Paige could make out mountains, a splash of yellow sunshine and a ginormous pink heart.

'I love it.' Johnny grinned as Paige's insides froze. She tried to breathe, felt the air catch in her throat. 'Is that me, your mum and you?' He pointed to the colourful scrawls.

'Yes!' Grace cheered, beaming.

'We need to talk,' Paige said, her voice barely a whisper. She took Grace's hand and steered her to Cora. 'I need a minute,' Paige croaked, and her mam paled as if she'd read her mind.

Then Paige stalked across The Book Barn. Blood was rushing in her ears as she whizzed past Agnes who was still greeting visitors, then what felt like another hundred people queuing outside. The sun was bright and she blinked, striding along the narrow pathway away from the library towards the high street. She stopped when she got to the bench facing the mountains – the scene of her embarrassing confession a few weeks before – then heard Johnny's footsteps behind her, and the patter of Mack's paws at his heels. When she turned Johnny was frowning, still holding Grace's drawing. 'What just happened?'

'Grace,' Paige moaned. 'I never expected…' She shook her head, remembering the huge pink heart, how her daughter's face lit up every time she saw Johnny. 'She's fallen for you.'

Johnny folded his arms. 'I'd say the feeling is mutual. Why does it matter?'

Paige shook her head fervently. 'It's one thing for me to take a chance on a stranger, one thing for me to make a mistake, but I never intended to risk Grace's emotions.'

'You think I'm a risk?' Johnny's face clouded.

Paige gave him an exasperated shrug. 'I don't know who you are. A month ago, we'd never even met.' She threw up her arms. 'Now you're asking me to stay, to leave the life I've built up in London. My career.'

Johnny's mouth pinched. 'A life that makes you unhappy.' His eyes scraped across her face. 'A month ago you were taking pills to get you through the day, you were losing weight because you were too stressed to eat. Are you saying you want to live that life again?'

'I don't know,' Paige hissed. 'At least it's mine. No one can ruin it, or make me feel like I don't deserve it. No one can walk away – physically or emotionally – just when I or Grace need them most.'

'What's this about?' Johnny asked quietly.

She shook her head. 'I made this mistake six years ago. Met a man I hardly knew, gave up everything. He didn't want me and he didn't want our daughter. I'm not making that same mistake again.' She blocked out the pain churning through her veins, the voice in her head telling her she was an eejit. Telling her it was time to take another chance. That Johnny was nothing like Carl, that she could rely on him. 'I'm going back to London to build a life for Grace and me, a life I can trust,' she murmured, steeling herself when Johnny's back stiffened and his expression shuttered. 'I'm sorry.' Her voice was lifeless. 'I'm not prepared to risk my daughter's heart, or my own.'

Johnny shook his head. 'You're being a coward, Paige. I should know because it takes one to know one. I've been terrified for the last three years. Too afraid to take a chance on anything, running from everything that might make me feel. Even Mack.' He looked down at the dog sitting patiently by his feet. 'You're looking for excuses because you're scared. I understand. But after three years, I've decided to move on with my life – I'd like you and Grace to move on with me… I will never hurt you,' he said softly.

'I'm sorry,' Paige said, avoiding looking at him. 'But I can't.'

Chapter Twenty-Seven

Paige shifted a suitcase along the floor in the small two-bedroom flat she'd rented and moved into over the weekend. It was a weekly let that she'd got via her estate agent, and they'd stay until she found another place to buy. It felt like months since she'd been back in London; she could hardly believe it had only been five days. Grace sat at the small white kitchen table which came with the property, colouring as Paws lay abandoned beside a pile of pencils, staring at the ceiling.

'How was the childminder today?' Paige asked, but Grace didn't look up. 'Did you play?' Her daughter let out a loud huff. 'I had a good day at work,' Paige lied. In truth, it had been strange being back. It was as if the world had closed over her head as soon as she'd gone. Other people had picked up her clients and events, and it felt like she was starting her whole job again from scratch, like she didn't belong. Even her brief meeting with HR had been unsettling. They'd handed her a pile of leaflets on managing stress, and sent her back to her desk. She'd felt so alone, and her mind had kept wandering to the warm chatter and laughter she'd grown used to in The Book Barn, to the way it had felt recommending books and knowing she was making a difference to people's lives. She remembered the Jam

Club, the friendships she'd started to make. Halfway through the afternoon, she'd found herself locked in a toilet cubicle, staring at the bottle of pills she'd unearthed from the bottom of her handbag, as her insides roiled. She'd recalled Johnny calling her a coward and wondered if he was right. 'What do you want for tea?' Paige asked, using her sing-song voice.

'Chocolate muffins.' Grace's frown deepened.

Paige sighed and hefted the suitcase onto the sofa before unzipping it. She'd packed the day after The Book Barn launch, knowing she couldn't stay in Lockton any longer. If she had, how long would it have taken her to seek Johnny out, to tell him she wanted to stay? She took a moment to watch her daughter, who was scowling at her drawing, feeling an uncomfortable lump rise in her throat. She lifted the red dress her mam had bought her from the suitcase and placed it carefully on the sofa, adding the matching cardigan before tugging out her favourite red silk bra. She took out the pink sparkly top, remembering her date with Johnny, and a tear tracked down her cheek as memories overwhelmed her. She swiped it away, taking out Grace's pink dress, and stopped abruptly when she saw the book lying on a pair of her grey pyjamas: *Home Is Where the Heart Is*. Paige batted at her tears again, as her body shuddered and she felt the sob climb in her throat. She looked around the cold, soulless sitting room, remembering Kindness Cottage with all its warmth, The Book Barn and all the wonderful people she'd met and helped in Lockton – then her mind shifted to Johnny. Something lay heavy in her stomach, an ache she couldn't control as she wondered for the millionth time since she'd arrived back in London if she'd made a terrible mistake. If she'd been a coward after all.

*

The garden at Kindness Cottage was buzzing as Paige angled her head, studying the pink fourth birthday bunting that her mam, Fergus, Charlie and Morag were hanging from a ribbon which led from her da's shed to the main house, while Agnes, Meg and Evie arranged a trestle table on the patio. It was laid with a pink chequered tablecloth and a selection of cupcakes, sandwiches, sausage rolls, crudités and crisps – a feast her mam had pulled together at short notice because Paige and Grace had only arrived late last night. A small pile of presents sat on a picnic rug on the lawn, and Paige happened to know they included a multitude of books, a set of new colouring pens, drawing paper and a powder-blue princess dress. She pressed a palm against her chest as everything inside her thrummed with trepidation and excitement. Grace and Marcus would be back from delivering the book to Johnny any moment now. Had he been at his house? Would he come strolling into the garden with them, smiling at her?

She chewed her top lip, staring at the gate leading to the front garden as her mam walked up to join her. 'It's good to have you back again, lass. I'm so happy your work let you leave so quickly…'

Paige shrugged. 'They've been wanting to restructure for ages. Given they'd moved all my clients to other people and I had nothing to do, they thought it would be best all round if I didn't work my notice.' The fact that the HR manager had seen the bottle of pills in Paige's bag when she'd pulled out her resignation letter had probably helped. She'd given her a steely look, then her face had softened and she'd told her there and then she could leave straight away if they didn't have to pay her for her notice period. 'I think they were worried I'd make myself sick again, which would open them up to all kinds of trouble. It wasn't strictly policy but I signed a waiver – I just wanted to get home.'

'Aye, well The Book Barn needs its librarian. We've been lost without you, what with all the extra members signing up after the launch event. Word spread and we've been overrun with people asking for the lass who knows exactly what to recommend.' Her mam's cheeks pinked as she gave Paige a quick squeeze, just as her da and Grace walked into the garden.

'No prince!' Grace exclaimed, her eyes lighting up when she spotted the banners and pile of presents on the lawn, and went running over to examine them.

'He wasn't there,' her da added, his ruddy cheeks blooming with rosy colour from the walk. 'So we left the book on the doorstep like you asked.' His face rumpled. 'I know we talked about this, but do you really think Johnny will understand?'

Paige nodded. 'I'm certain he will.' Her throat contracted – but would he come?

She watched as her da went up to the trestle table, saw Agnes bring him a mug of tea from the kitchen, then forced herself to end her surveillance of the gate as Morag came over.

'Looks good, lass.' She nodded at the bunting. 'I had a chat with your mam, and we agreed I should mention the party to some of my customers who have wee ones the same age.' She pointed at Grace. 'They said they'd pop in later; we thought the lass would need some playmates now she's moving here.'

'Thank you, that was kind,' Paige said. And it was true, everyone was so kind here.

Morag arched an eyebrow. 'Aye, lass. Well, I'm just glad you came to your senses. Aileen always said you'd return.' She looked up. 'Your mam, Agnes and I still like to imagine her looking down at us from somewhere. Watching, perhaps leaving books out for people in the library, nudging us along if we don't make the decisions we should.' She winked and turned before Paige could ask what she meant. Had it been the three women leaving the books out as she'd suspected, or had someone else had a hand in it? She'd wondered at times, but… she looked up into the blue sky.

There was a sound from the gate and Paige's pulse leapt, then Davey and Lilith came strolling into the garden carrying a hessian bag. Their arms were linked and for the first time since Paige had met her, Lilith was smiling. She remembered the book she'd loaned Davey on talking and was filled with an overwhelming sense of achievement. All the books, those small acts of kindness had the power to make such a difference in people's lives. Aileen had been right. 'We heard on the grapevine you were back,' Davey said to Paige, tipping his head in Morag's direction. 'I haven't had time to shop for a present, but here are some chocolate muffins and a tiramisu that was made this morning.' He dropped a quick kiss on Lilith's cheek, then drew out a Tupperware container from the bag and put it on the table with the other food as Grace beamed.

'Prince?' she asked, looking towards the gate.

'Not yet.' Paige ruffled her curls just as she heard a loud bark, then Mack came charging into the garden and sprinted up to

Grace. The toddler dropped to her knees to pet him as Johnny wandered in holding a cake carrier, with a book balanced on top. He wore jeans and a sky-blue T-shirt with 'Choose Kind' written across the front. He gave Paige a searching look, making her insides tumble, before he knelt in front of Grace and unclipped the top from the carrier. Inside was a masterpiece of icing technology. The three-tiered cake had been decorated in white royal icing and dotted with tiny handmade pink and purple buttercream flowers. There were large purple window arches and a bright pink front door. Johnny had added flags to the middle tier and a huge pink turret scattered with silver baubles at the top. Grace's jaw dropped as she stared at it.

'Castle.' Her voice was awed.

'Fit for a princess.' Johnny grinned, rising as Mack's nose began to twitch and he eyed the cake. 'Let's put it over here.' He led Grace to the table and laid it down. 'I've spent the last week making it.' His eyes met Paige's again. 'I was going to deliver it personally – your granda gave me your new address. I've just been to Morridon to put air in my tyres, ready for the trip.'

'You were?' Paige felt something inside her stir. Her da let out a short cough.

Two toddlers wearing princess dresses came running through the back gate and Morag clapped, looking excited. 'Aye, here are the wee lasses I was talking about.' She went to greet them, taking Grace as Johnny walked up to join Paige.

He held the book up, before grabbing her hand and leading her away from the throng, towards the shed where Braveheart was basking in the sun. The cat opened one eye then closed it. '*Home*

Is Where the Heart Is – how did you know I asked your mum to pack it in your suitcase?'

Paige shook her head. 'I didn't until I got back and she told me.' She smiled shyly. 'I was sending you a message, telling you I was home.' She looked at her pink sandals. 'I wanted to apologise and say I understood. I was a coward. I was too afraid to take a chance because I didn't want to be hurt again. I used Grace as an excuse.' She lifted her face. Johnny was watching her with a focus that made goosebumps dance across her skin. 'Carl hurt me so much, made me question everything about myself, made me feel so useless – I had to prove I wasn't. I wasn't ready to trust anyone. Going back to my old life was the safest thing to do.'

'Except it wasn't?' he asked.

Paige shook her head. 'No, because home is where my heart is now. You were right. It took the kindness of a stranger' – his eyes sparkled – 'the kindness of my parents and everyone in Lockton to make me realise that.' She looked around the garden. 'This is my home now, with my family, in the library amongst the books – and with you.'

She looked back at Johnny. He was grinning. 'Pleased to hear it, because driving to London to get you would have been hard work for a man whose mission in life is to take it easy.' His eyes crinkled at the corners and he stepped closer, before sweeping her into his arms. His lips were warm and familiar, and Paige pressed herself against him and wrapped her arms around his neck, giggled when he lifted her off the grass and twirled her. She heard a squeal of delight from Grace, the sound of clapping, but couldn't bring herself to break away.

*

'Happy birthday dear Grace, happy birthday to you.' The crowd finished singing the last verse as Johnny knelt beside Grace on the grass, where the cake had been placed on a low table.

'You need to blow out the candles and make a wish, princess,' he murmured, as she beamed at him before looking around at her audience, then down at the pile of presents she'd just unwrapped. She was wearing her new princess dress with white lace ruffles at the sleeves and Paige had never seen her look so content. A warm bubble of happiness expanded in her chest as she realised she felt the same.

Grace turned back to the cake and sucked in a breath before blowing out all four pink candles. 'I wish…' Grace blinked and looked around, then up at Johnny. 'I wish…' She shrugged as Mack came bounding up and she dropped to her knees to hug him. 'I wish for a doggy!' she yelled, clearly delighted she'd thought of something.

Johnny chuckled and stroked her hair. 'You can share mine,' he murmured, looking back at Paige and winking. She swallowed, glancing around the garden, at the sea of faces of her family and new friends. Her life had changed completely since she'd come back to Kindness Cottage, and she was just glad she'd been brave enough to return. And brave enough to listen to the books – all those small gifts of kindness – that had guided her here. She took Johnny's hand and squeezed it gently, before leaning in for a kiss.

A Letter from Donna

I want to say a huge thank you for choosing to read *Summer in the Scottish Highlands*. If you enjoyed it, and want to keep up to date with all my latest releases, just sign up at the following link. Your email address will never be shared and you can unsubscribe at any time.

www.bookouture.com/donna-ashcroft

This book took me back to the beautiful Scottish Highlands in the summer. When Paige Dougall is forced to visit her parents with her daughter Grace, she isn't expecting her whole life to change. But this story is all about kindness and how it can touch people's lives. How small acts can create giant ripples with the power to transform everything. I hope you enjoyed seeing how Paige's choice of books affected Lockton's villagers, and how the reads left out at The Book Barn for Paige helped to change her path. I hope you agree Johnny was the perfect match for Paige – a man with his own demons and a heart of pure gold, who had to learn to be brave enough to embrace the future he deserved.

If you enjoyed this summery, food- and book-filled escape, it would be wonderful if you could please leave a short review. Not only do I want to know what you thought, it might encourage a new reader to pick up one of my books for the first time.

I really love hearing from my readers – so please say hi on my Facebook page, through Twitter, or on my website.

Thanks,
Donna Ashcroft

DonnaAshcroftAuthor

@Donnashc

donnaashcroftauthor

www.donna-writes.co.uk

Acknowledgements

Thanks firstly to lovely Marike Verhavert who supported me so much at my day job when I was writing this book, listening patiently and stepping in to help when I got stressed. Thanks also go to my boss Ben Wigley as well as Alasdair Cox, Claire Hornbuckle, Kay Butt, Louise Patten, Lorna Fox, Olga Kukonova, Masha Rixon, Chris Nagels, Heinke Binder and Amy Bal for all of my wonderful years at Big Green Smile. As well as the wonderful and supportive Mel and Rob Harrison at Goodman Fox. I'm about to embark on a new, exciting journey but I will miss you all.

To Chris, Erren and Charlie – my fabulous family. Thanks for the tea, coffee, eclectic music at mealtimes, hoovering and (almost) endless patience. A shout-out as well to Erren, who is recovering from glandular fever but is working so hard to keep up with her studies. I'm lucky to have you all.

To Natasha Harding, my fabulous editor who brought me to Bookouture and helped to make me a better writer, I'm so excited to be working with you again. Thanks for keeping me going when I get stressed, for helping when I get tangled up in my own head, and for pointing me in the right direction with your brilliant edits. To Peta Nightingale, Saidah Graham, Noelle Holten, Kim Nash,

Sarah Hardy, Alexandra Holmes, Alex Crow, Claire Gatzen, Rachel Rowlands, and everyone else in the wonderful Bookouture team! Not to mention all their hugely gifted and very supportive authors.

No acknowledgements would be complete without a big Prosecco cheers to Jules Wake, who always has a life raft at the ready when I'm drowning in writerly angst, and to Jackie Campbell and Julie Anderson for all your support. To Anita Chapman, who sent me tulips at just the right moment. I'm missing you all so much in lockdown, but you guys keep me sane (thank you, Zoom). Thanks also to lovely mums Amanda Baker, Caroline Kelly and Giuilia Pitney Coope.

A particular thanks to Chris Cardoza for the anagram of Charlie Adaire; Claire Hornbuckle for the beetroot brownies she used to bring to work which inspired Johnny's dessert; to Jules Wake for the long walks, support and ideas when we discuss plots; and to Julie Anderson who gave me HR advice (which I then rewrote, apologies). Finally, I wanted to mention and remember Tony Davis, father of my dear friend Jackie Campbell, who passed away earlier this year. I gave 'Tony' Silver his name as a small act of remembrance – I think we all like to think of him eating good food, and drinking wine amongst mountains which he loved.

To all the people who message, support me or leave wonderful reviews – you cannot imagine how lovely it is to hear someone tell you they enjoyed your book. This includes: Fiona Morton, Alison Phillips, Eva Abraham, Wendy Smith, Jan Dunham, Catherine Hunt, Karen Philipps, Andy Ayres, Mirna Skuhan, Mags Evans, Claire Hornbuckle, Anne Winckworth, Kim Holt, Jan Dunham, Soo Cieszynska, Marilyn Messik, Hester Thorpe, Tricia Osborne, and anyone I may have forgotten. And to all the incredible bloggers who support me each time a book comes out, I am so grateful to you all.

As always, thanks to Katie Fforde, the Romantic Novelists' Association, Mum, John, Dad, Peter, Christelle, Lucie, Mathis, Joseph, Lynda, Louis, Auntie Rita, Auntie Gillian, Tanya, James, Rosie, Ava, Philip, Sonia, Stephanie and Muriel.

Finally, to the readers who have bought my books – many of whom have written reviews – I wouldn't be here without you. Xx

Lightning Source UK Ltd.
Milton Keynes UK
UKHW012005250521
384363UK00002B/106